WEEP IN THE NIGHT

Valerie Goree

WEEP IN THE NIGHT

Contact Information: titleadmin@pelicanbookgroup.com

All scripture quotations, unless otherwise indicated, are taken from the Holy Bible, New International Version[R], NIV[R], Copyright 1973, 1978, 1984, 2011 by Biblica, Inc.™ Used by permission of Zondervan. All rights reserved worldwide. www.zondervan.com

Cover Art by *Nicola Martinez*

Harbourlight Books, a division of Pelican Ventures, LLC
www.pelicanbookgroup.com PO Box 1738 *Aztec, NM * 87410

Harbourlight Books sail and mast logo is a trademark of Pelican Ventures, LLC

Publishing History
First Harbourlight Edition, 2014
Paperback Edition ISBN 978-1-61116-387-2
Electronic Edition ISBN 978-1-61116-386-5
Published in the United States of America

Dedication

In appreciation for his wholehearted and unwavering support, I dedicate this novel to my husband, Glenn.

A special thanks to my ACFW on-line critique group. Your suggestions, insight, and support are invaluable.

1

"Weeping may remain for a night, but rejoicing comes in the morning" ~ Psalm 30:5

She ran her finger across the white plastic nametag. Blue letters spelled out *Debra Johnson*, but that wasn't her name.

The bulb above the sink crackled and died. She hated the dark. Backing out of the bathroom, she leaned against the wall and flipped on the hall light. Shadows scuttled away, but left a trace of unease in her gut.

Tears blurred her vision as she pinned the nametag on her shirt. It took two attempts to snag the pin in place. *Get a grip, Sadie. You're safe.*

Although she'd been in the Federal Witness Protection Program for almost three years, she still thought of herself as Sadie Malone. Sometimes the past latched onto her soul and yanked her down to the depths of grief like a meteor plummeting to earth. Today would have been her husband's thirty-seventh birthday. She closed her eyes. The faces of Aaron, and Hannah, her four-year-old daughter, floated in and out of a gray mist. Gone. They were both gone.

A shiver took control of Sadie's body as ice crystals formed in her heart.

She would not succumb to despair.

Clenching her jaw, she hunted in the closet for a

new bulb and installed it. Light cascaded as she glared in the bathroom mirror, chest heaving, and the corners of her mouth pointing south. The hall clock chimed the hour. Nine o'clock. Sadie squared her shoulders and opened her cosmetic bag. No matter her emotional state, she needed to leave soon.

Miles Griffin, her local WITSEC contact, had found her the job and would be disappointed if she got fired. Dabbing on makeup, she paid special attention to her red-rimmed eyes. Couldn't have curious co-workers bugging her with questions.

Sadie brushed her hair and arranged the short blonde curls to cover the dark roots. Time to schedule an appointment with Yolanda, but it would have to wait until her next day off. Dyeing her hair took time and money, which she sacrificed without complaint to keep her whereabouts secret.

Satisfied with the makeup's camouflage, Sadie headed to the kitchen for her salad sack lunch. She'd much prefer to eat a burger and fries, but patted her flat stomach and closed the refrigerator. No way would she gain back the weight she'd lost since being in WITSEC. Dressed for work in blue jeans, aqua T-shirt, and sneakers, she slid the nonprescription glasses on her nose and glanced in the hall mirror. The wire-rimmed frames changed her appearance. She sure didn't look like Sadie Malone anymore.

When she stepped out of her corner, ground-floor apartment, she scanned the area for loitering strangers or anyone out of the ordinary. The whine of a power mower filled the air with the sweet smell of cut grass. Mrs. Gaffney watered plants by her front door; Lloyd Kaiser tinkered with his bicycle in front of his apartment, three doors down; Jodie Powers walked her pug. All familiar, all OK.

With a satisfied nod, Sadie took the sidewalk to the parking area and climbed into her white mid-sized sedan. The economical, inconspicuous vehicle matched her circumstances. In it, she could be as invisible as possible. At times, she missed her SUV, but with no little girl to buckle into a carseat and no husband to laugh and talk with, the smaller vehicle suited her needs.

As she drove to Rhodes DIY Headquarters, a local home improvement store, she fingered her nametag. Debra Johnson wasn't the only name change she'd had. Right after the trial in Los Angeles, still grieving for Aaron and Hannah, she'd been whisked to Seattle, known there as Sadie Mason.

She parked in the employee lot and glanced at her short nails as she removed the key from the ignition. At least in Seattle she had an office job. But her identity there had been compromised. Now, here in Austin, Texas, she worked at Rhodes in the garden center. Dirt under her nails, rough hands, aching back—nothing like her original job in technology. Computer expertise led to her placement in WITSEC. That meant no jobs in the computer industry for her ever again.

At least she had friends at Rhodes. She took a deep breath of the crisp morning air, still earthy from the overnight rain, and entered the store. Once in the break room, apron on, Sadie clocked in. Several people milled about.

"Hi, Debra. How was your weekend?"

Used to the name, she turned. "Hey, April. Great. It was nice to have two days off. How's Victor?"

"So-so. He took me to meet his parents yesterday. Then he asked me to move in with him, but I told him no." April, in her mid-twenties, a decade younger than Sadie, closed her locker and tied the apron around her slender waist. "I told Victor what your pastor said about marriage."

April still referred to Reece Patterson as Sadie's pastor, although she'd attended Hillcrest Church for six months. Sadie had only been going there a few months longer. Her church activities had ceased two and a half years ago when her family died. Attendance now wavered between enthusiastic and perfunctory, a result of guilt and a gnawing vacuum where her soul used to be.

"Good for you. Considering marriage is a serious commitment." *Stop, Sadie. Don't get involved in a discussion about marriage and family.* She closed the locker before adjusting the fake glasses. "Are you ready to go?"

With a nod, April held the door for Sadie, and they left the room together.

"Have you met the new guy? Ooh, *muy caliente.*" April fanned her face. "If I didn't have my Victor, I'd set my sights on him."

"No, I haven't seen this new, hot guy." After all that had happened, meeting men, good-looking or otherwise, was not high on Sadie's priority list. Since the car accident that killed Aaron and Hannah, she had little interest in a romantic life. Her routine consisted of work, developing a few friendships, and most important, staying safe.

A jab in the ribs brought her back to the wide store aisles. "There he is, Debra. Over there." April pointed to a group of men examining a stack of cedar fence posts.

To appease her, Sadie asked, "Which one? I

recognize Oscar and Greg."

"He's the one in the blue shirt."

The men concluded their discussion and the new guy turned, heading down the aisle.

Eyes on the approaching figure, Sadie had to agree with April. *Muy caliente,* indeed. About average height, thick black hair—a stray curl flopped on his forehead—and an athletic body. He beamed a hundred watt smile at April. "Hi." His deep voice complemented his physical appearance.

Before April could respond, her name echoed through the store. Paged by the appliance department, she shoved Sadie towards the new guy. "Got to go. Meet my friend."

Sadie frowned at April's retreating figure.

The man turned to Sadie. A dimple in one cheek enhanced his rugged face. "Hi, April's friend. I'm Sam." He extended his hand.

His name ricocheted through her heart. Automatically, she shook hands and mumbled, "I'm Debra."

Eyes as blue as a jay bird raked her face. "Nice to meet you. Which department do you work in?"

"Garden. And I'm sorry I can't stay and chat. I have a load of star jasmine waiting for me." She sent him a plastic smile she was sure never touched her eyes and hurried away.

Sam. His name was Sam. A lump of sadness slid down her throat. Because of her initials, her husband's nickname for her had been Sam—Sadie Aretta Malone.

Although the arrival of plants and other merchandise kept Sadie busy, she couldn't shake the recurring waves of melancholy that shadowed her. No matter how much she tried to avoid the new guy, he appeared at every turn, reminding her of happier days. Why did his name have to be Sam? He attempted to strike up conversations, but the early spring rush provided believable excuses for Sadie to escape.

Her ploy worked until lunchtime. She opened the break room door and scanned the crowded area. Oscar munched on popcorn, the charred, nutty aroma announcing he'd burnt it again, and someone had heated a fishy meal in the microwave. Sadie wrinkled her nose.

Where could she sit?

Sam sat alone at a small table wedged beside the counter. A pile of sandwiches spilled out of his lunch box. One foot rested on the single unoccupied chair. With eyebrows raised, he glanced her way. "Hey, Debra. Want to join me?" He set his foot on the floor.

She had no choice. "Sure." With great reluctance, she collected her sack from the refrigerator and sat in the chair he scooted out for her. "Thanks."

Salad bowl open, she mixed in Italian dressing. *Stay away from his eyes.* But she couldn't help it. Their blueness intrigued her. Were they real or did he wear colored contacts?

Focusing on her bowl, she chomped on lettuce, the tangy dressing enlivening her taste buds.

Sam picked up another sandwich and set his elbows on the table. "So, Miss Debra, how long have you worked here?" His dimple appeared again.

Always cautious when questioned, she kept the answer vague and brief. "A year or so."

"And where are you from? I don't hear a Texas twang."

Getting too personal, mister. She took a swig from her water bottle. "I moved around a lot as a kid. Don't claim any one state as home."

"I can appreciate that. My brother and I were raised in foster care, but I was born in Dayton, Ohio."

Thankful her eyes were focused on the last of the salad, Sadie kept her head down. First, his name brought back memories. Now, two more troubling coincidences. She'd been raised by foster families and moved more times than she could remember. And she had been born in Dayton.

She gulped hard to keep from choking on little bits of fear infused in her lunch. "You don't say." Salad bowl snapped closed, she gathered her things together. "Got a few phone calls to make before I return to the garden. Good-bye."

Anyone observing her exit would have thought Freddy Krueger chased her as she ran from the break room. Not knowing what else to do, she punched Miles Griffin's speed dial number on her cell phone.

Griff listened to her concerns about the new guy. "Good instincts, Debra. Glad you called. Find out his last name and any other personal information you can scrounge. I'll do a bit of checking." Talk about a Texas twang. Griff's words drawled out as if he had a limited number and had to make them last all day.

Sadie slowed as she neared the garden center. Sam did not have on a nametag. "I'll see what I can discover."

"In the meantime, young lady, stay cool and keep your eyes open."

"Always do. Thanks, Griff." She slipped her phone into her apron pocket.

Oh, joy. Now she'd have to talk to the new guy again or find another way of snooping for information. And she'd have to call him Sam—he couldn't be the *new guy* forever.

Opportunity came when Sadie clocked out at ten after six and had the break room to herself. Rhodes still used time cards, which were listed alphabetically in the metal holder. After returning hers to its slot, she checked for Sam's. It took a while but she located a card for Sam Boudine.

She tugged her purse and lunch sack from her locker and jotted down Sam's name. As she turned to leave the room, he entered.

"Hey, Debbie. Your shift over?"

The name grated like screeching metal. If she couldn't use her real name, then at least she'd have one she could tolerate. "It's Debra." With her purse in hand, she couldn't deny her intentions. "Yeah, I'm leaving."

"Sorry, Debra. I'm on my way out, too. Hold up, and I'll walk with you."

Every fiber in her objected, but she waited for him to clock out.

On the way to the exit, she fudged on the truth. "April told me your last name. There can't be too many Boudines in Ohio."

"My grandparents were from Louisiana."

While considering other questions she could ask to garner personal information, he continued the conversation and provided a cache.

"I really like Austin. Never lived in Texas, before. Got pink-slipped up north and thought I'd give the south a try."

"So you don't have any family down here?" Now outside, she elongated her stride to keep up with his long legs.

"Nah. It's just little ol' me." His shoulders

drooped, which caught her attention. "Had a wife and little girl."

Antennae now on full alert, Sadie rummaged in her purse for her keys. "What happened?" She expected to hear about a divorce, but his next words stunned her.

"They were killed in a car wreck."

Just like her family. Goosebumps pinpricked her arms. To hide her alarm, she pressed the car remote.

"Allow me." Sam opened her door.

"That's really sad." Sliding into the car, she threw her purse onto the passenger seat.

"Two years ago." Sam lingered by her door. "Want to see a picture?"

With his wallet already out, she had little choice. An attractive brunette holding a dark-haired toddler stared back at her.

Words clogged her throat. She glanced up at him and her heart twisted at his pained expression. Guilt for her earlier rudeness and for talking to him only to collect information needled her conscience. But her heart did more than flutter at his next words. It jerked to a stop.

"I still miss 'em. My baby, Paige, and my wife, Sadie."

2

Bowen switched the cell phone to his left ear and sank into the recliner. "I made contact. Today, in fact."

"Good, good. And what's your impression?" A note of excitement tinged the husky voice on the other end.

"Using your target words got a reaction."

"Like what?"

Bowen gulped a swig of soda before answering. "She flinched when I introduced myself as Sam. And when I told her my dead wife's name was Sadie, she bolted out of the parking lot like a NASCAR driver."

"Interesting. But *is* she Sadie Malone?"

"Can't say for sure. So far she's the most likely candidate I've found, but I've got two more women to check on."

"OK, but stay with Debra a while longer. I'm counting on you, Boudine. I have to find Sadie."

"I will." Bowen opened a manila folder on the side table and removed one of the photographs. "But she doesn't look much like the pictures you gave me."

"How so?"

Bowen squinted at the photograph in his hand. "Debra's kinda slender, has short blonde hair. Even her face. There's something different."

"It's been nearly three years. Could be she had work done. You know, plastic surgery." Bowen traced the outline of the woman's chin. "Maybe."

The client cleared his throat. "I don't mean to tell

you how to run your business, but should you be using your real last name?"

"I needed to get a job. It's much easier with legitimate I.D. If Debra checks me out, she'll find nothing on Sam Boudine. No one here knows my real name's Bowen."

"Sounds like you've made progress. Anything else you need from me?"

"Nope, not right now. I've got a few more tricks in my arsenal. Plan on spending time with little Miss Debra. Should have a definite answer for you soon."

After Bowen ended the call, he retreated to the small enclosed back patio and strapped on his boxing gloves. Each successive jab and thrust at the punching bag suspended from a beam mired him deeper in self-loathing. Although committed to a successful conclusion of this job, he could no longer ignore the guilt pricking at his conscience like an annoying leaky faucet.

Lies…jab…lies…thump. His cover story consisted of nothing but lies. He displayed a wallet photograph of an unknown woman and child to Debra—a fictitious wife and daughter. What kind of man did that? And he'd witnessed the blood drain from her face by mentioning the name Sadie. That hadn't been fun. Maybe the reason for her sudden departure had been legitimate, or maybe he simply came across as a little creepy.

Jab…one last upper cut before Bowen stilled the bag. "Doggone it. Wish there was another way." He tore off the gloves, threw them on the floor, and glanced around his makeshift gym. Bringing the worn punching bag with him when he'd left Los Angeles a month ago had been an afterthought. At least this furnished apartment had a place for it, and he needed the exertion more than ever.

A quick shower, then he dressed in blue jeans and gray T-shirt, and drove to Jerry's Café. He'd scouted the neighborhood for days and knew Debra's favorite haunts. Although she often ate at Jerry's, part of him hoped she wouldn't show up tonight. At this early stage of the hunt he usually orchestrated one encounter a day.

The waitress brought a glass of iced tea.

Bowen added sugar and stirred his drink before sliding a notebook from his leather case. He checked off trigger words the client had given him and found several he hadn't tried on Debra yet. He'd have to work them into their next conversation. Tomorrow. A gulp of cold tea slid down his throat. He smacked his lips as he set the glass on the table. Good thing he had electrical and woodworking experience. Having a job at the same place Debra worked sure made his investigation easier.

Next, he took out the folders of the other two candidates. The first, Mary Wolfe, lived across the street from Debra. The more he studied her photographs, the more he was convinced she couldn't be Sadie Malone. Something about her overall body build didn't match.

With the last folder open on the table, he examined a photo of Sandra Miller. Bowen knew people placed in WITSEC were usually given names with the same initials as their original name. That made Sandra a good possibility, plus she matched the physical characteristics—taller than average, with a little extra weight, long dark hair, oval facial structure. If Debra proved not to be Sadie Malone, he'd pursue Sandra next. He closed the folder. Debra Johnson. Mary Wolfe. Sandra Miller. The only one with Sadie's initials was Sandra. That meant if either Debra or Mary were in WITSEC, Austin was not their first relocation. That knowledge generated another set of questions he'd direct Debra's way at their next meeting.

Information given by the client placed Sadie living in an apartment on Monterey Oaks Boulevard in a large city in Texas. The client refused to reveal his sources, but for now Bowen accepted his position. The accuracy of the information mattered most. Bowen had already spent two weeks in Dallas chasing down leads, but the woman bearing a resemblance to Sadie in an apartment complex on Monterey Oaks turned out to be on the Dallas police force. He figured no one in WITSEC would be allowed to work in law enforcement.

The waitress set a plate of pork chops swimming in cream gravy, a baked potato, and mixed vegetables on the table. "Will there be anything else, sir?"

"Nope. This'll do for now. But I will take more tea when you have a chance. Thanks."

The waitress moved to the next booth as Bowen mixed sour cream into the steaming, fluffy potato. His closed folders lay on the table near his glass, but it wasn't Mary or Sandra who occupied his thoughts. A blonde, brown-eyed co-worker's face kept intruding.

Bowen took a bite of pork chop smothered in gravy. He had to keep the association with his target on a professional level. But after meeting Debra, he struggled not to think of her personally, which could be dangerous.

With tea glass in hand, he decided to turn up the charm level at their next meeting—for the sake of the job, of course. Shifting on the seat, he shook his head. He'd have to remember his assignment and forget about her pretty face—if possible.

His meal finished, Bowen gathered the folders, slid them in the leather case and zipped it closed. He left a tip on the table and paid for his meal at the counter. Behind him, a commotion at the entrance sent twitches to his stomach muscles and his breath quickened, as he separated Debra's voice from others. Should he acknowledge her presence or slip out unnoticed?

Oscar Santos made the decision for him by slapping him on the shoulder. "Hey, Sam. Want to join us?"

Sam? His cover name, of course. Bowen turned and recognized several people from Rhodes. "I've eaten already."

Debra paled and averted her eyes as she stepped behind April.

"We're here for pie and coffee." Oscar slugged Bowen on the arm. "Come on. We'll make room for one more."

Bowen could change his evening plans for an opportunity like this. "Guess there's always room for pie." He tucked the case under his arm and followed Oscar.

The waitress directed the group of six to a large semi-circular booth. Debra shadowed April, eyes downcast. The group's general camaraderie covered Bowen's intense observation and analysis. Debra, seated between April and Oscar, acted as if she'd never met him before. Bowen figured he had a long way to go to gain her trust. Maybe he shouldn't have mentioned his fictional dead wife so early in their acquaintance.

After coffee mugs were filled and assorted pie slices served, Bowen kept a stealthy eye on Debra while he chatted with Victor, April's boyfriend.

Greg shrugged out of his jacket and draped it in his lap.

Giggling, April pointed to his blue T-shirt. "Why do you have that silly horse on your shirt?"

With a pained expression, Greg clutched his shirt over the faded white outline of the animal. "It's not a silly horse. It's a mustang. My high school mascot." He stretched out his pecs and frowned down at the shirt.

April took a sip of coffee. "What high school?"

"Raul Medina in El Paso. The Medina Mustangs. It's an awesome mascot. What's yours?"

"A yellow jacket."

Almost choking on a bite of pecan pie, Oscar sputtered, "A what?"

"A yellow jacket. You know, a wasp." April flapped her arms like wings.

Oscar backed away. "Bzzz, real scary."

"That's nothing, you guys. My mascot was an owl and I nearly killed him one night."

"You're kidding." Greg tapped his fork on the plate. "What happened?"

Victor cleared his throat like he had an earth shattering announcement to make. "I ran into him during the Homecoming football game. Squashed him flat. Poor guy."

No one spoke for a bit while they cackled at Victor's expense.

Then Debra removed her glasses to wipe her eyes and set the frames on top of a menu.

Bowen stared at the print through the lenses—no

magnification. Her glasses were fake.

A jolt like electricity shot through his chest. He glanced away quickly so she wouldn't see his reaction. In his mind, a giant arrow pointed at Debra. Her glasses were part of her disguise. Why else would she camouflage her chocolate eyes with unflattering frames?

Greg elbowed him. "You haven't told us about your mascot. Where'd you go to high school?"

Unable to avoid participating in the discussion any longer, Bowen glanced at Debra across the table and blurted out the first thing that came to mind. "Dayton, Ohio."

Why'd he say that? He gave himself a mental thump when he realized the predicament he'd created. If Debra was Sadie, she'd know he lied. Why didn't he tell the truth about his high school in L.A.? He reeled in his lone excuse—his cover story didn't go back that far. Still, experience should have kicked in.

"What was your mascot?" Oscar asked.

Bowen stirred his coffee and then took a big gulp. When words did exit his mouth, he stammered, "It's so...so long ago, guys."

"Come on." Oscar gave him another thump. "You're not that old."

Bowen racked his brain. What were the odds he'd think of a real mascot for a real school in Dayton? "A cougar." Then to flesh out the lie he added, "Central High Cougars."

Debra's gaze locked on his. Cover story blown. But what she said next surprised his socks off.

Hands cradling her coffee mug, Debra corrected him. "Central High's mascot isn't a cougar. It's a panther."

3

Sadie couldn't believe she'd fallen for Sam's trick. Did he deliberately choose the wrong mascot or was he flying by the seat of his well-fitting pants?

Once safe inside her apartment, she lingered in the shower and tried to wash away the slip of her tongue. It had been a long time since she'd accidentally divulged details of her previous life. Why to Sam? Obviously he wasn't who he claimed to be. Although he'd covered his goof by saying he remembered the mascot as a cat of some kind. Still, his answer gave her further proof of his brand of truthfulness. She needed to maintain her guard around him.

At work the next day, Sadie kept busy in her department, surrounded by sweet scents from young spring flowers and primordial whiffs of damp earth. She hadn't heard back from Griff since supplying him with the new guy's last name, so she made a point of sitting with Sam at lunchtime.

Swallowing a bite of pasta, she studied him. In another blue shirt, his eyes mirrored the early morning sky. "You said you worked up north. Which state?"

"Indiana. Ever been there?"

She shook her head and stabbed a piece of chicken onto her fork. "What kind of work did you do?"

With his last meat filled sandwich in hand, Sam took a bite and chewed. "Construction." He drained his soda and then squeezed the can, collapsing the middle. "Where did you live before moving to

Austin?"

One more lie wouldn't hurt. "Miami." That was far enough away from Seattle.

And so the questions continued. By the end of the break, she hadn't learned much and had been extra cautious about what she revealed. If only her traitor heart would ignore his dimple, his eyes, his charm.

Immersed in purple verbena and blue plumbago, her cell phone rang. Caller I.D. indicated Griff. "What did you find out?" she asked.

"First off, I couldn't get anything on a Sam Boudine in Ohio. Are you sure that's the right name? Without a Social Security number or driver's license information there's not a whole lot I can do." Griff's slow drawl filled her ears.

"That's the name on his time card, but I'll try to get something else on him. Even though he was raised in the foster system, kids usually keep their family name. But I think he's lying about his background." She related the mascot incident from the previous evening, and Griff said he'd investigate further. Sadie terminated the call and concentrated on the gold lantana display.

The professionally landscaped yard from her home in Los Angeles flashed in her memory. Undulating rolls of nostalgia crashed over her, crushing her already weary soul and sapping her energy. All this business of keeping her guard up around Sam hurled her back to the past and made her stomach churn.

Julian Geis, the floor manager, found her sitting on bags of river rock with her chin resting in her hands.

His brow furrowed. "What's up, Debra?"

Embarrassed to be caught slacking, she jumped to

her feet and brushed dust off her blue jeans. A deep gulp of air helped ease the band squeezing her heart. "Sorry, I was taking a breather."

"No problem. I know you give a hundred percent every day. And that's what I want to talk to you about. Come to my office before you clock out today."

"I get off at three."

"See you then." Julian plucked a couple of dead leaves off a potted honeysuckle before departing.

One hour to wait. What did he want to discuss? Thinking up possible scenarios added to the volcano in Sadie's gut. Preoccupied with the meeting, Sam slipped from her mind.

Close to three o'clock, she knocked on Julian's door. He told her to enter, smiling from behind his desk.

He motioned towards a chair and opened a brown folder. "Have a seat, Debra. I see in your record you've been with us for a year. You get consistently good reviews. Why haven't you applied for a supervisory position?"

Of all the questions she'd considered he may ask, this one never made it to her list. For the moment, she couldn't speak. How could she answer truthfully? She wanted to stay under the radar with as little added responsibility as possible. Sadie wiped sweaty palms on her thighs. "I guess I don't think of myself in that role."

"I want you to apply. The next round of promotions is set for the middle of next month. That'll give you four weeks. OK?"

Refusing at this point would put her in a bad light, but she'd have to think long and hard about a promotion. "All right." She shifted uneasily. "Is that it?"

"One more thing. Tomorrow when you arrive, please set up a display close to the main entrance. You know, something colorful and eye-catching."

"Like the one I did last year?"

He nodded. "That's settled then. Thanks for stopping by."

Headed to the break room, she mulled over Julian's suggestion. Would a promotion be so bad? It would mean more money and more predictable shifts. Naturally, the money would be helpful, but she liked the odd shifts she worked. It gave her security knowing her comings and goings varied from day to day. Maybe a chat with Griff would help make up her mind.

On the trip home, she stopped at a grocery store and purchased items for the week. Since Griff had given her no information on Sam, she planned to spend the evening at an Internet café. She owned a laptop but had no Internet access. If family members of the man her testimony sent to prison ever found her, it wouldn't be because she left a cyber trail.

Refreshed from her shower, Sadie slipped into a sweat suit. The mid-March evenings still held a chill. Her meal of salad and mesquite flavored chicken took minutes to prepare. Although delicious, she left half of it uneaten, and drove to a café about ten miles away where she settled at a computer in the corner. Knowing Griff must have searched the usual places for information on Sam, she used her research skills to check sites with accessible backdoors. Hour after hour, she explored databases.

When she left the café, she had proof Sam Boudine was a liar. He'd never been married; no record existed of an accident in which Paige and Sadie Boudine died, and he hadn't graduated from Central High.

Although excited at the results of her research, a twinge of disappointment accompanied her home. The faint romantic stirrings Sam's physical appearance generated had been squelched. Too bad. She relegated him to a dark corner of her mind and then spent a restless night weighing the pros and cons of maintaining their friendship. Her rationale, however skewed, included the fact he lied about his past, but that didn't mean he came to Austin for the purpose of finding her. After all, she lied about her past all the time.

Early the next day at Rhodes, still groggy from lack of sleep, Sadie selected decorative pavers, bags of moss, and a variety of potted plants and flowers. With the dolly loaded, she proceeded to the main entrance.

Pavers arranged in various heights, daylilies, Mexican Heather, coreopsis, and tropical greenery strategically placed, moss covering the bare spots— finally the display met her expectations. Sadie gathered all her supplies and lugged the dolly towards the garden center.

Halfway there with clipboard in hand, April stopped her. "Julian wants me to update the list of employees' first aid skills. Check this out and initial what's appropriate for you."

Sadie took the pen and clipboard from April and scanned the page. She initialed next to care of minor burns, bleeding control, treatment for shock, CPR, Heimlich, and then hesitated. Infant CPR and Heimlich were the last items. No one had marked them yet. After a minor battle with her conscience, she initialed next to both and then handed the board back to April.

With an arm draped on Sadie's shoulders, April whistled. "Hey, girl, why do you know all this stuff for babies?"

How could she explain her knowledge of the infant Heimlich maneuver? The truth. "It's required for my volunteer work."

"No kidding. They teach you how to do that? Great. Got to go, *chica*. See you at lunch."

April disappeared down the next aisle, and Sadie turned to find Sam standing behind her. His eyes held a question, and she dreaded what he might ask. With her head down, she clung to the handle of the dolly.

"So, Miss Debra, you're full of surprises. Where do you volunteer?" Sam helped her steer the dolly towards the garden center.

She'd not shared her volunteer work with many co-workers. This would be one less thing to lie about. "I volunteer at the Travis County Children's Shelter. CPR proficiency is a requirement." Telling the truth felt good.

"Oh." His eyebrows shot up. "The children's shelter. That's interesting."

By now they'd entered the outdoor garden area, and she expected Sam to return to the lumber department, but he lingered.

"I'd like to volunteer. Do they need more help?"

His question sent her mind reeling.

"I suppose. They're always looking for people, but they do a background check." Did Sam blanch? "Come to think of it. They're doing renovations and could use your carpentry skills." Had she encouraged him to volunteer when she should have treated him like a leper? But if he passed the background check her suspicions of him would fade and she could relax. Her face heated as blood rushed up her neck when she realized she wanted him to volunteer.

He adjusted his apron ties. "Sounds like a plan. Whom should I contact?"

Sadie recited Carmen Rios's number and lifted a half-full bag of potting soil to hide her flaming cheeks.

"Here. Let me." Without hesitation, he took the bag from her and deposited it in the corner where she indicated.

She couldn't help but notice how the muscles of his arms rippled under his short-sleeved, tan T-shirt. His chivalry intensified her blush. Her ogling his arms hadn't helped either. "Thanks, I can get the rest."

"No problem. You sound like my Nana. She never let me help her either." He dusted his hands off on his pants, dug in his pocket for a pen, and wrote the shelter's phone number on his palm.

"Nana? I thought you were raised by foster families?" Sadie gathered her tools and returned them to the shelf.

He propped against the shelving unit and lowered his gaze. "Right. My brother and I lived with Nana until she passed away. Then the state took over."

Sam's chatting provided her with more information about his background, but could any of it be true? Although her heart ached for the lost little boy, she figured a little more probing couldn't hurt.

"You have a brother?"

"Yeah. Just the two of us. I'm the youngest. How about you? Do you have any brothers?"

A cold wave hit her, dousing the flush. She hadn't thought of Aaron's brother for months. He was the closest person she—Sadie—ever had to a brother. Cal Malone had been the perfect brother-in-law, but Debra

Johnson had no one.

"No. I don't have any family." She grabbed the handle of the empty dolly and focused on its rusty, scraped surface. "Thanks for the help. I need to get back to work."

With the dolly rumbling in front of her, she left Sam standing in the corner. She vowed to stay away from him. Every question he asked catapulted her into the past. True, she had to refresh her CPR skills to volunteer at the shelter, but she already knew how to do the infant Heimlich. She and Aaron had taken CPR lessons before Hannah's birth.

Hot tears pooled. But these skills couldn't save her precious child the day Aaron's car slithered off the bridge into the dark waters of the Santa Ana River.

4

Hairspray fumes and the fragrance of a bouquet of floral shampoos filled the Hair To Dye For Beauty Shop. While Sadie sat in the hot pink vinyl chair, a black rayon cloak covering all but her head, Yolanda's incessant chatter bombarded her. The petite, olive-skinned beauty shop operator had already touched up Sadie's dark roots and now trimmed her unruly curls.

The salon, around the corner from Sadie's apartment, had been one of her first stops after moving to Texas. At her initial appointment, Yolanda had chopped off her dark wavy locks. The resulting curls still surprised Sadie. She guessed the drier California climate and the weight of her hair had held them in check before.

Yolanda fluffed curls with her fingers. "There you go, honey. All set for another six weeks."

"Thanks." Sadie tilted her head to examine the curls in the large mirror above Yolanda's workstation. "You have magic fingers, Yolie."

She paid the receptionist and headed home. Plans for the rest of her day off included laundry, dusting—which she hated—and relaxing with a novel she bought last week at the book exchange.

Three washers were already occupied in the overheated and musty laundry room. Sadie piled her sorted clothes into the other two machines. When the water trickled into each one, she gathered detergent, fabric softener, and her basket, and sauntered towards her apartment. She once made the mistake of leaving her basket on the machine, only to have it disappear. Now she lugged her supplies back and forth.

Mrs. Gaffney, her neighbor, stuck her head out and called as Sadie approached her door. "Debra, dear, I need to talk to you. Can you come inside a minute?"

"Of course." She set the laundry basket by a stack of flattened cardboard boxes on Louise's living room floor. "What's up?"

Mrs. Gaffney motioned to the sofa while she sat in a plush maroon armchair rocker. "Sit, please."

Sadie sank into the chintz-covered cushions.

Intertwining her gnarled fingers, Mrs. Gaffney rocked back and forth. "Remember I told you my kids in Dallas want me closer?"

"Uh-huh."

"I'll be moving soon. My daughter bought a house with separate quarters for me." Her voice wavered and she hiked a bony shoulder. "I guess her heart's in the right place, but…"

"I'll be sorry to see you leave." They'd been neighbors for a year, and she'd mothered Sadie in many ways. "But I'm sure your grandchildren will love having you close by."

"I know. I know." Her gaze roamed the room. "I'll miss this place and my independence. Bonnie will hover and before I know it, she'll take my car keys away."

"Louise, she won't do that." But Sadie had met her daughter once and could sympathize with Mrs. Gaffney's apprehension. "You have many active years ahead of you. Show Bonnie how well you can manage."

Louise slumped in the chair as a tear channeled

26

down the wrinkles on her cheek. "You're right." She dabbed the moisture with a lace-edged handkerchief. "I should be grateful I have family who care about me."

Although her mention of family dampened Sadie's mood, she forced enthusiasm into her words. "You'll do fine."

"I suppose."

"When will you be leaving?"

Expelling a sigh, Louise tucked the handkerchief into her pocket. "Wednesday. Bonnie's hired a packing company. A young couple will take over my lease."

"Wow. That's quick."

"I know. Bonnie and Henry settled the house deal sooner than expected. I thought I'd have problems with the lease, but Cathy said a couple recently inquired about renting."

Cathy, the efficient apartment manager, no doubt jumped at the chance to raise the rent.

A dark cloud appeared in Sadie's mind. "I can't believe it." New neighbors meant admitting more people into her life. "Have you met the couple?"

Louise picked up a slip of paper from the coffee table. "Yes. They came by yesterday afternoon." She glanced at the paper. "Janelle and Pete Williams. And they have the cutest little boy, Zack. About eighteen months old. Cathy agreed they could move in the weekend after I leave."

"Interesting." A myriad of thoughts invaded Sadie's brain.

Mrs. Gaffney decided to leave and immediately a couple showed up to take over her lease. Why here? Why not the unit on the other side of the pool where two apartments stood empty? Why not the apartment complex across the street where the vacancy sign flashed every day?

"Are you all right, dear? You've gone a little pale."

Sadie tried to dislodge the doubts. "Yes, I'm fine. It must be the thought of losing you." She cleared her throat and stood. "Do you need any help? I'm off work today."

"No, thanks, dear. I'm packing my personal items. Then I have to organize a bit so when the movers come next week everything will be ready for them."

"Come and say good-bye before you leave." Sadie picked up the laundry basket.

"I will."

The thought of losing Louise bothered her, but knowing people were ready to move in concerned her more. Should she contact Griff or wait until she'd met the Williams family? Sadie decided to wait and give her paranoia a rest.

❧❧

Friday and Saturday zoomed by with customers scouring Sadie's department for items to spruce up their awakening gardens. Although still early in March, the warming temperature inspired amateur landscapers by the droves.

She had little contact with Sam. In her heart, she knew it best that way, but she couldn't help searching for his dark curls or listening for his deep voice.

The Sunday morning service at Hillcrest Church started at nine o'clock. She could attend and still make her afternoon shift at Rhodes.

Slacks and blue jeans comprised the bulk of her wardrobe, but today she picked out a pink swirly dress, a deeper pink sweater draped over her shoulders, and wore high heeled black sandals. After parking, she stepped onto the graveled lot and stumbled over a small rock.

A warm hand grasped her elbow. "Hey, watch out."

Her knees buckled. Not from the near fall, but from hearing Sam's voice.

"Thanks. What are you doing here?" Her gaze traveled over his striped tan shirt and khakis. She freed her arm and focused instead on where to place her feet as she made her way to the sidewalk leading around the stone building.

"Hi, to you, too. I'm here to worship. Is that all right with you?" The warmth in Sam's words diluted their sting.

"Yes. I'm sorry. Your presence surprised me. That's all."

He opened the heavy wooden door and waited while Sadie entered the vestibule in front of him. "April told me she attends here. I thought I'd give it a shot."

"I see." *You're not following me?* "I hope you find what you're looking for." Head lowered, she elbowed her way down the aisle to her favorite pew, five rows from the front. April worked early and wouldn't be joining her today.

When Sadie bowed her head, she shuddered at her rudeness. Here in this special place, how could she be so cold? She should have asked Sam to sit with her, but how could she encourage him to find what he sought when many Sundays she didn't even know why she came? And there was the matter of his lies. She still didn't know who Sam Boudine could be.

People filled the pews around her, and still she kept her head down. Often when she entered the hundred-year-old building, she cringed at her hypocrisy. She had no business coming to worship, because she lied every day, too, but she couldn't stay away. Something drew her most Sunday mornings.

"Dear God," she whispered. "Help me open my heart to You again."

Hymns echoed around her. Words of prayer gnawed at her soul. She and Aaron had operated a puppet ministry in Los Angeles. They wrote and acted out Bible stories for Sunday school classes, for vacation Bible schools, and for inner-city youth groups. They lived for their ministry.

Then the crimes she'd uncovered destroyed everything. Running, hiding. The accident that took Aaron and Hannah. The trial. WITSEC.

In Seattle, she avoided church buildings, and when she moved to Austin, she had no desire to visit either. But one Sunday morning, on what would have been Hannah's sixth birthday, Sadie passed Hillcrest Church on the way to a coffee shop. Words of a favorite hymn soared through the open windows, spilled out onto the sidewalk, and coaxed her in. How she needed light in her soul. She had to enter the building.

She'd attended almost every Sunday since, but some mornings, she sat like a stone in a rock pile, waiting for the Word to penetrate her apathy and ignite the passion that once burned so fiercely.

At the conclusion of the service, without a clue to the sermon topic, she shuffled out of the building with other parishioners.

Reece Patterson shook her hand at the door.

"Good to see you, Debra. How's the job?"

He always asked a specific question, and she gave a general reply. "Fine, thanks. How are the kids?"

"A handful, as usual. See you next week." Reece turned to the couple behind her.

Sadie moved to the shade of a live oak and berated herself. Why did she keep up the pretense? She wasn't a Christian. At least she didn't act like one. Her inner thoughts vanished when someone tapped her arm.

Sam beamed a smile at her. "Hey, why so glum?"

Flippant words pranced on her tongue, but she bit her lip and waited a second for her self-loathing to dissipate. "I'm sorry I was rude earlier. I should have asked you to join me."

"That's OK. I found another visitor and sat with him." Sam glanced over Sadie's shoulder. "There. That guy carrying his jacket over his arm."

Sadie turned, but didn't recognize the man.

"Said his name's Pete Williams. They're moving here next week, and he's scouting for a church."

Sam's words hit her like a ballistic missile. She blinked as the pain between her eyes blurred her vision. Rubber replaced leg muscles and she teetered. She gripped Sam's arm. "Did he say why he came to Hillcrest?"

The church was not exactly in the neighborhood, being a good fifteen miles from the apartment complex.

Sam frowned as he stared at her. "Are you OK?"

How could she share her skepticism with him? She chewed her lip and nodded.

The furrows eased, and he covered her hand with his. "Pete said friends told him about the church. He liked the service and wants to bring his wife and kid next week."

Sadie drew in a quick breath and removed her hand. It sounded plausible, but why did no one comment on the wary hackles she felt sure were poking through the back of her dress? "Gotta go. Good-bye." She turned and fast-stepped away.

Sam kept pace as she scurried down the sidewalk. "Um, can you join me for lunch?"

Surprised by his question, she slowed her pace a tad. "Sorry, I can't. Have to be at Rhodes in an hour."

"I have to be there at one. Maybe another time." He doffed an imaginary hat and then crossed the parking lot and climbed into his cream-colored pickup.

Her emotions in turmoil, Sadie staggered when she was tapped on the shoulder again. Behind her stood Grace and Tyrell Evans, Sylvia Guerra, and Kyle Nelson. The group, known as a dynamic foursome, inspired many of the innovative programs at Hillcrest.

Grace, her dark eyes sparkling, slid her arm through her husband's. "Hey Debra. We have a question. Can you sew?"

They all seemed to be waiting for her answer. Sadie pushed her glasses up on her nose and worded her answer with care. "I've handled a needle and thread before. Why?"

Kyle, the newest member of the group, adjusted the strap of his ever-present fancy camera. "You know our attendance has been climbing, and the number of children coming for classes is growing."

She didn't know, but nodded.

"We want to start a ministry for kids and need a couple of extra helpers." Kyle gestured to include the others. "We're aware that you volunteer at the children's shelter, and we've seen your interest in the programs the youngsters perform during services. And Reece told us you're good with words. Are you game?"

How had her editing the pastor's book become public knowledge? "What kind of ministry?"

Sylvia took a step forward. "A puppet ministry."

Blood deserted Sadie's brain. Air fought its way into her lungs. Sylvia's words roared in Sadie's ears but made no sense. She closed her eyes and wished she could disappear.

"Debra," Sylvia patted her arm. "Is everything all right?"

Forcing her shoulders to relax, Sadie exhaled. "I didn't eat breakfast this morning. I think it must be low blood sugar."

Sylvia seemed to accept the excuse and continued. "I've researched this puppet business and found a great website. Hands for Hannah."

Colored spots flashed before Sadie's eyes. Old wounds in her heart burst open. She and Aaron had helped develop the website. She blinked to dig herself out of the past.

Tyrell's voice helped. "And we're ready to start. Want to join us?"

Of all the programs she could participate in, a puppet ministry suited her skills the best. But could she overcome the precious memories and move forward? Was this the avenue God intended to use to awaken her spirit and generate the healing process? Pros and cons fought for supremacy in her addled brain. Why not do something worthwhile and get involved?

Sadie allowed a genuine smile to break. "OK. I'm in."

"Way to go, Debra," Sylvia said.

In unison, Grace and Tyrell let out a chorus of whoops, causing a blush to warm Sadie's cheeks.

Kyle grabbed his camera strap. His well-groomed sandy mustache twitched as he spoke. "So glad you agreed to be part of this venture. I'll walk you to your car and give you details of our plans." He took Debra's arm, leading her through the parking lot.

"I could see your hesitation. But don't worry. Sylvia's got a handle on things. That website is fantastic. You should check it out."

"I will." She had no intention of going anywhere near it.

When they arrived at her car, she punched the remote.

Kyle opened her door. "Our first meeting is this evening at seven. At my house. Can you make it?"

Her shift ended at seven. "I'll be a bit late."

"No problem."

Debra slid into the car and attempted to pull the door shut, but Kyle stepped closer and leaned towards her until his breath fanned her hair.

He held out a black business card with gold lettering. "Here's my address."

She grasped it, and Kyle held on for a couple of seconds before letting go. Odd. "Thanks. See you later."

Debra expected him to back away, but he straightened and said, "Interesting name for a website."

His slight delay confused her. Kyle had been friendly over the past few months, but his behavior now seemed strange.

"What name?"

"Hands for Hannah?"

After swallowing the cold lump in her throat, she shrugged.

His eyes stayed glued to her face. "Wonder who Hannah was?"

5

Bowen shook his head as he slid his time card into its slot. He'd been at Rhodes a week already. How time flew when he lived undercover. A large contract order awaited him. He adjusted his navy blue apron and trekked through the store to the outdoor lumberyard. Stacks of oak, pine, and cedar filled the air with remnants of their essence. Breathing deeply, Bowen flew back to childhood days when he'd helped his dad craft custom furniture.

The *beep-beep* of a forklift backing up wiped his memory slate clean. After strapping on his safety goggles, he measured and sawed two-by-fours and six-by-fours, mitered corners, and beveled edges until sawdust piled at his feet. But he couldn't keep his thoughts off Pastor Patterson's sermon. Bowen had visited Hillcrest Church because Debra attended services there. He had planned on quizzing people who knew her. But he hadn't planned on the pastor's words touching his heart.

The lesson from the book of Luke about a man named Zacchaeus clawed at his conscience. Patterson's exposition reminded him of his mother. He could hear her singing a chorus about Zacchaeus, a little man, climbing up a sycamore tree to see Jesus. The tune thumped over and over in his head. His mother had taken Bowen and his sister, Charlotte, to church when they were kids. On the way home, she would review the sermon and sing choruses. Her Christianity shone through her everyday life. What would she think of his lifestyle now?

At the flip of the switch, the saw stopped, and he removed his safety glasses. The last of the order lay stacked behind him, but he needed a break. He swung his arms back and forth to relieve the knot between his shoulder blades and then moved his head side to side and rubbed his neck.

Greg hauled a cart loaded with sheets of particleboard and stopped by the workbench. "How's it going?"

Bowen hiked one shoulder. "OK, I guess. And you?"

"Haven't slowed down all day. And the orders keep coming. I'd better deliver this load before I'm paged again. See ya."

As Greg maneuvered the cart, Bowen slapped sawdust off his apron and blue jeans. *I'm not OK. Not really.* His job—his real job—required him to lie, so why did words from a man behind a pulpit affect him so much?

In his real life he was a good person. A caring son and brother, an honest worker. He snapped the safety glasses on and picked up another length of wood. So why couldn't he focus on finding Sadie Malone?

The saw whined, and Bowen slid the wood in place. "I won't go back again. I can find out all I need without going to church." Smothered by the buzz of the saw, no one heard his words, but with the sentiment expressed, the tight band across his chest relaxed.

After the order had been cut, stacked, and labeled, Bowen headed to the break room. With any luck, Debra would be there, too. But she never showed. He ate his sandwiches in record time and then hurried to the garden center. Debra worked one of the registers where customers five deep waited in line. No chance to talk to her, so he leaned against a display of paving stones and watched her instead.

Frown lines creased her brow even when she offered each customer a smile. What troubled her? When the last customer paid for his bags of potting soil and flats of yellow flowers, Bowen sidled over and stood by her counter.

"Busy day, huh?"

Debra's head jerked up with the frown still etched on her forehead. "It's been nonstop ever since I clocked in."

"Had lunch yet?"

"I took my break about an hour ago."

Bowen studied her face. "What's up?"

Her shoulders slumped, and a heavy sigh escaped. With a quick scan of the area, she locked her register and glanced towards the woman at the other station. "Glenna. I'm closing for now. I need to check on supplies in back. Call me if you get busy." With a nod from Glenna, Debra motioned for Bowen to follow her.

They skirted rows of plants and headed down the last aisle where Debra straightened bags of potting soil and mulch.

Bowen replaced a fifty-pound bag of soil on the stack. "So, you gonna tell me what's bugging you?"

"It's nothing big." Debra slowed and shoved her hands in her apron pocket. "Something happened at church today after you left."

He raised his hand to touch her shoulder but decided against it at the last minute. He wanted her to confide in him without an invasion of her space. "What happened?"

By now, they were in the covered storage area at the back of the store.

Debra sat on a stack of cinder blocks. "Before I tell you, I have a question." She narrowed her eyes and tilted her head.

What now? Bowen sat next to her. "And what is that?"

"I know you didn't graduate from Central High in Dayton. Why did you lie about it?"

He'd been expecting this question and had an elaborate excuse ready but couldn't get through it under her intense scrutiny. Bowing his head, he poked at the sheet of thick plastic covering the blocks. "First off, I'm sorry for lying. But, you see, I'm ashamed of my past. I didn't attend a regular high school. Never graduated."

She shifted her weight and crossed one leg over the other. "Because you were raised in foster care?"

"Kinda. I was a troubled kid. Families passed me around like a stale Christmas fruitcake. Ended up at an alternate school for—" He slapped his knee and stood, keeping his back to her. "The other night when the guys discussed their mascots and pressed me to name mine, I had to come up with something. I couldn't tell them the truth." He sneaked a glance at her. The skepticism had left her gaze; a touch of pity replaced it. Good. He'd chosen the right strategy.

"In fact, if we had a mascot, it wouldn't have been a cute bird or big kitty-cat. It would have been that eternity symbol. You know, forever going nowhere." He hung his head when her movement caught his attention.

She came up behind him and briefly touched his

shoulder. "What do you mean?"

He knew by her soft tone he had her sympathy vote and turned, hands in his apron pockets. "No hope, no future. No one to care what happened to us." Maybe he'd milked it enough. He pulled a hand free and ran it across his brow. "But I moved on. Finally got my GED, attended trade school. Took a few computer courses."

Her gaze raked his face.

"And look at me now. I've done pretty good, even if I say so myself." He lowered his head a fraction. "But again, I'm sorry I lied. When they asked me and with you across the table, Central High was the first thing that came to mind. Will you forgive me?"

She stared at him a moment and then nodded. "Of course."

He thought that was the end of the inquisition, but a puzzled expression crossed her face. She must have another concern.

To forestall her inquiry, he asked, "Are you ready to tell me what happened at church?"

Debra pointed to the far corner of the storage area. "While I'm here I do need to check the outdoor furniture. Come this way. But before I explain my problem, I have to ask. Did you also lie about your wife and daughter?"

He followed her, glad she couldn't see his face. He hadn't prepared an answer for that question. But he improvised. "No. They did die in a car wreck." He almost gagged saying the words.

"Where?" Debra stopped at stacks of tables and chairs and faced him.

He had no time to wonder why she needed to know. "In Mexico." He ignored the jab to his conscience and elaborated on the lie. "We were on vacation in the mountains of northern Mexico." Lowering his voice, he added, "But I don't want to talk about it anymore." He hunched his shoulders and stared at the cracked concrete floor.

Debra moved a step closer. "I'm sorry. I know what it's—" She backed away and cleared her throat. "I have to count these items."

Bowen raised his head. Had she almost admitted to having lost a spouse and child? He kept his gaze on her as she counted the tables and figured he'd played his part well. But his conscience winched under an onslaught of jabs.

When Debra completed her task, she turned and rested against a glass-topped table. She rubbed her temples. "Can you stay a minute longer?"

Bowen glanced at his watch. "Sure."

She folded her arms and took a gulp of air. "I may be imagining a problem with a man who attends Hillcrest." She described her encounter with Kyle, what she knew of him, and ended with his odd behavior at her car.

"Why does that trouble you?"

As if she searched for the right words, Debra's eyes darted back and forth. "His reluctance to leave. The way he...leered at me, like he wanted to ask me on a date or something. And then his question about the..." She pursed her lips and shrugged.

"Question about what?"

"Never mind."

Bowen waited, but she didn't elaborate. "OK, so let's take the possibility of him asking you out. Is that something you want?"

Without hesitation, she said, "Definitely not."

The corners of his mouth twitching, Bowen lowered his head. He liked her reaction. "Sorry, but I had to ask."

"Kyle's fine as a friend, but nothing more."

The wheels in Bowen's brain chugged into action. He struggled to keep the smile from appearing again. "I have an idea, and before you say no, hear me out." He took a step towards Debra. "I liked the service today and want to visit again and get involved." The lies threatened to choke him. "I could join the puppet ministry, too. Maybe help build the set or whatever."

Debra's furrowed brow relaxed. Her eyes glowed as she took a step closer to him.

He focused on her face. "And we, you and I, could pretend to date so Kyle would get the message and leave you alone."

She jerked, and her eyes grew as large as a cartoon character's. Her hands flew to her hips.

Uh-oh. I'm in trouble.

"What did you say?"

He hesitated a moment, gauging her body language. "We could pretend to date."

Debra's eyes narrowed to slits. "How do we pretend something like that?" Her playful tone surprised him.

He took a step backward. "We, uh, we go out for a meal, or we sit together at church."

Debra sauntered closer. "But wouldn't that be dating?" She removed a loose thread from his collar, her fingers lightly brushing his neck.

At her touch, his skin tingled and his chest heaved as if a bolt of lightning struck red-hot into his flesh. Off-key words squeaked out. "I suppose it would."

Resting against the table again, she tilted her head.

"I'm sure the puppet ministry committee could use your help to build the stage."

Bowen had a hard time focusing on her statement. He rubbed his neck. "You can ask them tonight if they need my help."

An impish smile played around her lips. "Why don't you ask them yourself?"

"Huh?"

Debra stood, straightened her apron, and took three steps towards Bowen. "Why don't you come with me tonight and ask how you can help?"

With Debra an arm's length away, Bowen lost control of the situation. How had she turned the tables on him so fast? He planned on asking her for their first date, but she'd gotten the drop on him.

"OK. I'll come." Cogs churned. "We'll call this our first date. What time is the meeting? I'll pick you up."

She turned, shaking her curls, and the peachy smell of her shampoo drifted past. "It's at seven, but I don't get off until then. I'd rather meet you there. The address is in my car." Pointing towards the door, she added, "I've got to get back to work."

Bowen followed her out. "I also get off at seven. I'll meet you in the parking lot and tag along."

With her hands in the back pockets of her jeans, Debra strode ahead. He tried not to focus on her hands as they accentuated her swaying hips.

He almost bumped into her when she stopped suddenly and turned.

"Hey, Sam?" She eased a hand out of her pocket and prodded his chest. "Don't think this pretend dating business is going to lead to any handholding or kissing. Understand?" Without waiting for a reply, Debra sauntered away.

"A guy can hope, can't he?"

Only a customer in the next aisle heard his remark.

$\sim$

Kyle's house nestled in a tree lined suburb north of Hillcrest Church. Bowen and Debra approached the front door.

"Mr. Boudine, remember our arrangement," Debra said over her shoulder and rang the bell.

Bowen lowered his head and breathed in a whiff of her peachy hair. "Whatever you say, Miss Johnson. I'll take my cue from you."

Kyle opened the door, but his expression hardened when he shot a glance at Bowen. He made a quick recovery and welcomed them both inside. "Glad you could make it, Debra, and we can always use another volunteer." He shook Bowen's hand. "Come on in. There's tea and cookies on the table."

Debra picked up two glasses of tea, and then sat close to Bowen on the sofa. "Hi, everyone. This is Sam Boudine, a friend from Rhodes. He's a good carpenter." She then introduced the other people present.

Bowen acknowledged their greetings with a nod, sliding an arm along the sofa behind Debra. She didn't flinch, and he disguised his pleasure by taking a gulp of tea. Her curls brushed his shoulder. She relaxed next to him. How he wanted to draw her closer, but instead, he blew out a puff of air and repeated to himself, "You're playing a part. Stick to the script."

Sylvia, sitting cross-legged on the floor next to a sleeping baby in a carrier, picked up a three ring binder. "You're an answer to prayer, Sam. I downloaded plans for a wooden stage but had no idea who'd make it for us."

He inwardly balked at the prayer part but swallowed the guilt. "I'll see what I can do."

Sylvia flipped to the middle of the binder, opened the rings, and removed a section of papers. "See what you think."

Bowen had to remove his arm from the back of the sofa to accept the pages.

In the armchair next to Bowen, Kyle pointed to the binder. "Sylvia's done a lot of work already. The Hands for Hannah website has been very helpful. Our first order of business is to decide what kind of puppets to use. And do we order them readymade or craft them ourselves?"

While Bowen sorted through the stage plans, Debra's leg muscles tensed beside him. He stole a glance at her face, but she kept her eyes on Sylvia.

Kyle's voice droned on and on about hand puppets, stick puppets—people or animals?

Then Bowen sensed a change in Debra. She scooted forward as if engrossed in the discussion.

Sylvia peeked at her sleeping son. "I think we should use animals. Little ones love animals."

"But older kids would like people puppets," Kyle said.

Grace wagged a finger at the group. "Hold on. If we use people, then we need all skin colors. I want some like me."

Tyrell blew her a kiss. "You mean dark chocolate?"

She pretended to catch his kiss and giggled.

"Wait. Why don't we have both animals and people?" Kyle stood and lifted his empty glass. "I need more tea. I'll be right back."

Debra shook her head. "No. Having different puppets makes extra work for the operators."

At the table, Kyle stopped and turned. "What do you mean?"

Debra addressed the others. "To really engage the kids, each puppet needs to have a distinctive voice and mannerisms. If each operator has several puppets to personalize there's a greater chance for confusion."

The group fixed collective eyes on her.

Bowen reviewed all the information his client had provided on Sadie. A bell jingled in his head. Sadie and her husband were active in some kind of church work. He'd have to check his notes to see if it involved puppets. On alert now, he paid closer attention.

Sipping from a full glass of tea, Kyle returned to his chair. "Go on."

Debra scooted forward and rested her elbows on her knees. "I think we need one set of puppets to tell the stories."

"I agree with Grace." Kyle smoothed his mustache with thumb and forefinger. "But if we use people, how many different skin colors do we use? This could get out of hand."

Sylvia raised her arm like a school kid. "I've got it. We could forget about authentic skin colors. In fact it would be fun to use green, blue, and purple."

Nods of agreement abounded.

"Or we could use Hannah's favorite. Polka dots." Debra's eyes widened, and her hand flew to cover her mouth.

6

Heat rushed to Sadie's face. Everyone focused on her. She wanted to flee but her legs wouldn't cooperate. Instead, she sank into the cushion and shot a peek at Sam. Had she blown her cover?

He focused on the plans in his hands.

Sylvia snapped the binder closed. "Good idea, but how do you know Hannah liked polka dots?"

Please, earth, swallow me. Sadie had to come up with an explanation. And fast. "I...I checked out the website and read how Hannah wanted polka-dotted fabric for the puppets' faces."

"I must have missed that part," said Sylvia. "Where did you find it?"

Sadie hadn't visited the website in three years. And she didn't know if the current operators had changed it. She and Aaron used to have a link that displayed pictures of Hannah surrounded by puppets. Maybe since her death, they'd been removed.

By now Sadie's face no longer burned. "Some link at the top. I can't remember which one."

"It doesn't matter." Kyle took a sip of tea. "I think polka-dotted people will work. Let's vote."

Everyone voted for the polka dots and by the time Kyle exhausted his to-do list, his mantel clock chimed ten.

Sadie carried empty glasses to the kitchen. As she returned to the living room, she slowed when Kyle picked up his sophisticated camera from the side table.

His next words turned her feet to lead.

"Before any one leaves, I want to take a photograph. Come on, people, gather around Grace." Kyle removed the lens cover and fiddled with the dials.

Sylvia dug in her diaper bag for a blue pacifier and popped it into her son's mouth. "But, Kyle, my hair's a mess."

"Doesn't matter. So is mine. I want to document our committee's activities." He held a hand out to Sylvia. "Up you get."

People surrounded Grace in the armchair.

Sadie thought of taking a trip to the bathroom, but Kyle would wait to take the picture. She deliberately stood next to Sam and fingered the trim around the neckline of her T-shirt.

Kyle set the camera on the coffee table, joined the group and said, "One, two, three. Smile everybody."

Sadie turned her head towards Sam's shoulder and raised her hand to cover her profile. The flash caught her movement. Certain the photograph would not show her face, she scampered away from the group and picked up her purse before Kyle could check the camera and demand a re-take. "Sorry, guys, I have to leave. See you next time."

She and Sam were the first to leave. He'd been the perfect, attentive date, and once she overcame her blunder, she had enjoyed his company.

They stopped at her car, and he opened the door. "This has been great. We need to do it again. Soon."

"You mean work with the puppet committee?"

"No. Go on a date."

Sadie glanced at Sam to see if he was kidding. The dimple hovering near his lips confused her. "But this was a pretend date, remember?"

"It didn't feel like one to me. So, what do you say? I'll still take my cue from you about the handholding and kissing part."

A giggle bubbled up and a surge of warmth radiated from her midsection. Maybe it was time to let down the drawbridge of her heart. A teeny bit. Passion had been locked away for so long. Eyes on his face, she slid behind the wheel. "Fine. But we'll take it slowly."

The streetlight accentuated his dimple. "Great. I'll go as slow as you want—within reason." He removed a small card from his wallet. "Here's my cell number."

She took the card on which he had scrawled numbers, and caught a glimpse of the photo of a woman and child in his wallet. Sadie's euphoria subsided. She'd almost forgotten her initial doubts and suspicions. But he'd explained why he lied, and if they dated, she could keep an eye on him.

"Thanks. I'll check my calendar and pencil you in."

Sam returned his wallet to his back pocket. "Hope you can find a spot for me." He closed her door.

After she turned on the ignition, she lowered the window. "Are you working tomorrow?"

He rested his forearm on the opened window. "Yeah. You?"

Sadie glanced at the dark curly hair on his arm and nodded.

"See you then." He straightened and then lowered his head again. "By the way. When did you check out that puppet website?"

When, indeed? They'd come straight to Kyle's from work, and Sam knew employees had no access to personal computers at Rhodes.

Another lie. "At home after church." Sadie dared not look at Sam, so she fussed with the seatbelt.

He patted the roof of her car. "OK, then. Drive carefully. See you tomorrow."

As she drove away, the weight of her deception lay heavy on her soul.

ॐॐ

Louise Gaffney came by the next morning while Sadie consumed her second mug of coffee.

She sat across the small dining table from Sadie, her white hair wrapped around tiny green sponge rollers, her feet engulfed by fluffy mauve slippers. "Heard you up and about, dear, and came to visit."

"How's the packing?"

Before Louise could answer, her cell phone chirped. She slid it out of her housecoat pocket.

While her visitor chatted, Sadie drained her coffee mug, finished off a bowl of granola, and then carried her dishes to the kitchen.

A frown added to the deep wrinkles on Louise's forehead as she ended the call. "Drat. That was Pete Williams. He's right outside and wants another look at the apartment." She patted her rolled hair, blue eyes wide. "I can't let him see me like this."

"I'll meet him while you take the rollers out."

She shuffled to the bathroom and said over her shoulder, "Thank you dear. Tell him I'll be right out."

As Sadie closed her front door, a tall, redheaded man in a dark suit strode across the lawn. He straightened his tie and slowed as he neared the building. Furrows marred his freckled brow for a second.

Sadie moved closer to Mrs. Gaffney's door. "Hi, are you Pete Williams?"

"I've come to see Louise Gaffney."

"She'll be out in a minute. I'm Debra Johnson." She extended her hand, which he clasped in a quick shake. "I believe you plan to move in right away."

"Yes. We've been staying with Janelle's folks in San Antonio and can't wait to get our own place. I started my job here two weeks ago."

Sadie took note of his black leather briefcase.

He glanced at his watch. "I don't have much time, but I need to take measurements. The in-laws bought us a bedroom suite with an enormous headboard and oversized dresser. Need to make sure the pieces can be maneuvered down the hall and into the bedroom."

Louise's apartment had the same floor plan as Sadie's. The short narrow hall and sharp turn into the bedroom could pose a problem. She crossed her arms and gave Pete a reassuring nod. "She won't be long."

Right on cue, Louise joined them, her hair now in soft curls. "Thank you, dear." She took keys from her pocket. "Come on in, Pete."

He seemed to be a nice enough guy, and his reasons for moving so quickly made perfect sense. No need to worry.

Sadie returned to her kitchen and cleaned up. Dishes washed, sack lunch of left-over chicken and salad prepared, she still had an hour before she needed to leave for Rhodes.

Sadie wandered through her small abode, straightening a cushion here, closing a magazine there, and ended up in the bedroom. On the nightstand lay Sam's card with his handwritten phone number. She plopped on the bed and picked up the card. She'd already programmed the number into her cell phone but couldn't throw away this connection to him. It conjured up his face, his voice. But the photograph of his deceased wife and child interrupted her musing.

An elephantine weight plunged her spirit into an arctic lake. Associating with Sam took her on a wild ride of pleasant possibilities to dark reminders of the past.

Sadie jumped to her feet and threw open the closet door. Shoving aside hanging blouses and slacks, she located the small gray door of the apartment's electrical control panel. Her hand shook as she popped it open. She eased off the laminated instruction sheet from inside the door and hesitated.

But she had to see it one more time. The dog-eared picture of her, Aaron, and Hannah slid into her hand. Her darling little girl. Her wonderful husband. The only photograph she had of them. Against orders, she'd secretly kept it. If Griff or anyone from WITSEC knew, they'd destroy it and reprimand her for her foolishness. But she couldn't let it go. It was her one link to the past.

The last time she'd looked at the photo had been about eight months ago. Hannah's birthday. The same day she'd visited Hillcrest Church for the first time. With hands that trembled, Sadie held the photo to her chest for an agonizing moment. Then she planted a kiss on the picture and returned it to its hiding place. She closed the gray door and scooted the hangers back in place across the rod.

Sadie backed out of the closet and tromped to the bathroom to splash cold water on her face. But Mrs. Gaffney's green rollers filled the sink. The sight brought on the giggles, and Sadie collapsed onto the tiled floor.

When the mix of mirth and grief subsided, she scrambled up and examined her face in the mirror. Good thing she had time to repair the damage. While removing mascara streaks, she analyzed her reaction to seeing the photo again. The old haunting pain hadn't paralyzed her this time. Instead of wallowing in self-pity, she'd focused on the good times they'd experienced. If levelheaded Aaron could talk to her now, he'd probably advise her to move on. He wouldn't want her to grieve forever.

Makeup repaired, curls tamed, she gathered the rollers together and found a plastic bag in the kitchen.

After Sadie knocked several times, Louise opened the door. "So sorry, dear. I was on the phone with Bonnie. Come in."

Sadie held up the bag. "I don't have time to visit, I have to get to work. But I brought these back."

"Oh, my rollers. Thanks, dear." She took the bag. "I forgot all about them. Pete kept me busy. He asked a lot of questions about you."

Although Sadie had already stepped away from the door, she stopped at Louise's words. "Really? What kind of questions?"

"Oh, you know, the usual. What sort of neighbor are you? How long have you been here? Stuff like that."

Sounded harmless enough, but Sadie's caution meter kicked into gear. So much for her earlier complacency. She'd have to keep alert around the new neighbors. "See you tomorrow."

Sadie collected her lunch sack, jacket, and purse. With keys in hand, she rounded the corner of her apartment unit, but a movement by the maintenance

Valerie Goree

shed caught her eye. Two men conversed in angry tones. One pointed to the other then threw his arms in the air. Meandering between vehicles, Sadie kept her eyes on the men. They looked familiar. Then she recognized the dark suit—Pete Williams. Who was his companion? Near her car, she punched the remote. The *beep-beep* alerted them, and they both glanced towards her.

In that instant, she recognized the other man. Kyle Nelson from Hillcrest church.

They locked gazes across the parking lot for a few seconds before the two men slipped out of sight behind the shed.

7

The sight of Kyle arguing with her new neighbor stuck with Sadie all the way to work. Were they friends? Did Kyle invite Pete to Hillcrest? Paranoia had free reign in her mind until she parked in Rhodes' employee lot. She told herself to get a grip. Two men arguing—but Kyle's odd behavior the night before and Pete's questions to Mrs. Gaffney hung in the air.

April's knock on Sadie's window yanked her back to reality, and she climbed out of the car.

While they entered the store, April regaled Sadie with Victor's latest request to live together. "But I'm sticking to my principles. I told him if he's serious, then he better start thinking about our future."

Approaching the break room, she drew Sadie aside. "We're going to the South by Southwest Music Festival this weekend. Want to join us? Oscar's coming."

"Sounds like fun. I'll get back to you after I check my work schedule."

By the time they clocked in, Sadie had relegated Kyle and Pete to the back of her mind.

New plant arrivals kept her focused on the job for several hours. On her way to the break room, Oscar waylaid her as she passed through the plumbing section.

He fell in step beside her. "How was your weekend?"

"Good." Remembering Sam's attentiveness from

the previous night sent a mini-quiver to her stomach. "How about you?"

Oscar didn't seem to hear her question. He cleared his throat and focused on the floor. "Um, Debra, I've been wondering. Can you, I mean, would you care to go out for coffee or something?"

Sadie had been expecting this for a while. She'd often caught him watching her with interest or found him included in the group when April invited her places. Like the recent request.

At the end of the isle, she stopped and turned, hoping her smile conveyed sincerity. "Oh, Oscar, I'm sorry. I don't think so." She stuck her hands in her pockets and focused on the collar of his shirt. "You see, there's someone else."

Who would have thought she'd be thankful for Sam's pretend date? She liked Oscar, but her pulse didn't race at his invitation.

"It's the new guy, isn't it? It's Sam." Oscar hit his palm to his forehead. "I knew it. I'm too late."

Agreeing wouldn't be a lie. She and Sam had one date, and he'd hinted he wanted to ask her out again. "I'm sorry, Oscar."

His sad puppy-dog eyes snagged a piece of her heart.

"He's a lucky guy." Oscar loped off around the corner.

Sadie continued to the break room, deep in thought. As she turned down the last aisle, Sam popped up in front of her.

"Hello."

"Hi."

"I hear you were asked out on a date."

Try as she might, she couldn't take her eyes off his

dimple-creased cheek. Or the dark curl that fell across his forehead, or the tiny razor nick marking his firm chin.

Her face tingled, and she self-consciously adjusted her glasses. "How do you know?"

With his hand on her arm, Sam accompanied her to the break room. "I overheard Oscar."

She swatted his hand but said nothing.

"So, Miss Debra, am I the *someone else*?"

Freeing her arm, she ignored his chuckles and entered the room.

৵৵

The evening chill sent a shiver slinking through Sadie.

Sam slipped his arm around her shoulders and escorted her into El Capitán, a Mexican restaurant several blocks from Rhodes. His shift had ended two hours before hers, and he'd gone home to change into brown slacks and a blue shirt.

However, she still wore jeans and a rose pink T-shirt.

At lunch he'd invited her, and she agreed to meet him at the restaurant. They were directed to a table along the mural-covered wall. Once seated, they perused the menus, surrounded by hints of chili and cinnamon.

During the meal, Sadie took the opportunity to pump Sam for information. Although he shared few personal stories, Sadie did learn a little more about him. He loved football, kept in shape by kickboxing and pummeling a punching bag, and knew how to make a girl feel special. She appreciated his attentiveness. This pretend date wasn't so bad after all.

Sam set his knife and fork across his empty plate. "Those enchiladas were real good, but I prefer Calif..."

Sadie wiped her mouth and waited for him to complete his sentences, but he took a gulp of tea and examined the mural. "Prefer what?"

He cleared his throat. "You know, Mexican food differs from state to state."

"I agree, but when were you in California?"

Sam's shoulder muscles looked tense. Why would her question about California affect him so?

"Remember I told you I was raised in foster care. One family I lived with took us on vacation there." He gulped the last of his tea. "So, when do you think the puppet group will want the stage?"

Well done, Sam. He'd answered and changed the subject without blinking. Sadie understood his reluctance to discuss his time in foster care. He must be telling the truth.

"You can ask them on Saturday night. Kyle wants to meet again, and everyone is coming over to my place."

Sylvia had called Sadie as she left Rhodes and she'd reluctantly agreed to host the meeting.

"Sounds like a plan."

When they finished their decaf coffee and chocolate cake, he followed her to her car.

"I had a good time. Thanks, Sam."

He took her hand. Nothing as dramatic as electric sparks traveled up her arm, but the heat from his touch radiated through her. He gazed at her face and slowly lowered his head. A kiss? She wasn't ready.

But he drew her hand to his lips and kissed her fingers. She relaxed and sighed, the soft touch of his lips sending a shiver of pleasure down her spine.

He released her hand and raised his eyebrows, as if he knew the effect his action had caused. "See you tomorrow?"

"I'm working a half day. I'll be in about three." She slid behind the wheel.

Sam gave her a nod and disappeared across the parking lot.

Sadie slumped against the seat and rubbed the hand he'd kissed. Whew. She'd have to lasso her heart and keep a tight rein on it.

On the way home, she fantasized about another date, but by the time she parked, she'd shaken the scenarios away and reminded herself she knew little about Sam.

Although still early, Sadie prepared for bed and snuggled under the covers with her laptop balanced on her knees. In the morning, she'd visit the children's shelter. For each trip, she took along a story she'd written, featuring characters named after children at the center. The kids loved to hear their names. She had a few more pages to compose for tomorrow's visit.

The hours slid by and at midnight, she turned off the light.

Dreams featuring Rhodes' co-workers and long ago foster families peppered her night. She awoke and dressed, disappointed Sam hadn't made his way into her subconscious.

Eager young faces greeted her at the shelter.

Carmen Rios, the director, gave her a list of newcomers so she could include their names in the story.

On the way to the indoor play area, Sadie asked, "Has a Sam Boudine ever called you? He may want to volunteer."

Carmen frowned and shook her head. "Sorry. Name's not familiar."

Interesting. Maybe he changed his mind. Sadie would have to quiz him at their next meeting. Once seated, she wrote the names in gaps she'd purposely left blank and then gathered the kids around her.

They squealed and clapped as she read, and then they wanted the story repeated. After the third rendition, Sadie gave the pages to Carmen and joined the kids in outdoor games.

Close to noon, she hugged each child and then returned home for a salad lunch and a quick visit with Louise.

At Rhodes, time hung heavy on her hands. Dreary, gray skies must have kept shoppers at home since few people visited the garden center. Sadie took the opportunity to pick up a promotion application packet from Julian and tucked it in her locker.

Sam entered the break room, his mood as gloomy as the weather. The nod he gave her served as his greeting. He pounded the bank of lockers with his fist. The metal fixtures rattled like a dragon's loose teeth. "Blast." His back to her, he hung his head.

"Sam?" She took a hesitant step his direction. "What's wrong?"

A mammoth sigh escaped, and he turned. The muscles along his jaw clenched. "I almost got fired because I'm late, but you'll never believe what happened." He paced liked a trapped lion.

Sadie sat at a table and patted the chair next to her. "Come sit. Tell me about it."

He hauled the chair out and sank into it, his posture rigid. "I should have been here hours ago, but I had two flat tires." He thumped the table. "Two."

Sadie flinched at his action but concentrated on his face. "What was wrong with the tires?"

At first, Sam glared at her as if he'd forgotten he had an audience. Then his mouth softened and his eyes focused. "I'm sorry for ranting, but it's so strange. One tire had a nail in it. OK, I can buy that, but the other had been slashed."

"Are you sure?"

"Of course." He rested his elbows on the table and twisted his silver watch band. "Seems someone didn't want me to drive my truck today. I had to wait for the tow truck and buy two tires. Nearly cost me my job."

She touched his forearm where dark hair curled over taut skin. "Did you tell Julian why you were late?"

"Yeah, but since I'm still on probation, he said he would be justified in firing me." He thumped the table again, sending the salt and pepper shakers trembling. "Two tires. I can't believe it."

"But he didn't fire you?"

"No. He gave me a warning and said I should have phoned him, but to tell the truth, I was so mad I didn't think of calling." His shoulders slumped as he rested his forehead in one hand.

Sadie's desire to offer him comfort by wrapping her arms around him almost overtook her common sense. To distance herself from the temptation, she pushed back.

Sam straightened, his lips curled enough to reveal the dimple for a second, and then it disappeared. "I better clock in. Have to make up the hours. I'll be here until closing." After he punched his time card and tied his apron, they left the room together. "I wanted to ask you out again tonight but can't now."

"There's always tomorrow." She couldn't believe she made the suggestion.

"Suits me." Sam flashed his knee-bending smile her way. "I'm off tomorrow. What time should I pick you up?"

At the end of the aisle, she froze. Would it be OK for Sam to know where she lived? After all, he'd be coming with the puppet group on Saturday. "Six thirty. I live at 7523 Monterey Oaks Boulevard. Apartment 117."

"Can't wait."

She shoved her hands in her jeans pockets and took a meandering route to the garden department, hoping the heat in her cheeks would dissipate by the time she had to face Glenna.

Few customers braved the cool evening, and Sadie spent the rest of her shift in the covered storeroom doing inventory. On the way to her car, her cell phone rang. "Hey, Griff, what's up?"

"Where are you?" His familiar twang sounded stressed.

"Leaving Rhodes, heading home. Why?"

"I've got a bit of troubling news."

He's found out something sinister about Sam.

"What is it?" She popped the remote and slid into the car.

"I heard through agency channels that someone has been attempting to access your old financial records."

She locked the door and whispered, "You mean Sadie's records?" Paranoia nibbled at her gut. She glanced around to make sure no one eavesdropped.

"Yes."

"What does that mean? There's nothing there, right?" When she'd entered WITSEC, Cal, Aaron's brother, liquidated their assets, paid debts from the proceeds, and the rest—not much to show for an upper-middle class lifestyle—was funneled to her.

"Right. There's no money, but we left a paper trail to prove to anyone who checked that Sadie Malone was dead."

The damp chill seeped into her bones, and she shivered. Griff's words about Sadie pierced her heart. She wanted to scream, "I'm not dead. I'm here. I'm alive."

Griff's anxious voice penetrated her pain. "Debra?"

"I'm trying to process what you said."

"No need to panic. Your new identity has not been compromised, but we thought you should know."

Oscar passed by her car and waved. Acknowledging his greeting with a nod, Sadie so hoped she wouldn't have to move again, adjust to another new name, new job, new friends. "Is there anything I need to do?"

"Be alert and careful. And if anything or anyone acts suspicious, give me a call."

She decided to tell him about Pete and Janelle Williams' eagerness to move into her apartment complex.

"I'll check them out. Go straight home, and call me when you get there."

"OK." She ended the call and drove out of the parking lot. Her stomach ached as she turned onto the road. Bile pulsated up and down her throat and a tight band constricted her chest.

Breathe.

The drive home wouldn't take long. She relaxed her grip on the steering wheel.

Then headlights on high beam glared in her rearview mirror. They stayed behind her for miles. She turned left. The vehicle turned left. She slowed. It slowed. Panic ate through her like acid.

Debra knew better than driving home and flew past her apartment complex. What to do? Then she remembered a police station a few blocks away.

With a safe destination ahead, she sped up. So did the other car. She screeched to a stop in front of a row of police cars and watched the vehicle glide past—a cream-colored pickup truck.

And the man behind the wheel looked a lot like Sam.

8

Bowen helped a customer calculate how many two-by-fours he needed for a patio roof and then directed him to where he could locate the other supplies on his list.

With fifteen minutes left in his shift, he cleaned up his workstation. The tire incident still rankled. Who would have destroyed two of his tires? Neighborhood kids, or someone who didn't want him to work at Rhodes?

Oscar's face flashed into his mind, but he shook his head. Surely not. He seemed like a decent guy, and when they'd spoken yesterday, his congratulations on dating Debra sounded sincere. Must have been kids.

Bowen clocked out and then trudged to the store exit.

"Wait up, Sam." Greg caught up with him. "Want to join me at Aces for a beer or two?"

Slowing at the use of his cover name, Bowen jingled his keys and tried to ignore the tightness in his throat as he recalled the bitter, but familiar taste of a cool beer sliding down. "No, thanks. Something I got to do at home."

"Maybe another time." Greg thumped Bowen's shoulder.

Bowen unlocked his truck and climbed in. He fastened the seat belt and muttered, "Sorry, Greg, but there won't be another time."

He gritted his teeth as the truck's speed increased. No, there'd be no beers at Aces or anywhere else. He'd been sober for eleven years and although the urge to indulge hadn't left completely, he wasn't about to break now. His drinking had cost him plenty—several jobs and a family. Liz divorced him after four years of marriage. A high price to pay. He wouldn't let booze destroy anything else in his life.

At a red light, he stopped and glanced down at the small vehicle next to him. It reminded him of Debra's car, and he checked the time. Nine fifteen. He dialed the cell number she'd given him the previous night.

When she answered he said, "Hi. Hope I'm not calling too late?"

"I'm wide awake." Her voice held a hint of unease.

He concluded from a murmur in the background that she had company. "Did I call at a bad time?"

"Yes. No. I'm still a bit rattled. Someone followed me home from Rhodes."

"What? Are you all right?" Bowen made a U-turn at the next corner. Although she said she was fine, he needed to see her. In a matter of minutes, he swung into the parking lot and bolted to Debra's door. He'd scouted the complex previously and knew where to go.

She opened the door at his knock. He read the surprise in her face.

"Hey, Sam. Since you're here, come in and meet my, uh, friend."

Taking his arm, she led him into the living room. "This is Griff."

Bowen extended his hand. "Sam Boudine."

The men shook hands and eyed each other, saying the usual inane greeting words. *Nice to meet you.* Were they ever sincere? Bowen studied Debra's friend. He detected a bulge under his jacket where a shoulder holster might be. Friend or law enforcement?

Debra released Bowen's arm and glanced at Griff. "Thank you for coming, but you don't have to stay. I'll be all right."

"Are you sure?" Griff's question had an edge to it.

"Yes. Sam had a bad day and worked the late shift. He won't stay long." She pointed to the sofa. "Have a seat, Sam. I'll be right back."

Debra and Griff moved to the door and spoke in low tones. Bowen couldn't make out what they said. After Griff whispered in Debra's ear, he left.

She returned to the sofa and sat near him.

How could he find out more about her visitor? Before he could formulate a question, she provided a bit of information.

"Griff has been a good friend for a long time. That's why I called him."

"You could have called me. Julian would have—"

"I did phone Rhodes. Greg said you'd been busy all night, and when I called you were with two elderly ladies."

Bowen remembered them well and raised his eyebrows. "Ah, yes. The lovely Cooper sisters. They had a two-page list. Took me thirty minutes to help them locate everything. But enough of work. Do you know who followed you?"

She wiped a hand across her forehead. "No, but I did get a partial license plate number. Griff's going to check it out."

He nodded. So this guy could be a cop.

Debra nudged him in the ribs. "Why so serious? What are you thinking about?"

His Sam persona firmly in place, Bowen tapped

her arm. "You. I'm thinking about you and how I don't want anything bad to happen."

The look she gave him pricked his conscience. Trust filled her eyes.

Before he could say or do anything he'd regret, he stood and yawned. "Glad you're all right, but I can't stay. I only stopped by because of the concern in your voice. Anything you need before I go? I have to make a quick trip to the grocery store."

Debra eased off the sofa and ruffled her curls. "Thanks for taking the time to come, but I'm fine."

On his way to the door, Bowen said, "This is a nice place you have." He noted the clean lines of her simple decorating, the functional arrangement of furniture, and the lack of photographs. "How long have you been here?"

"About a year. It suits my needs, and I like the location."

Reluctant to cut the visit short, he scrambled for a reason to stay. "I just thought of something. Why don't you give me that partial plate number? I'll see if I can track it down."

A frown creased her brow. "How?"

Bowen scoured his brain for an explanation, and then shrugged and told the truth. "I've got contacts." He hoped his nonchalance would satisfy her.

She pulled a scrap of paper from her jeans pocket. "Here it is."

One glance at the scribbling and his mind raced. "A California plate. Interesting."

Debra had a good eye to make out the state and some of the characters. His pickup's tags were from California. He'd better make up a good cover story if she ever asked about them.

"Interesting, indeed." He tucked the paper into his shirt pocket. "Are we still on for tomorrow night?"

"Yes."

"Stay safe." He wanted to hold her, but she backed away and crossed her arms.

After she closed the door he waited to hear the lock click before jogging to his truck.

Conflicting emotions surged through his chest. Desire for her ran smack into fear that someone else from California had found her. And a touch of elation. He was seventy-five percent certain she was Sadie. Earlier he'd checked notes from his client and sure enough, Sadie and her husband had been involved in a puppet ministry. But if she was Sadie, he'd have to make the phone call that would end their relationship. This dating game was simply part of the job.

For the rest of the drive home, he thought about Griff. Was he a cop? Maybe a U. S. Marshal? He might be Sadie's local WITSEC contact. Hours of research awaited him. Good thing he had tomorrow off.

৵৽

Bowen had no luck tracing the California plate number. Even his research into Griff turned up nothing. But his gut told him the man worked in law enforcement.

He closed his laptop and stretched. What a way to spend his day off. With Debra's friend fresh on his mind, he reviewed the events of the previous evening. The memory of Griff's left hand on her shoulder came to mind. A wedding ring. Great. Griff was married.

Bowen assumed his association with Debra did not involve romance. Thinking of her spurred a phone call. After he ascertained she'd suffered no ill effects, he confirmed their date and ended the call. Hunger pangs rumbled and he checked his watch. Twelve forty-five. Time for lunch. He examined the contents of the refrigerator—a bag of shriveled carrots, leftover lasagna, and an almost empty carton of milk. Anxious to get home last night and begin the research on Griff, Bowen had canceled the trip to the grocery store.

"I see another visit to Jerry's Restaurant in my future."

On his way to his truck, Bowen disposed of the carrots. His drive took him past Debra's apartment where a moving van commandeered a large chunk of the parking lot. He slowed and watched two workers carry a sofa to the ramp. Right. Debra mentioned her neighbor would be moving out today.

A familiar figure crossed the lot towards Debra's unit. Bowen parked along the curb, donned a pair of sunglasses and an old black baseball cap, and climbed out of his truck. Keeping a close eye on Kyle, he crouched behind vehicles and followed the man.

Kyle stopped at the corner of the unit and glanced over his shoulder. Bowen ducked behind a sport utility vehicle and peeked through the windshield. Kyle disappeared, and Bowen crept to the unit. Shielded by a clump of sage bushes, he eyed Kyle as he knocked and then fiddled with the doorknob of Debra's apartment.

Two men in coveralls exited the neighbor's apartment carrying a large dresser.

Straightening, Kyle stroked his mustache, pivoted and strode off with big steps around the corner. He crossed the parking lot and disappeared. Strange.

Bowen could have sworn Kyle attempted to pick

Debra's lock. And he sure acted as if he'd been caught with a handful of cookies.

Driving to Jerry's, Bowen tried to recall Kyle's last name. Newman. Newcomb. Nelson. That's it. He ordered meatloaf, mashed potatoes, and a salad and ate in record time.

Once home, he checked his Internet sources and discovered a few interesting details about the man. Kyle Nelson rented his house three months ago. He worked as a freelance journalist and drove a vintage muscle car. But Bowen could not find information on Kyle before he moved to Austin. Bowen decided to use the puppet group meeting Saturday to ply Kyle with questions.

The afternoon flew by. At six, Bowen showered, dressed in black jeans and a white shirt, and set out for Debra's apartment. Two young boys with long-stemmed roses in a bucket had a table set up in an empty lot. Bowen parked at the curb and bought a red rose.

When Debra opened the door, he held the rose in both hands and bowed. "For you, *chère*."

A playful smile brightened her face, and she accepted the flower. "Thank you." She sniffed it. "Mmm, beautiful. Come in."

Bowen followed her, admiring the sway of her hips. No jeans tonight. She wore a straight dark skirt and red top. He exhaled a slow breath. *Job. It's only a job.*

"I'll get a vase." Debra opened a kitchen cabinet. From an array of assorted glasses, she chose a tall, fluted goblet. "This will have to do." She filled it with water and set the rose on the counter. Her features relaxed, and then her lips quivered. With moisture ready to escape her eyes, she glanced away.

Jacket and purse in hand, she pointed to the door. "Let's go."

"I know you've given me a little information on Kyle, but is there anything else you can tell me about him?"

"That's not a question I expected. Let me see, he's involved in Hillcrest Church activities. He's a widower, about forty-five. Always carries his monstrous camera. That's it. Why?"

Bowen helped Debra into his pickup, climbed behind the wheel, and then described his observation of the man earlier.

"What was Kyle doing at my apartment? Maybe he had a question about Saturday's meeting."

Bowen slowed and swung into a parking lot. "He could call you."

"He doesn't have my cell number. I'm stingy in sharing it." She glanced out the window. "Where are we going?"

After helping Debra out of the truck, Bowen took her hand. "I'm taking a chance here. Hope you like jazz." He pointed towards a low purple building. "We're going to eat while we listen to The Saxy Trio."

Debra squeezed his fingers. "I like jazz. Good choice."

His chest tightened. What if he ascertained without a doubt she was Sadie Malone? A cold wave of regret washed over his heart. Maybe he could keep...

Mouthwatering aromas and the cacophony of downtown traffic jerked his mind back to the parking lot.

They approached a dark blue sports car close to the entrance and he pointed. "Nice wheels."

Debra glanced at the car and stopped. Her fingers vise-gripped his hand as she tensed. "That looks like Kyle's."

9

Sadie took a step backward. "What's he doing here? Is he following me?"

A pickup maneuvered into the next row, the headlights emphasizing the somber lines of Sam's face. "His car was already here, and I didn't tell anyone where we were going. Could be he also likes jazz. We can go someplace else."

Sam's reasoning made sense. Sadie nodded towards the entrance. "I'm acting like a ninny. Let's stay. I'm looking forward to the music."

Subdued lighting in the restaurant made it difficult for them to check out the other patrons. With the car that looked like Kyle's parked close to the building, she assumed Kyle came inside. But he could also be in any of the neighboring clubs or restaurants.

Although the music touched her soul and the dill-covered salmon pleased her palate, worrying about Kyle's strange behavior kept her from completely enjoying the evening. Sitting close to the entrance, she kept a wary gaze on everyone around her.

When they left, another vehicle occupied the spot where the car had been.

While Sam drove her home, she struggled to concentrate on what he said. She eyed the side mirror, searching for Kyle's vehicle, but they arrived home with no one tailing them. In the parking lot, she rested her hand on the arm Sam offered, taking note of his serious face. "Sorry I wasn't much of a conversationalist tonight."

"I understand."

They stopped at her door.

"What if it wasn't Kyle's car?" Sam asked.

Sadie leaned against the door and pursed her lips. "Your use of logic is working. I'm going to forget about him."

Sam boxed her in, hands on either side with the door to her back. He lowered his head towards her face. "Good, but remember I'm as close as a phone call."

She nodded, making every effort to keep her mind on his words. The faint scent of his woodsy cologne wafted past and her self-control flew south. With her eyes closed she leaned closer and allowed him to fold his arms around her. How safe. Safe and right.

He nuzzled her neck and whispered, "Remember, I'm taking my cue from you, but I think we're long passed the pretending stage."

She slid her arms around his body. Solid, warm. "You're right. But we need—" The phone in her purse jingled. She ignored a few chirps but then backed away from Sam to check the number. Recognizing it, she said, "Hi." What a time for Griff to call.

"Good news. The pickup that followed you a few days ago belongs to a guy who recently moved here from California. Has no arrest record, but he does have a few citations for reckless driving." Griff's words merged together. Sadie hadn't heard him speak so fast before.

"He sure was reckless the night I saw him."

"I think that explains it. He's no threat. How are you doing?"

Her gaze centered on Sam's face. "Fine, thanks.

Been on a date with Sam."

Griff's voice lowered. "Aren't you concerned anymore?"

With Sam's blue eyes devouring her and his fingers massaging her shoulders, how could she answer any differently? "It's all good. Thanks for the information and for your concern. I feel very safe with Sam."

After another reminder to be observant, Griff hung up.

"Someone's checking up on you." Sam's mouth widened into a broad grin. "And I make you feel safe?"

She peeked at him through her eyelashes and nodded.

"I'd like to build a wall around you so no one can harm you."

His fingers released the tension in her shoulder muscles, but his reference to building reminded her. "By the way mister, I volunteered at the children's shelter yesterday. Carmen says you haven't called yet. What gives?"

He stopped the massage. "Um, I kinda forgot. Sorry. I'll call next week."

"You don't have to. Only volunteer if it's in your heart."

With his eyes on her face, he said, "You have no idea what's in my heart."

Brought on by the intensity of his gaze, heat traveled to her face.

They stood in silence for several beats.

Sam's reluctance to leave made her think he wanted to come in, but she needed time to evaluate her chaotic emotions.

He seemed to read her mind and brushed his lips

across her cheek. "Better be going. I'll see you at work tomorrow. Open the door, and then I'll leave."

She still felt the prickle of his whiskers on her cheek as her hands shook a bit. She managed to unlocked and opened the door.

Once inside she turned. "Thanks, Sam. Good night."

He saluted and left.

Sadie locked the door. In the kitchen, Sam's rose drew her to the counter. She sniffed it and touched its velvety petals. This was the first flower she'd been given since Aaron's death. Holding her emotions in check, she retreated to her bedroom.

⋙⋘

The next morning a commotion in Mrs. Gaffney's apartment woke Sadie. She threw on a sweat suit and peeked out the door. The maintenance crew hauled equipment into the vacant apartment. Right. Paint, repair, shampoo carpets for the new tenants' arrival.

Later, while dressing for work, Sadie took extra time applying makeup and fixing her hair. Starting the day in anticipation of seeing Sam sent butterflies prancing in her stomach. A few touched her heart. She arrived at work at the same time as Julian.

He accompanied her into the store. "Started on the promotion application yet?"

"I have the packet at home. I'll complete it tomorrow since I work half day."

Julian slowed at his office door. "Good deal. Let me know if you have any questions."

"Will do. Thanks." Once in the break room, she clocked in. Sam hadn't arrived yet. He wouldn't be given fulltime status until he'd completed his probation.

Filling orders from Yard Art, a local landscape company, occupied Sadie's morning. Right before noon, she received a text from Sam. He and Greg had a huge contract order to fill, and he wouldn't take his break for several hours.

Sadie missed him at lunch, but the afternoon sped by with her answering customers' questions or helping them to locate the right shade of flower.

Sam visited the garden center at three thirty. He didn't ask for another date, and she was a little disappointed. Even when they realized their shifts ended at the same time, he didn't volunteer to wait for her.

As he left, Sadie studied his retreating figure. His behavior puzzled her. During the first week he'd been at Rhodes he'd done everything to attract her attention. Was he getting cold feet? Maybe he really didn't want to be involved in the puppet group and this was his way of bowing out. Or he'd changed his mind about her.

A slew of customers kept Sadie twenty minutes after her shift should have ended. She rushed to the break room, but Sam had already clocked out. After sliding her time card into its slot, she collected her things from the locker. A note fell to the floor. It was from Sam. She scanned the scrawled words in eager anticipation.

He apologized for not waiting for her. His brother called with a minor crisis, and he had to act as mediator. He'd phone her later.

With his note clutched in hand, Sadie left work and climbed into her car, relief bubbling through her like a mountain stream on a mad dash for the ocean. That evening she ate leftovers with her phone on the table.

But he didn't call.

She invented a dozen excuses for him while working on the application. In bed at eleven thirty, she tossed and turned, weighing her conversations with him. What had she done wrong? It had to be her fault. She straightened the covers and closed her eyes. At their next meeting she'd have to scrounge up enough gumption to ask him. Or she could forget about him and go out with Kyle. She buried her head in the pillow and screamed. "Yuck."

An early half-day shift had her up and dressed by seven forty-five. The gray skies matched her mood. She hoped it wouldn't rain since Pete and Janelle Williams expected to move in today.

As soon as Sadie entered work, she sought out Greg at the customer service counter in the lumber department. She propped her elbows on the scarred surface and rested her chin in her hands. "What time is Sam coming in today?"

Greg checked the computer on his desk. "Let me see. Sam Boudine. Ah, yes. At noon. Works 'til six." He cleared the screen and stepped over a pile of binders on the floor. "I heard you and Sam are dating." At the counter, he scribbled notations on a legal pad.

"Who told you?"

"Word gets around." He arched his eyebrows. "So, are you?"

She shifted her elbows and shrugged. "Sort of. I think."

"What does that mean?"

How could she answer him when she had no idea

what was going on? "Never mind. Talk to you later." She turned and jogged through the store to the break room. Would she even see Sam today?

Sadie's half-day shift crawled by. She checked her phone a dozen times but received nothing from Sam. Calling or texting him would be her last resort. She'd give him a few more hours.

On the way home, she stopped at Jerry's and ordered a taco salad and a pecan pie to go. She ate lunch on her back porch, watching clouds scurry by. Her mood brightened with each fresh patch of blue sky. After her meal, she took the pie next door.

Pete, in jeans and T-shirt, invited her in and accepted the bakery box. "This looks delicious. Appreciate your hospitality."

"You're welcome."

Furniture and boxes covered every inch of floor space. "I'll clear a chair for you."

"Thanks, but I won't stay long."

"At least wait to meet my wife and son. Janelle's changing Zack's diaper."

While Pete set the pie on the counter, Sadie took advantage of his wife's absence. "How do you know Kyle?" The fact they knew each other still bothered her.

"Who?" He pivoted, his face taking on a darker hue. Was he blushing?

"Kyle Nelson. The man I saw you arguing with the other day."

Harrumphing, he picked up a large box with 'bedroom' written in thick black letters. "Oh, him. I don't know the man. Only met him that day." He set off down the hall. "Honey, we've got company."

At that moment, Janelle, with a chunky redheaded

toddler on her hip, brushed past him and entered the living room.

Sadie introduced herself and added, "Is there anything you need?"

"Time. It's so hard to get anything done with this little ball of fire." She planted a kiss on Zack's head. Her dark brown hair was tied in an untidy ponytail and poked out every direction. Her yellow blouse hung loosely on her slender frame. Dark circled eyes and a pale, drawn face completed her tired look.

"Are you sure I can't help?"

"We can manage." She bounced Zack on her hip. He kicked his plump little legs and gurgled.

It had been a long time since Sadie had held a baby. Not since— "I can see you're busy, so I won't take up any more of your time. Please let me know if I can help." She swallowed the urge to cry and opened the door.

"Thanks for stopping by."

Sadie entered her apartment but hung by the door for a minute. Should she offer to babysit? But she *had* asked if they needed help.

Although suspicious of Pete's response to her question, she fell asleep on the sofa. Later that afternoon, a deep voice vibrated through the wall and shattered her dream.

Dear Mrs. Gaffney had been a quiet neighbor. Sadie hoped this noise wasn't a sign of things to come. Then the voice reverberated around her back porch door.

Sliding the glass door open a fraction, Sadie listened to Pete's end of a phone conversation. She would have closed the door and ignored the intrusion, but his words held her captive.

"I've met the blonde." "No, not yet." "Give me time. I'm still unpacking." All uttered in a booming voice.

But it was his final whispered statement that tore open a fissure in her chest.

"Listen, Lonnie, I'll do it when I'm ready."

A chill grabbed Sadie's neck and slithered down her spine. The man her testimony sent to prison had two children. One was a son named Lonnie.

10

Bowen dialed Debra's number. The call went to voicemail again. He left another message as he stalked across the parking lot to his truck. Time to pay her a visit.

Why hadn't she responded? True, he'd failed to contact her the previous evening, but surely she wouldn't hold that against him. His reasons for not following through were legitimate. The note he left her indicated family business required his attention. That part was true.

His mother resided in the Alzheimer's unit of a San Diego nursing home. Charlotte had called with several concerns. None of this could be shared with Debra, so before he arrived at her apartment he had mapped a plausible story.

As he neared Debra's building, her voice drifted over the wooden fence surrounding the tiny garden at the rear of her apartment. He took a detour. She chatted with her neighbors over the wooden fence.

He intended to make his presence known, but the conversation intrigued him.

Pete said, "Sorry for the disruption."

A woman added, "Pete usually loses his temper when he talks to Ronnie. I promise we won't be noisy neighbors."

End of conversation. Doors slid closed.

Bowen sprinted to her front door and knocked.

Instead of the pleasant expression he expected, she

greeted him with a frown. "What are you doing here?"

"I've called you a dozen times. I came to see if you're all right. May I come in?"

"I suppose."

Crumpling into the armchair, Debra tucked her legs under her.

Not wanting her to know he eavesdropped, Bowen settled on the sofa and waited.

She toyed with the laces of her sneaker. "I was talking to my new neighbors out back. I didn't have my phone with me."

"For an hour?" He flinched as her head shot up and her dark eyes challenged him.

"What's wrong with that?" She dipped her head and mumbled, "And it wasn't an hour."

Still unsure of his footing with this feisty Debra, Bowen met her gaze. "Any problems?"

A mini-frown creased her forehead, and then disappeared. "Not anymore." Her tone did not match her words.

His neck muscles tightened.

Debra shifted in the chair, extending her legs.

"Is there anything I can do to help? Want to go out for a meal?"

Debra kicked off both shoes and then rubbed her temples. "Thanks for the offer. All I want is a shower, headache meds, and sleep."

He cocked his head and arched an eyebrow. "Alone?"

She glared. "Of course, alone."

"Just teasing. I hate to see you so blue. I had to do something to bring the sparkle back to your eyes."

"Thanks for your concern, but I'll be fine." Debra stood.

"What hours do you work tomorrow?" Bowen followed her to the door.

"Ten to four. You?"

"I think noon to six again. I'll try not to be late for tomorrow night's meeting."

She slipped her hands into her pockets and traced a circle on the tiled floor with a white-socked toe.

"See ya." He ached to hold her and waited, but she didn't move towards him.

"Good night," she said, and closed the door.

He stood still a moment. Instinct told him Debra's conversation with Pete concerned more than the volume of his voice. How could he get her to trust him?

Later, while whipping up an omelet, he contemplated his future actions. Almost positive Debra was Sadie, he decided to check out the next best candidate, Sandra Miller, real soon. Tonight, in fact. He knew where Sandra lived—two blocks from Debra.

Bowen grabbed his digital camera, along with Sandra's folder, and set off for Monterey Oaks Boulevard again. He parked along the curb with a view of Sandra's second story apartment and waited. Previous scouting had revealed she worked at a clothing boutique and got off at eight. With any luck, she'd be home any minute.

He didn't have long to wait. A woman grimacing in pain limped towards the stairs. Bowen couldn't see her face, so he climbed out of his truck.

She made it up the stairs where a boy, at least ten or eleven, greeted her. "Hi, Mama. Does your knee still hurt?"

Arm in arm, the pair continued to the far end of the complex.

Bowen ducked behind a privet hedge. After a few minutes, the *tap-tap* of high heels announced the approach of another woman. A peek confirmed it as Sandra. She struggled up the stairs with two brown paper grocery sacks. As she neared the top of the second flight, one bag slid from her grasp. A string of colorful words escaped her lips.

The perfect opportunity. Bowen left his hiding place and darted to the stairs. "Need help?"

A smoker's raspy voice yelled back, "Of course."

He took the stairs two at a time. The sack had split, spilling cans and boxed items. He picked up the groceries.

Her flowery perfume couldn't disguise the strong whiff of tobacco that drifted out of her long, dark hair. "Thank you. Can you carry them for me?"

"Sure." Although aware of her apartment number, to play his role he asked, "Where is it?"

"Follow me." She led the way and unlocked her door.

Stale cigarette odor spilled out of her apartment.

After Bowen deposited the groceries in the kitchen, Sandra called from the living room. "Come on in."

What a perfect situation to find out more about her. "My name's Sam."

She draped herself in the loveseat. "I'm Sandra Miller. Join me." She patted the seat next to her.

His gaze drifted to a long narrow table against the wall where framed photographs covered the surface. Debra had none. Bowen examined the display. "Nice bunch of pictures. Family?"

She pointed to a ten by eight frame in the middle. "That one was taken at my parents' thirty-fifth anniversary. Those are my two brothers and sister."

Bowen picked it up. "Do they live in Texas?"

"Here in Austin." She pointed to the next picture of five young children. "My nieces and nephews."

Other photos appeared to be of Sandra's siblings or their children. If she was in WITSEC she wouldn't have contact with family members, and she certainly wouldn't have their pictures displayed.

"Hey, Sam, be a darling and get my purse."

He found it on a table by the door and handed it to her.

She pulled out a pack of cigarettes and a lighter. As she lit the cigarette, he took note of the abnormally short pinky finger on her left hand.

Sandra took a long draw and blew smoke to the side. "Now, Sam, tell me about yourself."

"Not much to tell." Then he exaggerated a look at his watch. "Wow, I didn't realize how late it is. I have to go."

She fluttered her eyelashes. "Are you sure?"

He had to stay in character. "As inviting as that sounds, I need to leave. I'll see myself out. Good-bye, Sandra." Bowen closed the door and ran down the stairs. The blood on a high-speed chase through his body had nothing to do with Sandra's offer. She couldn't be Sadie.

According to his information, Sadie did not smoke. Sandra had the deep-throated voice of a habitual smoker. Sadie wouldn't display recent family pictures. And the client would have mentioned an odd-sized pinky.

No doubt about it. Debra Johnson was Sadie Malone.

11

In preparation for the puppet group meeting, Sadie cleaned her apartment. As she dusted around the vase holding Sam's rose, she recalled his brief visit the evening before. It had been a long time since someone cared enough about her to check on her like he did.

With the duster poised over the table, she bit her lip. How she wished she could tell Sam why she'd been out back talking to Pete and Janelle. Initially, at the mention of Lonnie's name, she'd staggered inside, but when Pete kept talking, she realized she'd been wrong. He'd used the name Ronnie over and over.

Although she'd been mistaken, the thought of Lonnie Levasseur still had the power to coil her innards like a cobra set to strike. And Pete's questionable association with Kyle added to her unease.

Shrugging off the image, Sadie stowed her cleaning supplies and then left for work. Her ten to four shift would get her home in time to bake a batch of brownies.

She placed the completed promotion application in the mail holder on Julian's door. Saturday shoppers kept her too busy to make a side trip to the lumberyard. At twelve thirty she received a text from Sam. Could she meet in the break room for lunch? She checked with Glenna and took off. When she entered, Sam waved a welcome over his lunch box.

Sadie poured honey mustard dressing over her

salad. "What's with you? Did you win the lottery?"

"You could say that."

She studied his face. The harsh lines had softened. His smile turned his eyes into warm blue pools of liquid sky.

"What you looking at?"

A tiny blob of mayonnaise clung to the comer of his mouth. She used it as her excuse and pointed. "Right there. Mayo."

He grabbed his napkin and wiped it off. "Thanks."

She nibbled a bread stick.

Sam covered her hand with his and cleared his throat. "Tonight, after the others leave the meeting, I need to talk to you."

His hand dwarfed hers, but she liked the feeling. "We have time now."

"No. What I want to say needs privacy and will take more than a few minutes." He kept a firm hold on her hand while sipping bottled tea.

Privacy? Her salad forgotten, Sadie couldn't take her eyes off his face. "Can you give me a hint?"

He squeezed her fingers and whispered, "What I have to say will change your life. It will—"

"Sam, there you are." Greg barged to their table and thumped Sam on the shoulder. "Come on, buddy. We received a mega order. I need your help. Is your brcak almost over?"

Sam hiked a shoulder and raised his eyebrows at Sadie. "Sorry. Our talk will have to wait." He gathered his trash. "Coming, boss."

Slumped in the chair, Sadie kept her eyes on him as he left the room. What could he possibly tell her that would change her life? She took a bite of salad. An outlandish idea struck her, and she almost choked.

Could he be ready to declare his feelings for her? Coughing and spluttering, she shook her head. No way. They'd only known each other two weeks. But stranger things had happened. She removed her glasses and used her shirttail to wipe off a finger smudge. What was he up to?

She placed her lunch bag in her locker. On the way to the garden center, she couldn't help smiling. At ten after four, Sadie dashed home and made brownies. Then she showered and dressed in a black, scoop necked top, cream slacks, and black, sling back sandals.

Kyle arrived first and commandeered the armchair.

Sadie chose one of the straight-backed chairs she'd hauled over from the dining table.

He unzipped his laptop case. "Do you have Wi-Fi here?"

"No, sorry. Why?"

"I want us to check out the Hands for Hannah website while we're together." Kyle plugged in his computer. "Don't worry. I brought my wireless card. I'll log on in a minute."

His words twisted a knife in her heart. She knew the group used the website as a guide, but that didn't stop the pain as memories scuttled for cover.

When Sylvia sans baby, Grace, Tyrell, and Sam were seated, Kyle pointed out various features on the website.

Sadie ducked behind Grace. She couldn't bear to look at the screen.

Kyle followed the website excursion with a thorough examination of Sylvia's notebook. By nine o'clock, they had chores divided and timelines set.

Determined to be the perfect hostess, Sadie

arranged brownies on a floral plate, but as she brushed off a few crumbs, the lights went out. Apprehension niggling at her gut. She clung to the counter. "Hold on, everyone. I'll find a flashlight." She located one in a kitchen drawer and flicked it on. With its beam aimed at the group, Sadie stifled a giggle. "I did pay the electric bill. I promise." Her eyes adjusted to the dark as her guests scurried about.

Sylvia stepped to the window. "Street lights are on. So are the lights in apartments across the way."

At the open front door, Tyrell added, "Lights are still on in the next building. I think it's only your unit, Debra."

Her hand shook, sending the gold beam dancing. Her electricity was off. That meant a fuse may be blown again.

Sidling next to her, Sam reached for the flashlight. "Where's your control panel?"

"Do you want me to contact the manager?" Kyle unplugged his laptop and coiled the cord.

Sadie shrank away from Sam. She couldn't relinquish her source of light. "It's happened before. If my electricity goes out, I can count on my neighbors' going out, too. This is an old complex, and I'm sure the wiring needs updating."

Sam nudged her shoulder. "But where's your control panel?"

Keeping a firm grip on the flashlight, she pointed with her chin. "It's in the bedroom closet. I'll take care of it." But she couldn't leave her guests in the dark. Shining the light into a kitchen drawer, she located a box of matches. "Tyrell, take these and light the candles on the coffee table."

While he lit the candles, Pete hollered from

outside.

Sadie opened the front door. "Your lights out, too?"

Still in his suit, he rubbed his chin. "Yeah. And we can't find matches or a flashlight."

"I have another one in the bedroom. Come in."

A soft glow from the candles spilled across the living room. Sadie headed down the hall and cringed at the footsteps behind her. How could she ask Sam and Pete not to follow without sounding like a prude? Struggling to keep her voice even, she said, "I'll get the other flashlight." She usually kept one in the bedside table drawer. Its silver casing glinted next to a stack of magazine and papers. She handed it to Pete. Her light now shining into the closet, she moved clothes aside to expose the little gray door.

Sam held his hand out for her flashlight again. "Let me help. It will be easier if I hold the light."

With great reluctance, she complied.

As he opened the door, the beam illuminated the switches inside.

But Sadie's eyes flew to the laminated sheet on the inside of the door. A corner of her photograph stuck out the bottom. She gasped and immediately covered her mouth.

"I found the problem. The circuit probably got overloaded and tripped the fuse." Sam flipped the switch and cheers erupted from the living room as the lights came back on.

"Fantastic," Pete said. "Hope our problem is that easy to solve."

Debra's gaze fixed on the little metal door. She averted her gaze but not quickly enough.

"That's odd." Sam touched the corner of the

photo. "There's something behind this instruction sheet."

"No, don't."

Too late. He slid out the picture.

She tried to grab it, but he held on. "Who are these people?"

"Give it to me, please."

He avoided her hand again.

"Please, Sam. Let me have it."

"Have what?" Kyle, at the opening of the closet, smoothed his mustache.

Why had he followed them?

"Hi, Kyle." Pete slapped him on the back." Didn't know you were here."

"What's the hold up?" Kyle didn't acknowledge Pete's greeting.

Sam turned off the flashlight and set it on the side table, and then closed the panel door. "Nothing. We're coming."

He passed the photograph to Sadie, but her hand trembled. The photo landed at Kyle's feet.

Sadie bent to retrieve it, but Kyle picked it up.

"Nice looking family. Who are they?"

Snatching the photograph from Kyle, Sadie marched out of the bedroom.

Someone had arranged the plate of brownies on the coffee table. Grace poured lemonade into glasses, a scene straight out of a *Good Housekeeping Magazine*.

Ripples of nausea tickled the back of Sadie's throat. How could they continue as if the world hadn't exploded? The photo burned her fingers. She tucked it inside her blouse.

With flashlight in hand, Pete opened the door. "Thanks, Debra."

Kyle closed his laptop and slid it into its case. "Can't stay, guys. See y'all at church tomorrow." In less than a minute he was out the door.

With two glasses of lemonade in hand, Grace stood by the coffee table. "Why did Kyle rush out of here?" She *tsked* and set the glasses down. "That's just like him. Always on the run."

"Excellent brownies." Sylvia, mouth covered with chocolate evidence, glanced at Sadie. "What's wrong?"

Head down, Sadie fussed with a pile of yellow paper napkins. "I'm fine. I just don't like being in the dark."

"Where's Sam?" Tyrell blew out the candles. "Did he get lost?"

Sadie shrugged and kept her eyes on the napkins. She didn't care where any of them were. She wanted to be alone.

Chomping on a brownie, Tyrell hollered from the hall. "Sam's in your bedroom on his cell."

Great. Why is his call so important? Sadie hadn't forgotten what he'd said at lunchtime, but she couldn't think of anything that would change her life more than people seeing her—Sadie's—photo with Aaron and Hannah.

In a minute, Sam joined the group and took a brownie.

Sadie searched his face but could read nothing there.

Although she tried to be congenial, Grace, Tyrell, and Sylvia didn't stay long.

Sam took another brownie and inched to the door. "There's something I have to do, but I'll be back in an hour or so. Don't go anywhere. I need to talk to you." His gaze lingered on her, and he hesitated. "Please. It's very important." Then he left and the door latch clicked behind him.

Slumped on the sofa, Sadie reviewed the evening's events. Had her life turned upside down, or was her imagination running wild? After all, what had really happened? Sam, Kyle, and Pete saw a photograph. By her reaction, they might assume it belonged to her. Rats. Why didn't she let them believe she'd never seen it before?

But none of the men acknowledged that they recognized her. The picture depicted a woman, a man, and a child. They didn't see Debra Johnson. Think. How had they responded?

She jumped up and paced, reliving the moment. Pete returned to his apartment to fix his lights. Kyle left abruptly, but that wasn't unusual. There was no notable change in their demeanor. And Sam? His actions were a little more suspect. He left, but he said he'd return to tell her...what? Something that would change her life?

Sadie focused on the three brownies on the plate and reviewed everything she knew about Sam. Sure, at first his questions and the similarities to her—Sadie's— —life concerned her, but nothing negative had transpired. If he recognized the photograph, why leave her alone for an hour or more?

Another image bombarded her brain. Pete, in her bedroom, greeting Kyle like a buddy. He'd lied about their relationship. Was he a threat?

Maybe she should call Griff. But what would she tell him? She couldn't very well say, "I kept a photograph of Aaron and Hannah. Three people saw it tonight."

Keeping the picture violated the conditions of her

contract. If she told Griff she had it, he'd have reason to void her agreement with WITSEC, and then she'd be on her own with no protection. She knew the risks when she'd saved the photo.

With robotic motions, she cleaned the kitchen. After placing the brownies in a plastic container, Sadie retreated to the sofa and pulled the photo from her blouse. She should destroy it. Turning it over so she couldn't see the faces, she prepared to rip it in half.

But she couldn't. Her fingers shook. Tears pooled. Her throat burned.

She threw the picture across the room and then collapsed on the sofa. "I can't."

12

Close to midnight, Sadie hauled herself up and plodded to the bedroom. *You're late, Sam. I'm going to bed.*

A knock penetrated her bumbling thoughts. She trudged to the front door and checked the peephole.

Sam waited with a quirky grin on his face.

She opened the door.

"Sorry I'm so late, but you'll understand in a minute." He brushed past her and motioned for her to follow him to the living room. "Let's sit." The same softness she'd detected earlier eased the lines on his face, but this time his calm and assured manner intrigued her.

He took her hand. "What I'm going to tell you will come as a shock. I was almost positive before, but after seeing the photo tonight, I'm certain. I know you are Sadie Malone."

The room swirled. Blood roared through her head. No! No! No! She jerked her hand away. With all her strength, she shoved Sam and bolted for the door.

But he grabbed her from behind. "Debra, Sadie. Wait. I'm not—"

"Let me go." She squirmed out of his grasp. What now? Run. Get out of here. She turned the doorknob.

He grabbed her and clasped a hand over her mouth. His other arm encircled her waist, dragging her away from the door.

She kicked and twisted. Her lungs begged for air.

She expended one last burst of energy and clawed at his hand. But she couldn't break free. *This is it. This is the end.* Memories of Aaron and Hannah hurtled through her mind in a kaleidoscope of colors.

Sam's breath heated her neck. "If you promise not to scream, I'll remove my hand."

Anything to get his hand away. She nodded and quit struggling. Hope blossomed for a second.

He slid his hand down to her throat.

Great. He's going to strangle me. Drawing on hidden wells of strength, Sadie dug into his flesh again. Then she threw her head back, striking Sam in the face. She kicked out, hitting his shin, and elbowed him in the gut.

He groaned and slackened his grasp enough for her to twist free. But his hunched body blocked the front door. The locked porch gate made that escape route impossible.

She spun and raced back to the bedroom where she jabbed the button lock. Her fingers scrambled through her pockets for her cell phone. She punched Griff's speed dial number. Busy.

No, no. Griff, I'm in trouble. She disconnected and punched it in again only to get the same result. With the phone back in her pocket, she eyed the high window above her bed. Could she squeeze through it?

A thump sounded in the hall.

Her breath caught. Blood pulsed through her body, hammering inside her skull. The cheap lock wouldn't keep Sam out for long. She searched the room for something heavy to shove in front of the door. A rustic six drawer dresser sat on the other side of the room. No way could she maneuver that.

Sam pounded on the door. "Debra, open up. I'm

not the bad guy here."

Her heart thudded. *Am I supposed to believe you?* "I've called Griff. He's on his way." One more lie didn't matter in the grand scheme.

The door shuddered as Sam threw his weight against it. Once. Twice.

What could she use as a weapon? The flashlight. Her fingers gripped it hard. She hid it behind her back as the wooden frame splintered, and Sam crashed in.

Blood caked beneath his nose. Good. She'd inflicted some pain. She expected to see his blue eyes smoldering, but they were gentle.

He ventured a few steps closer. "Please, Debra, hear me out."

She stood her ground. She had one shot. Didn't want to waste it. The flashlight hung as heavy as lead dumbbells in her hand.

Sam held his arms out, palms open as if he wanted to show her they held no weapon. With the strength of a bull, he needed nothing but his muscles.

"Don't come any closer. Griff will be here soon."

"Listen to me—"

Sadie swung the flashlight at his head with all her might. It caught him square on the temple, and he staggered. She lunged past him, out the door, but he seized her blouse, propelling her backward.

He pinned her arms behind her back with one hand, groaned, and rubbed his head. "Nice shot, but it'll take more than that to stop me."

She struggled but his steel grip held. Spent, she whimpered, "What do you want? Get it over with, please."

Without relaxing a muscle, he dragged her back into the bedroom and shoved her onto the bed. *No,*

Sam, not this. But he stayed near the doorway and pointed to the side table. "Give me the box of tissues."

She threw it to him, keeping her gaze on his face.

He tore out a couple of tissues and wiped blood from his nose. "Now, listen to me. Yes, I've been sent to find you, Sadie Malone, but—"

"I'm Debra Johnson." She set her feet on the floor, ready to run at the first opportunity.

Shaking his head, he ripped out another tissue and held it to the welt on his left temple. "No, Sadie, that boat sailed. And sank. I know you're Sadie. Your little attempt to flee confirmed it."

"So, you work for Lonnie Levasseur. Big deal." The flashlight lay eight or nine inches from her feet. Maybe she could use it again.

"No, I work for Caleb, your brother-in-law."

Tufts of beige carpet seemed to come alive. Patterns swirled and twisted, making her eyes cross. She blinked and stared at Sam. "What did you say?"

He planted his feet wide and stuck his hands low on his hips. "Cal sent me to find you. He has—"

"Why should I believe you? Everything you've ever said to me has been a lie." She held his gaze but moved the flashlight closer with her foot.

He rubbed the goose egg on his temple. "I agree, I've told my share of lies."

"Is your name even Sam Boudine?"

He lowered his head.

Sadie grabbed the flashlight, and before he faced her again, shoved it behind her back.

"You're right. My name's not Sam. I used it because it was Aaron's nickname for you."

She closed her heart to his words. They slithered over her like frozen rain. Keeping the weapon concealed, she stood on rubbery legs and took a step closer. "Who are you?"

He removed his wallet and held it out to her, exposing his driver's license on one side and the photo of his wife and child on the other. The one he showed her before.

Without looking at the license, she asked, "Is that your wife?"

"Don't know who she is. But here, check my license. I'm Bowen Boudine."

Another step closer. She glanced at it. "Is that supposed to make me trust you, *Bowen*? Is it real?"

He snapped the wallet shut. As he slipped it into his back pocket, she lashed out with the flashlight. This time she hit him on the back of the head. The blow sent him staggering into the wall. She raced out of the bedroom, down the hall, and made it to the front door before his groans followed her.

Out the door, across the lawn. The slick soles of her sandals lost traction on the damp grass, and she landed on her knees. Scrambling up, she scanned the area. Where could she hide? She ran on blind instinct. With her car keys still in her purse on the dresser, she had no fast escape. She rounded the corner of the unit and collided with Kyle.

"Where're you going in such a hurry?" His voice sounded thick and strange.

"Kyle. What are you doing here?"

He held onto her arm and jerked his head in the direction of her apartment. "I left my wireless card on...on your coffee table. I need it for work tomorrow."

Staring at his twitchy mustache, she frowned. "I didn't see it when I cleaned up. Are you sure?"

His grip on her arm tightened. Alarm bells clanked in her brain. She struggled. "Let me go." She didn't like the tone of his voice nor the way his eyes narrowed to dark slits. Why was he really here? Had she missed something in his reaction to her photo? "Let me go, or I'll scream."

He jerked her closer. A hard jab in her ribs. "If you scream, it'll be the last thing you do. Now, keep your voice down and tell me where you're going?"

The gun digging into her side froze her vocal chords but spurred her brain. Kyle meant no good, for sure. Sam, uh, Bowen hadn't tried to hurt her. Maybe she could pit one against the other.

"I left something in my car," she whispered,

Kyle, taller by at least eight inches, lowered his head until his hot, garlicky breath seared her cheek. "You won't need anything from your car—or anywhere else. Turn around."

She complied.

His left arm circled her throat. The gun poked her lower back.

"Keep walking." He forced her to her door.

They entered the dark apartment. Had Bowen turned off the light? If the open door surprised Kyle, he didn't comment on it.

Sadie listened for Bowen, but her heart pounded so hard, she heard nothing but the *tick-tock* of the hall clock.

With the gun digging into her flesh, Kyle thrust her into the dark living room and stopped.

"Turn on the light," he hissed.

She raised her arm.

Kyle moved the gun a fraction.

Before she could flip the switch, a slight noise to

her right made her hesitate.

Then Kyle spun away, grunting and cussing.

Sadie turned on the light. Bowen had Kyle in a headlock. She couldn't see the gun. Kyle twisted free and aimed the weapon at Bowen, who swung his leg in an arc, knocking the gun across the room. He threw several hard punches at Kyle's head, but the taller man ducked and stepped sideways. Bowen didn't give up. Kyle avoided each thrust, dodging furniture as he maneuvered around the room.

Light bounced off a metallic object on the floor. "He's after the gun!"

Her words distracted Bowen enough for Kyle to land a solid blow to his jaw. She'd meant to warn Bowen, not to give Kyle the advantage. The men locked arms and struggled. They fell to the floor and rolled, first Bowen on top, then Kyle, thuds and moans accompanying their movements.

Could she retrieve the weapon? She'd have to step over the flailing bodies. She decided not to risk it. The action moved closer to her. She jumped onto the sofa in time to avoid their entangled, thrashing legs.

Kyle groaned and rose to his feet, his eyes unfocused. Bowen knocked him into the coffee table. Candles and candleholders flew in all directions as the table disintegrated.

Avoiding the debris, Sadie slid off the sofa and staggered to the wall.

Bowen punched Kyle three times in quick succession and then held back.

Kyle lay among the broken table pieces as still as if asleep.

After feeling for a pulse, Bowen flipped him over and twisted his arms behind his back. "Get something to tie him up. He won't be out for long."

Leaning against the wall, Sadie stared at the men on the floor. She was glad Bowen had overpowered Kyle, but she still didn't trust him.

"Come on Deb...Sadie, I'm the good guy here. Help me tie him up, and I'll prove it." His chest heaved in and out from the exertion. "Hurry. Do you have any rope?"

She shook her head.

He pointed with his chin. "Then hand me that lamp. I'll use the cord."

Giving Kyle a wide berth, she reached for the plug. "Wait. How about extension cords? I have three or four."

"They'll do. Hurry."

She scrambled in a kitchen drawer and withdrew a tangle of cords which she deposited near Bowen.

While he lashed Kyle's wrists and ankles, he said, "Get me something for a gag."

A dishtowel lay on the counter. She threw it to Bowen.

After he tied it around Kyle's mouth, he sank back on his haunches and rubbed his head. "Sadie, girl. You sure have good aim. Kyle's jabs didn't help, either. Now, please, we need to talk." He pulled himself to a stand and examined his grazed knuckles.

With Kyle safely out of the way, Sadie still had questions for Bowen. "Go wash your hands, and I'll get you some ice."

"I'll wash, but I don't need the ice. Promise you won't run?"

Sadie nodded. She wanted to know why he said Caleb sent him. But now she'd have an advantage. Kyle's gun lay on the floor behind a potted plastic ficus. She picked it up and held it out of sight by her side.

When Bowen returned, the hair around his face damp, she aimed the gun at him and motioned for him to sit in the armchair. "Now prove to me you've come from Caleb."

Hands help up in mock surrender, he stood by the chair. "We need to move to another room. Don't want Kyle to overhear us."

"But—"

"Let me check on him. I'm sure he's still unconscious."

Taking a step backward, Sadie lowered the gun a fraction. "OK. No tricks."

Bowen lifted one of Kyle's eyelids and then felt his pulse. "Out cold, but I don't know for how long."

"The bedroom." Sadie wiped her clammy palm on her slacks. "Move slowly."

He held his hands high and walked down the hall.

She followed with the useless weapon aimed at his back. She'd never fired a gun, but holding it gave her a bit of confidence. "Sit on the stool by my dresser."

After Bowen sat, she closed the door and leaned against it. "Start talking."

He sucked in a breath and kept his gaze fixed on her face. "Cal sent me to find you because he has important news."

The gun was heavy. She supported her wrist with her left hand and aimed in the general direction of Bowen's chest. "You've already said that. Where's the proof?"

"Cal gave me a code word. He said you would know it and accept me. The word is cooterpeter."

Sadie's arms trembled. The gun wavered as an icy

shudder skated through her. Cooterpeter. That's how Hannah pronounced computer. Caleb would know that. Lonnie Levasseur would not.

She sank onto the bed, gun forgotten. Cal sent Bowen to find her. Why? A hoard of reasons collided in her brain, but none made any sense.

The gun dropped from Sadie's numb fingers. Her voice came out in a tight whisper. "What does he want to tell me?"

Sliding next to her on the bed, Bowen placed an arm around her shoulders. "Brace for it, Sadie. Cal thinks Hannah is alive."

13

Bowen caught Sadie before she slipped off the bed. He cradled her head on his shoulder and stroked her cheek.

"Sadie, wake up." His heart still clenched at her pain-filled moan. What was going through her mind? He couldn't imagine.

Her eyelids fluttered, and she brushed his hand away. "Sam?" She raised her gaze to his face, eyes heavy with confusion. "Bowen, did I hear you right? Hannah may be alive?"

Although he wanted to wrap his arms around her and somehow convince her to trust him, all he did was touch her arm. "Yes. Cal sent me."

"I heard that part, but what about Hannah?"

Bowen rubbed the lump on the back of his head and flinched. "My assignment was to locate you. Cal didn't give me details about your daughter." Why hadn't he demanded more information from Cal? Here he was, flying blind and causing misery, when all he wanted to do was comfort.

Sadie stood, steadied herself, and paced to the door and back. "I must talk to him. I need to get back to California. Now. I must go now." She moved about the room fidgeting and pacing like a hyperactive kid.

"Where's my phone? What...I've forgotten his phone number. How can I call him?"

Bowen caught her in mid-stride and gently squeezed her shoulders. "Sadie, calm down. I'll give you the number I have for Cal. I agree we need to get out of here. But first, we have to take care of Kyle. It appears he was after you, too."

"You mean after me as Sadie or as Debra?"

"You, Sadie. Kyle came after you. He saw your photo with Aaron and Hannah and must have recognized you."

Swallowing despite the tightening in his throat, he rubbed his thumbs on the soft skin of her neck. He'd come close to botching this assignment. The face of a client who died while under his protection years ago slammed into his memory. Why did he dismiss the holes in Kyle's background so cavalierly? His blunder almost cost Sadie her life and he wouldn't let that happen again. "Your identity has been compromised."

She pulled away and moved to the door. "I know—you found me."

"Cal hired *me*. No one else. We can't take a chance on Kyle's motives."

Anxiety tightened her face. "I must call Griff—"

"He's your WITSEC contact, isn't he?"

She brushed the curls off her forehead and nodded.

Bowen didn't want her to contact the U. S. Marshal, but he would understand if she did. "Is that a good idea? Will he allow you to visit Caleb in California?"

Sadie flopped on the edge of the bed, her hands kneading her thighs. "But he can't stop me. If I leave Austin, it will break my contract and—"

A thump from the living room interrupted her.

"Stay here." Bowen picked up Kyle's pistol, opened the door, and moved down the hall.

He found Kyle conscious and thrashing about. "Sa...Debra, come here and help me." If Kyle was after Sadie, Bowen didn't want to confirm her identity.

As Sadie entered the living room, a knock sounded on the front door. She and Bowen exchanged glances.

Bowen whispered, "Quick, help me get Kyle out of here. Let's take him to the bathroom." He placed the pistol on the kitchen counter and then picked up Kyle's head and shoulders. "You get his legs."

They carried the thrashing man down the hall and dumped him in the tub.

Eyes wide, breathing hard, Sadie hurried to the front door and peeked through the peephole. She turned to Bowen, who'd followed her, and mouthed, "It's Pete, my neighbor."

Bowen mouthed back, "Open it, but don't let him in." He stepped out of the line of sight, picked up the pistol, and positioned himself for another fight.

With the safety chain on, Sadie cracked the door. "Hi, Pete."

"Came to check on you. We were up with Zack——he's coughing a bunch—and heard loud voices and strange noises."

"I'm sorry. You know I had company, earlier. While cleaning up, I knocked over a chair."

"So there's nothing wrong?"

"No. Sorry I disturbed you guys. See you tomorrow." With the fake smile still plastered on her face, she shut the door.

From the kitchen, Bowen motioned for her to come. "Good job. Now let's get out of here." He set the weapon on the counter and stepped towards the hall.

Sadie remained glued to the door. Her face was pale, her breathing shallow, and her gaze darted back and forth. Bowen couldn't decide if she was contemplating her next move or if she was frozen in shock. But he had no time to be gentle.

He held out his hand. "Come. I have a plan, but we must hurry." Bowen put a finger to his lips. "We need to keep our voices down. We don't want Kyle to know what we're doing. You should pack a suitcase."

"I've changed my mind." Gone were the erratic eye movements and bloodless cheeks.

"You don't want to see Cal?" What now?

Determination firmed her jaw. "No. Yes. I want to leave right away, but I'm going to call Griff."

Here it comes. His plan could fall apart in the next second. "Go ahead. Where's a suitcase? I'll get it ready for you."

Sadie pointed to the hall. "In the closet. Get the big black one." She punched a number on her phone.

"Stay in here while you talk so Kyle can't hear you." Bowen hovered in the doorway.

She sat on the sofa, ankles crossed and one leg bouncing up and down. "Hi, Griff. Sorry to bother you so late, but I've got a big problem."

Bowen joined her on the sofa, watching her face as she listened. Her eyes narrowed, and she bit her lower lip. What was wrong?

Her voice lowered and she frowned. "All right. I'll be in touch." Sadie's eyes glazed over. All color drained from her face

Bowen slid closer. "What's wrong? Why didn't you tell him?"

But then her eyes sparked with fear as she tensed.

"I'm in serious trouble. Griff used our code word. I can't believe...code words, twice in one night. He....I must leave Austin."

"I know that, but why didn't he come here and tell you?" Her words were making no sense. What could Griff have said to cause such a reaction?

She stood and moved to the hall. "I have to pack."

"No." Bowen reached to restrain her. "Tell me here. Kyle—"

"OK." She entered the kitchen and opened a cabinet. "How will we travel to California? Fly, drive?"

"Drive. Flying will leave a paper trail. Now what about Griff?"

"That'll be a long drive." Sadie snatched items from the shelves. "We can take these."

Bowen caught the bottled water six-pack before it slipped off the counter. "We'll have to share the driving."

Since it seemed Sadie intended to take several items, he found a cloth grocery bag next to the refrigerator and packed the water and boxes of snack bars. "Tell me what Griff said."

Sadie opened the refrigerator. "We had a plan. We had a code word to use if either of us were in danger. Should I pour out the milk? It'll turn—"

"No. You have to leave everything in place, like you stepped out for a minute. In fact, when you pack, take the hangers too so it doesn't look like clothes are missing."

She closed the fridge and fled to the bedroom. "But Kyle—"

Bowen set the bag of snacks by the front door and then followed Sadie. As he passed the closet, he retrieved the suitcase and unzipped it on the bed. After closing the bedroom door, he folded his arms and kept out of Sadie's way. "Kyle doesn't know we're leaving together. He can assume. Please tell me more about Griff."

Sadie snagged items from her dresser drawers and dumped them into the suitcase. "He didn't want to talk. There may have been someone with him."

On the sidelines, Bowen chomped at the bit. Why had Griff used the code word? Frustration at not being able to help the marshal churned in Bowen's gut. But he had to make getting Sadie safely back to California his first priority.

She gathered clothing from the closet and then haphazardly folded T-shirts, slacks and jeans into the case. Sneakers and a pair of brown shoes topped the pile. Plastic hangers lay in a colorful mess on the bedspread. "That's it. Except my makeup and toiletries. They're in the bathroom."

"Leave them. We'll stop along the way and purchase what you need. Are you ready? What about the hangers?"

She placed her hands on her hips and surveyed the room "I'll throw them in the dumpster. Yes, I'm as ready as I'll ever be. Can we stop at an ATM on the way out?"

"No. You don't want to leave a trail."

"Oh, yeah. I understand. There's not much in my account, anyway." She raised her strained face to his and held up a finger. "Wait. One more thing."

Bowen heard her rummaging in the closet. She came out holding a thick brown envelope.

"Ever since I entered WITSEC I've dreaded being at the mercy of others. So I keep a stash of cash for emergencies." Holding up her treasure, she quirked an eyebrow. "And I think this qualifies as an emergency." She shoved the envelope deep into her large purse. "I'm ready now."

Bowen zipped the suitcase and carried it to the small foyer.

Sadie followed with her purse, jacket, and the jumble of hangers. She took one last look around the living room. "You said I must leave everything in place, like I left to run errands. What about the smashed coffee table? That's not normal."

"Right, but we can't change what happened here. Kyle will talk." He held out his hand. "Give me your phone."

"Why?"

"You need to leave it here. You don't want anyone to track your whereabouts."

Sadie dumped the hangers on the floor and slid the slim phone from her pocket. "But I need phone numbers from it."

"Like who? You're not going to be calling April or Julian."

She stared at the screen. "You're right. And I know Griff's number."

Anxious to be on the road, Bowen shifted his weight from foot to foot. "Delete the numbers and your call history. Authorities can get your records from the phone carrier, but erasing information now will prevent Kyle from accessing it."

"Right." She thumbed the keys and then set the phone next to the rose he'd bought her, which sat on a pedestal side table.

When she raised her head, a hint of regret hovered in her eyes.

He had no idea what thoughts raced through her

mind, but he had a job to do. "We need to leave."

"I'll never be back here." Her shoulders heaved as she blew out a slow sigh. "Another life I have to leave behind."

Bowen shrugged as he separated a plastic grocery bag from the stash next to the fridge. "Debra Johnson is gone forever." He stuffed the discarded hangers into the bag and moved to the door.

She scanned the living room. "My photograph." She found it behind the ficus. "I can't leave my picture here."

"You should burn it."

"It's all I have right now. If Hannah's alive—"

"Bring it then. We must leave."

After burying it in her purse, she adjusted the glasses on her nose. "Guess I don't need these any longer." As she removed them, Bowen shook his head.

"Uh-uh. Debra wouldn't leave the apartment without them. Take them with you." He twisted the doorknob, but a muffled thud emanated from the bathroom. "Better check on Kyle."

Bowen dropped everything and lunged down the hall with Sadie on his heels. They found Kyle on the bathroom floor, the cord around his ankles unraveling, and the shower curtain ripped from the plastic rings.

"Doggone it." Bowen grabbed Kyle's feet and lashed the cord tighter around them. He checked the cord around his wrists, threw the curtain aside, and then hefted him back into the tub.

"Will he be OK in here?"

"For now." Bowen closed the door and ushered her back down the hall.

On the way past the kitchen, he stopped at the counter. Kyle's pistol lay next to the container of brownies. Should he take it? Although he'd fired a variety of weapons many times in his line of work, he'd never killed anyone, and he loathed carrying a gun. But he was headed into an unpredictable, and perhaps dangerous, situation.

He shook his head. No sense courting problems with the law by carrying a weapon without a permit.

Once outside, Bowen and Sadie approached the brightly lit parking area, but he slowed at the corner. "I've changed my mind. We need to destroy your phone. Keys?"

Sadie handed them over.

"Dump the hangers, and then come back here and wait. I won't be long." Bowen left the suitcase and snacks with her and sprinted back to the apartment.

In his haste to seize the phone, he knocked over the vase. Glass shattered on the floor. Water splattered his jeans, and three rose petals lay in the debris like large drops of blood.

His fingers tightened on the phone. The damaged rose reminded him again that this was a job. But the admonition had no effect on the fist-sized knot is his chest.

Giving himself a mental kick, he crushed the phone under the hell of his boot, removed the exposed data chip and exited the apartment.

"Some night, huh?"

He flinched at the voice coming from the open doorway next to Sadie's apartment. Pete.

Bowen quirked his eyebrows up and down, and hoped guilt wasn't written all over his face. "We got a little wild."

"Good for you." Pete gave him a thumbs-up sign.

Bowen waited for him to close the door before

running back to Sadie. So much for leaving no trail, but maybe Pete didn't know his name and wouldn't assume Sadie, um, Debra left with him. They needed to get out of Texas, and fast.

He directed Sadie to his truck. She climbed in while he placed her suitcase in the backseat.

"What about Kyle? What if he can't get free?"

He slid behind the wheel and switched on the ignition. The engine roared to life. "Don't worry about him. I'll make a phone call later today. Ready?"

She buckled her seatbelt. "Yes. Are we going to pick up your stuff?"

Bowen turned onto Monterey Oaks Boulevard and hit the accelerator. "I already packed. When I left the meeting, I went straight home. All my things are in the back."

She peeked at the backseat and obviously saw his computer case, punching bag, and the two suitcases.

After a few miles, he approached a fast food joint. From under his seat, he extracted two baseball caps. "Put on this cap and hide your hair if you can. Turn your head while I order coffee. Do you want anything?"

He donned the black cap and pulled it low over his eyes.

"Nothing for me. How's this?" She turned to him as she stuffed her curls under the tan cap.

Bowen had to admit even with the stressful events of the night, she could still look cute in a baseball cap.

∽◅

Once on Interstate 10, Bowen threw the data chip from Sadie's phone out the window, then set the cruise control, and turned on the radio. "Do you have a preference? I've got satellite. Anything you want to listen to?"

From the dim corner where she rested her head on her wadded up jacket came a small voice. "Jazz. Something soft and soothing."

He punched a button. "Contemporary jazz. How's this?"

"Fine."

She was his responsibility now. He had to keep her safe. "Are you warm enough?"

"Yeah."

The strains of clarinet and saxophone floated around the cab. Bowen took a sip of coffee. "Why don't you try to sleep?"

She let out a low moan.

"Sadie, I..." Bowen placed the cup in the holder. He had no idea what to say. Did she need his comfort or should he back off and be silent? She'd shown remarkable courage and strength in their struggle and in her handling of Kyle, but she'd withdrawn from him emotionally.

Sadie shifted in the seat. "I can't sleep. All I can think about is Hannah."

"Do you want to call Caleb?" Bowen glanced at the clock. "It's two here. Midnight in L.A."

"Yes." Her voice held a hint of enthusiasm.

Bowen slid the phone out of his shirt pocket and handed it to her. "Cal is speed dial number seven."

She took the phone, punched the number, and waited. "He's not answering. It's going to voice mail."

"Don't say anything. Hang up." He held out his hand for the phone. "One never knows who's going to listen to messages."

Disappointment oozed from her hunched body. She hadn't spoken to a family member in three years.

Could he survive such isolation? "I'm sorry you didn't reach Cal. You can call again in the morning."

"Fine, but I'm going to try Griff again." Straightening, she punched in a couple of numbers.

He snatched the phone. "No, you can't." She didn't seem to realize the danger. He'd have to coach her in the intricacies of escaping undetected.

"Why?"

Bowen concentrated on the road but softened his voice. "A call to him from my cell phone can be traced. They can locate where you called from and will easily deduce you're on your way west. And it will lead them to me and my vehicle." He sent her a quick glance. He could kick himself for being so abrupt, but he couldn't let her use his phone. "If Griff's in trouble then all that information could fall into the wrong hands. I want this trip to California kept between you and me. And Cal."

Sadie's silence bothered Bowen.

"You understand, don't you?"

"Yeah."

Miles of tarmac flashed by. The song ended and Bowen turned down the volume. "Sleep will do you good. It'll be your turn to drive before you know it."

"I can't sleep." She removed her glasses and stuffed them into her purse.

Bowen drummed his fingers on the steering wheel. Questions to ask Sadie swirled through his brain. Since she was awake and couldn't escape, he broke the silence. "Are you up to talking about your past?"

"I suppose." She tucked one leg underneath her

and rubbed her knee.

He cleared his throat. "From what I know about your situation, your husband and daughter drowned when their car slid off a bridge. Why would Cal think Hannah might still be alive?"

A ragged breath rumbled from Sadie. "You're right. Aaron's car crashed into the Santa Ana River, a concrete-sided section through the city. He'd picked up Hannah from daycare. Witness statements indicated he was involved in a car chase. A dark SUV followed him and shots were fired." Her voice broke, and she sucked in air. "There had been unprecedented heavy rain that week. When they landed in the water, Aaron must have loosened Hannah's car seat strap, or told her to. His body was found wedged between the front seats, Hannah's jacket in his hand. The rear passenger windows were down."

"He must have opened them." Inwardly Bowen shuddered at the vision of a father trying to help his young child. Did Sadie think about the last minutes of her husband's life? Did she ever sleep soundly without horrific nightmares?

"Aaron died from head wounds. Hannah's body was never found. Authorizes believed it floated downstream. They searched for days…"

Even in the dim interior, he could see the anguish on her face. He brushed the back of his hand across her cheek. "She could have survived." He would have clung to such a hope if it was his child.

She rested her cheek against his hand. "Someone could have pulled her out."

Moisture trickled over his fingers and he longed to stop the truck. His reply seemed so inadequate. "That's a good possibility."

"I've wondered about it every day for two and a half years, and in a few hours I'll know for sure."

And when Sadie had Hannah safe by her side, she'd have no further need of his help. Could he turn her over to the U. S. Marshals and say good-bye?

14

Fatigue invaded every pore. Sadie blinked against the early morning sunlight as Bowen stopped next to a gas pump. The crick in her neck indicated she'd slept several hours.

Easing her head back and forth, she turned to Bowen. "Where are we?"

"Fort Stockton." He rubbed his hand over his face. "We need gas, and I need coffee."

With a grunt, he opened his door, set the black cap low on his head, and handed the tan one to her. "You go in and don't talk to anyone. Want coffee?"

Purse and jacket in hand, she jumped out of the truck. "I'll get it."

Stiff muscles objected as she slung her jacket around her shoulders. A few minutes later, she set two cups of coffee in the holders and climbed into the truck. She sipped the strong brew while Bowen completed the transaction at the gas pump. Although their stop had been quick, she was anxious to call Cal. She yawned and then checked her watch. Seven fifteen. Too early? Tough. She needed reassurance he had knowledge of Hannah.

Bowen returned from the convenience store. "I'll drive to El Paso where we'll stop for breakfast. Can you wait another three hours to eat?" He slid behind the wheel.

"Of course." If they'd flown from Austin they could have been in L.A. by that time.

121

"You can take over from there." He started the truck and steered around a sedan at the next pump.

Sadie sniffed steam escaping from the tiny opening of her cup. Even the vapors revived a few brain cells. "Somewhere along the way I need to buy toiletries."

He merged onto the freeway and accelerated. "Sure. But I have a plan. As far as we know, no one is aware you left Austin with me. We have to keep it that way. Kyle might assume we're together, but if he's involved in anything illegal, he won't blab. I e-mailed Julian my notice this morning, so folks at work might not connect your disappearance with me."

"You quit this morning?"

He ignored her question and continued. "I want you to buy a wig before we have breakfast. Wear it whenever we're in public. That way if my vehicle is tracked, the description of the woman with me won't match Debra Johnson."

Another sip of coffee. Her brow scrunched in a major frown. "Why a wig? Why not dye my hair again?"

"We don't have that kind of time. And you need a complete change in appearance. A wig's the fastest and easiest way."

"Hmm…in that case, I think I'll be a redhead."

"I like redheads." He grinned and wiggled his eyebrows. "I've seen photographs of you and you were a beautiful brunette. Right now, you're a stunning blonde. So why not be a knockout redhead?"

Heat traveled up her neck and touched her cheeks. She finished her coffee and set the cup in the holder. "I want to call Cal. It's five thirty in L.A. Can I use your phone, please?"

He placed his cup next to hers and handed her his phone. "The charger is in the glove box. The battery is low, so plug it in. Hope we get service out here."

Under a pair of sunglasses and clump of folded maps Sadie located the cord, plugged it into the receptacle, and attached the phone to the other end. She punched speed dial seven and waited, her heart bouncing.

A hoarse, but familiar voice said, "Hello."

"Caleb, it's me." She swallowed hard to hold back tears.

Silence, and then a sharp intake of breath. "I'm so glad you called. Did you call last night? I recognized Bowen's number, but there was no message."

"Yes. We're on our way, almost out of Texas."

"Great. How long will it take to get here?" He was taking great care not to say her name.

"I don't know. You can ask Bowen in a minute, but tell me about...about my daughter, please." Anxiety and excitement chewed at her insides, but she made sure not to say names, either.

"Sure. I first saw a child four months ago—"

"Four months? Cal, why'd you wait so long?"

"Give me a chance to explain."

"Sorry. Carry on."

"After seeing the kid that day, I returned home and examined H...her picture. You know the one you took at Disneyland?"

With eyes closed Sadie visualized Hannah in a long, blue princess dress standing next to Cinderella. "I remember."

"I was pretty sure the child was her, but I couldn't just start a conversation with her."

"Where'd you see her?"

"I've been dating a woman who lives in Santa Clarita. Reyna Perez. We're engaged."

"That's good news, Cal. Where is Santa Clarita? I can't place it."

"Northwest of L.A., about thirty miles. Anyway, Reyna's daughter, Francesca, plays soccer. We were watching a game one Saturday and...Ha...the girl was on the opposing team. After the game, both teams shared refreshments, very civilized. I asked Reyna if she knew the little girl with brown pigtails. She said she'd seen her at games."

"Does she attend the same school as Francesca?" Hope nibbled at Sadie's heart.

"I don't know. The soccer league is privately sponsored. Kids from any community can participate."

"Are you basing your assumption on looks alone?"

"No. One Saturday I didn't join Reyna at a game. Instead, I waited until it was over and followed the woman to a small house on the edge of town. I didn't speak to her, but I talked to her neighbors. They said she's lived there ten years or more. She was never married as far as they knew. One day about two and a half years ago, a child appeared. A little girl, maybe four years old. The woman said the child was her niece."

Sadie stared at the vast stretches of flat Texas flashing by. Her baby could be alive. "Were the neighbors convinced?"

"She told them her brother and sister-in-law died, and she took the child. But here's the kicker. The next week I returned with a small photo and asked neighbors if they recognized it."

"And?"

"They said it resembled the child she brought home."

"What name does she use?" Tears gathered in Sadie's eyes and blurred her vision

"They call her Penny. Penny Adams. The woman is Evelyn Adams."

"Do you think the neighbors warned her in any way?"

"No, I explained to them I was investigating a missing child report, and that we didn't want to cause a problem if there was no need, so I asked them to keep it confidential. Thanks to television shows about missing kids, they complied."

Despair, tinged with anticipation, tightened Sadie's throat and rendered her speechless. She handed the phone to Bowen.

"We're driving straight through, Cal. We'll be in L.A. by midnight or early Monday morning. I'll contact you when we get close." After listening for a few seconds, Bowen said, "Uh-huh. I'll give a full report when I see you." He secured the phone in the dashboard holder.

Sadie appreciated his silence. She closed her eyes and prayed silently. Since the accident, she'd voiced few petitions to a distant God. But in the past few months, she'd arrived at the point where she sensed His presence more and more. Would He still listen to her pleas? *Oh, God. Keep us safe. Let me find my baby. Please, God.*

"We'll be in El Paso soon. Do you feel up to giving me the details of how Cal found Hannah?"

Light reflecting off the barren land speared her tear-sensitive eyes. She scrambled in her purse for the fake specs and clipped the sunglasses in place. He deserved to know the full story. Sadie repeated what Cal had shared, and by the time the words had drained her soul, Bowen pulled into a mall parking lot.

He stared out of the window. Then he turned tired eyes to her and said, "You should be able to find everything you need here. The marquee advertised a wig store, too. Go there first." Bowen undid his seat belt and withdrew cash from his wallet. "Don't use your money. I'll expense this all to Cal." He handed her the slew of twenty-dollar bills. "Is that enough?"

She had no idea how much a wig cost but nodded and climbed out of the truck, baseball cap squished down on her head.

As they walked towards the entrance, Bowen rolled his shoulders and moved his head side to side. "I'll be glad to sleep a bit after breakfast. While we're in the mall, I'll keep my distance. I don't want us seen together. Get everything you need, but hurry. And do your best to keep your head down in case of cameras."

The automatic doors hissed open, and she entered, leaving the sunglasses on to hide swollen eyes. Wendy's Wigs didn't open for another twenty minutes. Sadie paused at the door, hoping Bowen would understand why she went to the drugstore first.

After her basket overflowed with toiletries and makeup, she added a fancy pair of sunglasses with large, dark lenses. If she had to be in disguise, she'd do it with style, and she could ditch the clip-ons and fake glasses.

At Wendy's Wigs, Sadie tried on two auburn pieces. Neither suited her. The clerk suggested a platinum blonde number. Shoulder length, straight, with bangs.

"This is the one." Forget being a knockout

redhead.

Bowen's cash didn't quite cover the cost, but the wig looked too good to pass up. Sadie pulled a few bills from her stash and then sauntered out of the store, right past Bowen, whose mouth hung open. She exited the mall and waited at the pickup.

He whistled as he approached. "Wow. I can't keep my eyes off you."

"In that case, give me the keys."

Sadie slid behind the wheel and moved the seat forward. "Hop in, mister, or you'll be hitching a ride to L.A."

"Stop wherever you want for breakfast. I'm going to sit here and admire the view."

She couldn't help smiling at his banter, but there were too many questions about his behavior in Austin for her to take his attention seriously.

Although much bigger and more powerful than her little sedan, the pickup reminded her of the SUV she'd owned in L.A. Shaking off the painful memories, she concentrated on the traffic.

On the outskirts of the city, she pulled into a gas station next to a restaurant advertising the best pancakes in Texas.

After Bowen topped off the gas tank, Sadie parked in front of the café.

Cap tugged low on his brow, he hauled his computer case over the backseat. "I do need to check my e-mail and a few sources."

With wig and new sunglasses in place, she climbed out of the truck. The disguise injected a bounce of confidence in her step.

They were seated at a booth near the back and had coffee served right away.

After ordering, Bowen plugged in his laptop, inserted his Wi-Fi card, and concentrated on the screen.

Dark stubble covered his chin, and his eyes drooped in weariness. She'd let him sleep all through New Mexico if she lasted that long. Her whole body ached from the scuffles with Bowen and Kyle.

The waitress served their pancake orders and left a tray containing four syrup varieties. She ate and drank in silence, eager to get back on the road.

Bowen drained his coffee mug and pointed to the computer screen to his right. "I'm checking *Austin American-Statesman's* website. Maybe you're in the newspaper's headlines." But then his eyes widened and he pulled the screen closer.

"Sadie." He hesitated before turning the computer so she could read the news story. "You're not going to believe this. Griff's been murdered."

15

Heart galloping, and with pancakes and coffee threatening a return trip, Sadie buckled her seatbelt and started the truck.

Bowen opened his laptop again and drummed his fingers while waiting for the newspaper website to load.

Gripping the steering wheel, she peeked at the computer screen. "Tell me exactly what the article says. How did Griff die? When?" After reading the headline in the restaurant, they'd paid the bill and left. She wanted—needed—details.

"I need to scroll down a bit. Here it is. He was found in his car at a convenience store. Shot twice—in the chest and head. Robbery not considered a motive. He still had his wallet. Evidence of a struggle. And evidence of a passenger." Bowen paused a moment. "When you called him last night, did you get any sense he was in danger?"

Strident tones of the brief conversation from the previous evening echoed through her head. "He used our code word indicating I was in danger. His voice was even, but I heard a sound in the background, like someone else talking. I remember thinking he had company."

"There's more." Bowen scanned the article. "Authorities checked his phone records. They say the last call he received was at midnight. The caller is wanted for questioning."

Sadie had called Griff at midnight. She may have been the last person to talk to him, other than the killer, of course.

Blinking back tears, she argued with herself about whether to turn back or not. She couldn't help Griff now. If she returned to Austin, she'd have nothing to contribute to his case and would forfeit the opportunity to find Hannah. That settled the argument. She must find Hannah.

Bowen closed his laptop, slipped it into its case, and returned it to the backseat. "Are you OK?"

"No." Sadie tightened her hold on the steering wheel. "But there's nothing I can do about it."

"You're right and I'm sorry. I'm—"

"Stop! Just stop. I don't want to talk about him."

He held up his hands as if to ward off her rant. Lowering the cap over his eyes, he slumped in the seat. "I really am sorry about your friend. Wake me when you need a break."

❧❦

New Mexico real estate flashed by in a blur. Straight black ribbons of tarmac stretched as far as she could see. Yellow lines zoomed by, as in a surreal daydream. With cruise control on and a jazz radio station that never faded, Sadie felt as if she'd slipped into autopilot. Turn the wheel here, pass a vehicle there. Good thing she had a gazillion images dancing through her brain to keep her awake.

Would Hannah recognize her? How tall would she be? Sadie pictured Hannah in a soccer uniform. Had the Adams woman treated her well? Who murdered Griff and why? What about his wife and children?

The tarmac shimmered in the midday sun. Sadie adjusted the oversized sunglasses. She longed to share the troubling thoughts. But Bowen's heavy breathing signaled deep sleep. She glanced at his clasped hands, knuckles grazed and swollen, tiny scabs from her raking nails. Her champion.

They entered Arizona and Sadie stopped at a rest area.

Bowen stirred and shifted in his seat. "Want me to drive yet?"

"No. I need a restroom break." She took the keys from the ignition and opened the door. "Are you getting out?"

Bowen adjusted his cap and yawned. "Guess so."

They went separate ways, and when Sadie returned to the pickup, Bowen leaned against the door with arms folded and the cap bill shading his face. He stood so still, for a moment she thought he was asleep.

The *beep-beep* of the vehicle remote startled him.

"I'll keep driving, at least to Tucson. You need more beauty rest."

He stretched and climbed in. "Great. We're making good time, but I don't think any amount of shut-eye will help my looks." His one-dimple smile disappeared quickly.

Once on Interstate 10 again, he resumed the almost prone position and fell asleep.

Sadie envied people who could fall asleep so quickly. It always took her forever.

Although she enjoyed the variety of jazz, she experimented with the array of satellite stations. She found one with music that carried her back to college days and the first time she met Aaron. Alone with her memories, the miles streaked by.

Close to Tucson, Bowen woke up. He squinted at the scenery, flexed his fingers, and groaned. "This bed is not comfortable."

"Want to stop and stretch?"

"No. Let's wait until we get through Tucson. You OK with that?"

"Yeah. I'd like to wash off, too."

He leaned over the seats and extracted two bottles of water from the sack. After opening them, he handed one to her.

"Thanks."

"Let's find a truck stop where we can shower and change clothes." The contents of his bottle disappeared in one gulp.

"Good idea. My slacks will never be the same." She'd added a splotch of coffee to the grass stains from her failed escape attempt.

He glanced at his watch. "Slept about three and a half hours. Not bad. I'll take over on the other side of Tucson. But first I need to call about Kyle. If he's still trussed up in your tub, he'll need rescuing."

Bowen opened his wallet and slipped out a small card. He punched a number on his phone, and after a few seconds, said, "This is Boudine. Echo Bravo Charlie, five-four-seven-nine. I need a sweeper." Then he read a series of numbers off the card and added Sadie's Austin address. "You may have to clean up some. The usual. And one more thing. Can you check on the murder of Miles Griffin, a U. S. Marshal? Thanks."

With the phone back in his pocket, he shoved the small card into his wallet and eased out the photograph of the woman and child.

Good. The perfect opening to pummel him with

her barrage of questions, but first she had to know. "Who'd you call and what's with the Echo Bravo sweeper bit?"

After donning a pair of mirrored sunglasses he'd retrieved from the glove box, he chuckled. "It's best you don't know, sweetheart. Kyle will be taken care of."

"You don't mean taken care of as in…killed, do you?" She checked for a reaction.

He folded his arms, biceps bulging, jaw muscles clenched. "No. That's not our style. But he won't carry any tales to the cops."

Traffic increased, and she concentrated on the vehicles around them.

But before they stopped to shower, she needed other questions answered.

She pointed to the photo he'd placed on the console between them. "Why did you tell me her name was Sadie? Did you do that on purpose?"

"Sadie, dear, everything I did was deliberate. Except…"

"Except what?" A mile sped by, and she gave up. "Your job at Rhodes, attending Hillcrest—all designed to break into my life, right?"

"Yup. And it worked."

A troop of motorbikes passed the pickup, the roar of the engines filling the cab.

Sadie wanted to throw accusations, but how could she? She owed him her life. "How much of what you told me about your background is true? I know you're more than a carpenter."

He pointed to a billboard advertising a truck stop. "Look at that. Remember the exit number. They have showers." After a pause, he continued. "I was born in

San Diego and lived there until I attended UCLA. After I graduated I worked overseas, in Washington D.C., and in Virginia. I've been back in L.A. now about three months. My father passed away last year and my mother lives—"

"Whoa. Your father and mother. So, were you raised in foster care?"

"No."

Sympathy his story had generated in her heart melted and turned to indignation. How dare he prey on her childhood memories of life without parents? Words clawed at her throat. She shot him a glance she hoped conveyed her disgust.

"I'm sorry, Sadie. It was cruel but necessary."

"Humph." She swallowed the anger. "I assume since you graduated from UCLA that your story about an alternate high school was also a lie."

"I had to make up something to cover my blunder with the mascot." He shifted in his seat. "Pretty much everything I told you was a variation of the truth."

Silence wedged between them.

Sadie tapped her thumbs on the steering wheel. "Fine. Now tell me the rest of your real story."

"My mother and Charlotte still live in San Diego."

"Who's Charlotte?"

"My sister."

"Sister? Why'd you lie about her? You said you had a brother. Oh, now I get it. You needed to get me thinking about brothers."

"My cover story, Sadie. It wasn't meant to hurt you. I used trigger words to elicit responses."

She applied the brakes to disengage the cruise control and focused on the mud flaps of an eighteen-wheeler in front of her. "Your strategy worked. It

134

resurrected my past in living color."

"I'm sorry, but everything I did had a purpose. To reconnect you with Cal and possibly Hannah."

His words seeped into her mind and slowly vaporized her hurt feelings. His soft tone and gentle pressure on her arm sent tingles to her heart. She may see Hannah very soon.

Traffic slowed as they eased through downtown Phoenix. The warmth of Bowen's hand reminded Sadie of other answers she needed. She shook off thoughts of Hannah and lowered her arm, forcing Bowen to remove his hand.

"A few more questions while you're in a disclosing mood. I know Cal hired you, but who do you work for?"

"I'm a private investigator, of sorts. That's all I can tell you, for now."

"OK." She pointed to the photo again. "I know she's not your wife, but are you married?" Why did every inch of her being wait in limbo for his answer?

"Divorced eleven years ago. No kids." His flat tone hung in the air.

A flicker of hope sparked in her heart. "Why'd you divorce? Was it related to your job?"

He folded his arms, and by the set of his jaw, Sadie thought he wouldn't answer, but one word slipped out.

"Booze."

"What did you say?"

"I drank too much. Liz handled it as long as she could. Then she left me." The fingers of his right hand drummed on his left bicep. "She filed for divorce, and I quit drinking."

Sadie veered past a large pothole. "I'm sorry."

What else could she say? Although she and Aaron seldom had more than an occasional glass of wine, she'd had several foster parents who overindulged. She knew firsthand the devastation alcohol could cause.

Removing his sunglasses, he slipped them into his pocket. "Been off the stuff for eleven years."

A car horn blared somewhere behind them. Sadie gripped the wheel and stole a look at Bowen. He slumped in the seat, arms folded again.

"That's something to be proud of."

He snorted and relaxed his arms. "But it cost me."

They drove the next miles in silence until she turned into in the truck stop parking lot.

"Take in whatever toiletries you need and a change of clothes. We'll shower first and then eat." Bowen slid out of the pickup and opened the back door.

Sadie located sneakers, jeans, underwear, a pair of socks, and a blue T-shirt and stowed the items in the bag with her drugstore purchases.

With a small duffle bag and computer case slung over his shoulder, Bowen asked, "Got the keys?"

In answer, she tossed them to him.

He caught the key ring and closed the door. "Let's be quick. The sooner we're back on the highway, the better." Once inside the facility, Bowen paid for two showers and they entered separate areas.

Sadie left her sandals on and hoped they'd survive their dunking. The warm water pounded tension off her stiff muscles. But as much as she wanted to linger, she dried off on the thin, scratchy white towel and dressed. After using the blow dryer on her short curls, she positioned the wig in place. A touch of makeup, all items stowed in the sack, and she was ready. She'd neglected to purchase a toiletry bag so everything jumbled together.

Patrons' chatter, the clinking of silverware, and whiffs of grease, coffee, and stale tobacco smoke led Sadie from the showers to the restaurant.

Clean-shaven Bowen in cowboy-cut jeans, boots, and a black T-shirt, waited at the entrance. No cap, no sunglasses. Damp curls slicked back. Eyes wide and innocent, searching for her. Sadie drew in a breath and glanced in the bag so he couldn't read her expression. *He lied. Everything he ever said was a lie.*

But Cal sent him. She would have to forgive Bowen's methods if they led to a reunion with her daughter. Her heart softened a little, and she joined him at the hostess podium.

While they waited to be seated, he leaned close.

Wisps of a citrusy aftershave tickled her nose. Sadie inhaled deeply but kept her eyes lowered.

"At first I thought that style of wig was a mistake. But you look nothing like your old photos. Observers will notice the hair, your figure, your confident air. They won't see you—if that makes sense—and they certainly won't pay me any heed."

For nearly three years, she'd worked hard at being invisible. The wig gave her a measure of anonymity and the boldness to stand next to this man.

A young waitress with a braided black ponytail directed Bowen and Sadie to a booth. They scanned the menu and ordered quickly.

Bowen opened his laptop, punched the power button, then attached the wireless card. When the newspaper website loaded, he turned the computer so they both could see the screen.

"Griff's story has been updated." He scrolled down and pointed to the last paragraph. "What do you think of that? Authorities are close to releasing the name of a suspect."

The words danced around her brain. Did this mean they wouldn't trace her phone call?

After closing the computer, Bowen took a long drink of iced tea. "Hmm, I feel like a new man. Shave, shower, ready to conquer the world." He took Sadie's hand. "And you, sweetheart, you have admiring glances from all the men in here."

"Stop lying, and don't call me sweetheart."

His grasp tightened, and she couldn't pull away. "Go with the flow. There really are two guys eyeing you. Don't make any obvious movements, but they're at the counter."

She flicked a quick glance at the two burly, bearded men and caught their leers. "Ugh. OK, if holding your hand will keep them away, fine, but don't insult me with any more lies."

"There are a few things I didn't lie about."

"Really? Your punching bag is in the backseat, so I guess that wasn't a lie."

"Right. That was true, and I love football." His gaze dropped to their clasped hands where his thumb rubbed circles on her knuckles. "And that's not all. I hated deceiving you because developing a relationship with you was more than a job. It was real."

She jerked her hand free. "That's not fair. I—"

The waitress approached the table and set down Sadie's small chef's salad and Bowen's tacos. "I'll be back with more tea. Will there be anything else?"

Bowen dolloped salsa on his tacos and flashed his dimpled smile at her. "Nope. This looks good.

Thanks."

Sadie shook her head, and the waitress left. After he'd delivered her to Cal and located Hannah, Sadie wasn't sure she wanted to see him again. His mysterious past, the way he'd found her, made her think there was more than a private investigator here. Her heart whispered an anguished plea that he was trustworthy. She sipped tea and stared out the window. Eighteen-wheelers chugged away from the diesel pumps. A scrawny blackbird pecked at the gravel along the sidewalk.

A dark blue sports car like Kyle's pulled into the lot.

Her blood turned as cold as the tea in her glass. Sweat gathered under her wig.

She set the glass down and tapped Bowen's hand. "Look out the window."

"Is it Kyle?" He stared. "We have to get out of here."

Grabbing the bag of clothes and her purse, Sadie slid out of the seat.

But instead of following her, Bowen pointed. "It's not Kyle."

An Asian man climbed out of the car.

"Can we still leave? I—"

"Of course." Bowen motioned to the waitress and after she gave him their ticket, he slung his bags over his shoulder.

They hurried out of the restaurant, dumped their belongings in the pickup, and set off with Bowen behind the wheel.

Although Kyle had not found her, knots of curdled fear filled Sadie's stomach. Her gaze drifted to Bowen's strong hands on the wheel. He held her life in those hands.

His phone beeped and he answered. "Yes, she's here. I'll put it on speaker."

Once he set the phone in its holder, a male voice filled the cab. "It's all over the news. Debra Johnson is wanted as a person of interest in the murder of Miles Griffin."

16

Tension sizzled in the cab.

"You're safe," Bowen said.

"But the whole world's looking for me."

"No. They're looking for Debra."

Although previous assignments had landed him in precarious positions, his face had never been plastered on a wanted poster. He had no idea what that was like. What could he say to reassure her? "We've been careful since we left Austin. No one's going to find Debra."

Still no response from her.

"I have many faults, but one thing I'm good at—my job. Keeping you safe." Why did he keep putting his size elevens in his mouth? "Please, Sadie, give me a chance. Yes, this is a job, but like I told you, my feelings for you aren't part of the assignment."

Silence from her side of the vehicle.

"I promise." He shot a glance at her. "Talk to me. Please."

"At this point in my upside down life, I don't care what you say. We have to be together, and I appreciate your help. But know this, Bowen Boudine. I'm sick of lies—yours, mine—all of them. Whatever the outcome of this venture, our paths will take opposite directions. After I talk with Cal and find Hannah, I'm not sure I want you around. I...you lied to me. I know you did it because of your job, but..." With arms folded, she sat back and faced the side window.

Bowen let twenty miles pass before stealing a glance at her. Her fingers twitched, and although half concealed by a curtain of hair, her jaw clenched.

Cal had supplied few details of the events leading up to her placement in WITSEC. But to protect her he needed as much information as possible. He cleared his throat and focused on a line of charter buses ahead. "You didn't get a chance to eat much. Are you hungry?"

"No. I can wait until we stop for gas again."

"Let me know. I'll stop anytime."

A minute of thick silence passed.

"I'm sorry for my tirade. I really appreciate what you're doing for me."

"I'll do everything in my power to keep you safe." Everything. Was she ready to tell him about her life? His cell phone rang again, and he pulled it from the holder. "Hello."

"This is Bravo Delta Tango, six-three-one-seven."

"Go ahead. What's the situation?" Bowen mouthed to Sadie, "This is about Kyle."

"Nelson was not at the location you provided. A neighbor—Pete Williams—was instrumental in releasing him."

"No kidding?" Kyle and Pete in cahoots? Bowen shook his head. "And were the authorities notified?"

"Nope."

"What about the U. S. Marshal's death. Discover anything?"

The voice on the line hesitated and then continued. "Don't know what you got yourself into, but this is a big mess. Sources told me the Austin Marshal's office has a major leak. Your murdered agent had several witnesses whose identities were compromised."

Bowen whistled. That might explain why the authorities wanted to locate Debra Johnson.

His caller asked, "Anything else I can do on this end?"

"No. That's all for now. If you hear more, give me a call. Thanks." Bowen returned the phone to its dashboard holder. "Bad news from Austin." He repeated the information his contact had provided.

Her eyes widened when he mentioned Pete Williams. "Do you think he and Kyle were working together?" She told him about her concerns regarding the men.

"They could be in cahoots. But what concerns me more is Griffin." After Bowen related the problems discovered with Griff's witnesses, Sadie's skin paled. "I know you considered him a friend, but could he have turned traitor?"

"Never. He's been my contact in Austin for over a year. Why would he betray me now? No. I won't believe it."

"I was going to suggest you contact the WITSEC office in L.A., but who knows how far the leak has traveled."

"I trust Cal, and he trusts you. We're on our own until I find Hannah. Then I'll make contact."

"Speaking of your past, I'd like you to tell me what happened. What led to your identity change? I was out of the country at the time and didn't keep up with U.S. news. Are you up to it?"

A heavy silence permeated the space. Had he asked too much?

"The details are never far from my mind, no matter how hard I try to bury them."

"Take your time. L.A. is four hundred miles

away."

She took off her sunglasses and rubbed her eyes. "Five years ago Aaron and I opened a technology consulting business. Our graduate degrees are in software engineering, but we had experience in many areas. We could handle pretty much anything in the industry." She shifted in the seat and picked at a thread on her jeans. "August three years ago, Brady Holdings hired us to revamp their accounting system."

"I've heard of Brady Insurance. Big office building on Wilshire, right?"

"Uh-huh. Beautiful glass façade hiding a mountain of corruption. Reminds me of a Bible verse about the Pharisees being like whitewashed tombs that look good on the outside, but inside they're full of dead men's bones."

"Nasty image." Bowen massaged his temple. Sadie's mention of this scripture struck like a javelin at his heart. Didn't that describe him? All right on the outside but full of sin and guilt on the inside? He gave Sadie a nod. "Go on."

"One evening I worked late—Aaron had already gone home. On my way to the employee exit, I overheard Hank Otis and Duke arguing. Hank was Brady's Chief Security Officer."

"Duke?"

"Levasseur. The owner of Brady Holding. He insisted he gave Hank a thumb drive pouch, and Hank denied it. Anyway, they bickered back and forth and finally Duke said that if the Malones got a hold of it, Hank would suffer severe consequences."

Bowen glanced at Sadie. Her rigid body told him plenty. "I'm sorry, Sadie. You don't have to carry on."

"It's OK. I left without them seeing me and fled

home and told Aaron. The next day there was a malfunction in the tech room. While working on the problem, I found a small black zippered pouch half hidden under a metal cart."

"It contained the missing thumb drive?"

"Two of them. I should have left the pouch there, but Duke's threatening words spurred my curiosity. I took it to the office we'd been assigned and plugged one of the drives into the computer."

"And you found—?"

"The mother lode. With Aaron keeping watch on our office door, I scanned the information. The first drive listed financial transactions that had nothing to do with accounting programs we'd had access to. The second one contained names, dates, and dollar amounts going back years. It also had transactions in code. Too much for us to decipher at my desk, and too dangerous." She glanced at Bowen, her eyes sad and lackluster.

"I always carry extra flash drives. I copied all the files, erased any trace of my actions, and continued about the day's work as usual."

"I can't believe it. Little Debra Johnson, the plant expert, is really a cyber-spy. What was in code?"

"Aaron and I concluded Duke had two accounting systems. One auditors had access to, and the one I'd discovered. When we deciphered the code, we found transactions detailing major drug deals, arms shipments, pays and owes—"

"Pays and what?"

"Pays and owes. Records of money laundering."

"I learned something new today. Please continue."

"The worst information we found was details of his importation of underage girls from Latin America."

Sadie shuddered. "The whole operation still gives me the creeps."

"All of this was conducted out of Brady Holdings? Who was running the show?"

"The Levasseur family. Duke was in charge, but his kids, Lonnie and Nicole, were involved."

"What happened next?"

Sadie poked at a spot on her jeans. "We checked with an LAPD friend at church who worked for the OCID, the Organized Crime Investigation Division. He said they already had Brady Holdings on their radar. We gave the flash drives to them, and they asked that we stay in the company to gather more information. We delayed the completion of the project so we could tape conversations, take cell phone pictures, and gather more evidence. Because the crimes crossed state lines, the FBI got involved."

"And that's how you ended up in WITSEC?"

A quick nod.

Bowen slowed as the traffic through Phoenix increased. "Duke's in prison, right? What happened to his kids?"

"Duke was sentenced to fifty years in prison, but there wasn't enough evidence to tie Lonnie and Nicole to the illegal activities at Brady Holdings. Lonnie's still in charge of the above board company—insurance and stock trading."

"So you're in WITSEC because of Lonnie and Nicole?"

"Yes. Although they stayed out of the spotlight, I received numerous threats during the trial. I'm sure they came from Lonnie, but we couldn't prove it."

The setting sun shone right into the vehicle. Bowen lowered the visor and sat a little straighter.

"Can you fill in the details on what happened to Aaron and Hannah?"

Sadie nibbled a nail and then clasped her hands. "Aaron and I completed the job at Brady, we thought without Duke becoming suspicious, but afterward he kept calling our company office. He even called the house."

"Did you report his harassment?"

"Of course. During the investigation, additional police patrols were sent to our neighborhood in Culver City. Aaron and I took extra precautions, but…"

Anger burned in his gut. No wonder she slumped in the seat. He hated to prod, but he needed the last chapter. "Tell me the rest, Sadie."

She placed both hands over her heart as if to prevent its escape. "You already know bits and pieces, but I'll tell you the whole story. Hannah was four and a half, in a pre-school program close to the office. Aaron picked her up, and witnesses stated his vehicle was followed by a dark SUV. He called me and said he was being forced off the road, and that's the last time I spoke to him. His car smashed through the bridge railing and landed in the rain-swollen Santa Ana River." Sadie shuddered and air rattled out of her lungs as she exhaled. "Dark blue paint transfer on scrapes and dents indicated he'd been rammed from behind…" Her voice faded. After a long pause, her dull, flat words barely reached his ears. "I was immediately given federal protection, but it was too late for my family."

Bowen let the silence between them act as a balm.

"Did they ever find out who rammed Aaron's vehicle?"

She drew in a jagged breath as if she'd been

sobbing. "No. But during the trial someone slipped an envelope under the door when I was in the ladies' restroom. It contained a blurred photograph of Hannah with a terrified expression, staring out of the window of Aaron's car."

17

Bowen pulled up next to a pump and turned off the engine. The harsh lights of the gas station filled the cab with a sharp fluorescent glow. He glanced at Sadie as she stirred. She'd slept through their entry into California, and another border patrol stop.

She squinted and stretched. "Where are we?"

"This is Blythe—a few miles across the California border." Bowen ran his fingers through his hair and then jammed the cap on his head. "Please wait for me, and then we'll enter the store together."

"OK." Her discarded sunglasses lay on the console. She placed them in her purse.

Bowen climbed out of the pickup and entered the convenience store to prepay. Rubbing his tight shoulders, he tromped to the pump and filled the gas tank. He returned to the store with Sadie. After using the facilities, they purchased barbeque sub-sandwiches, bottled water, and large cups of coffee, under the cold-eyed stare of the elderly clerk. Bowen kept his head down and trusted Sadie's disguise would thwart anyone searching the store's surveillance footage.

As they returned to the pickup, Sadie asked, "Want me to take over?"

"No. I'm fine. We'll be in L.A. in three or four hours." Bowen opened the door for Sadie and held her cup while she buckled herself in.

He maneuvered back onto I-10. When he'd

finished eating his sandwich, he crumpled up the wrapper and tossed it over the seat. "I appreciate you telling me your story. I'm sorry if it opened old wounds."

"Being with Cal in L.A. again will probably sling me back to the past. It's inevitable."

"You have no other family in L.A., right?"

"Cal is all I have. And Hannah, if she's…" Her voice trailed off.

"It'll be close to midnight when we reach the safe house. We—"

"What safe house? Aren't we going straight to Cal?"

"You said you trusted me, so this is the plan, and you have to promise to follow it. OK?" Sadie would not end up like Patricia.

"Promise."

"Once in L.A., I'll take you to a safe house. In the morning, we'll contact Cal and arrange to meet in a secure location. After I check out the story of the Adams woman, I'll figure out how to get you to see Hannah."

"Why all the secrecy with Caleb?"

Bowen glanced at her. In the muted light from the instrument panel he noted the tight line of her lips and the furrow between her eyes. "Please listen with your head and not your heart. I have no idea what you're going through, but be patient a few more days. We have to make sure no one knows you're in California." For a moment his role as protector and friend blurred. He funneled his thoughts back on the job. Keep Sadie safe. "By now people at work have realized something's wrong. And who knows what your neighbor Pete will do? We have to take all precautions."

"And Hannah? When can I see her?"

"Depends on what my contacts have discovered about Ms. Adams. We have to be positive about identification. Maybe tomorrow."

Yanking off the wig, she threw it on the floor. She shook her head, freeing her curls. Deep groans erupted and she pounded her knees.

"Sadie, I'm sorry." He had no words of comfort. An intense desire to hold her and press his lips against hers hit him broadside. Gripping the wheel with one hand, he slid the other over her shoulders. "You've got to be strong a while longer."

Sadie took the discarded wig and straightened it on her head. She scrunched up in the corner, her misery evident.

Bowen punched a radio button, selecting a pop-rock station. He drummed his fingers on the steering wheel in time to the beat.

"Please turn it down. I want to talk to you."

He turned off the radio. "Sure. What's on your mind?" *Stupid question.* "I mean—"

"You don't have to walk on tiptoe around me. I'm so used to being independent, but I need your advice."

"How can I help?"

Her head was bowed, and she twisted her hands in her lap. "It's about Griff. I feel responsible for his death somehow. When he used the code word, I should have…" Her voice cracked.

"What could you have done? The news report indicated he was shot soon after receiving a call, which we assume came from you." Bowen took her hand. "He knew the risks his job involved. He gave you a warning, and you heeded it."

A heavy-duty sigh whooshed from her lips. "I know, I know." She pulled her hand away and brushed the hair from her face. "And now, do I contact WITSEC in Los Angeles? I don't know what to do. I can't think straight."

"That's why I'm here. My job is to deliver you safely to Cal. Once we meet him and you're certain the girl is Hannah, then you can contact WITSEC. You need to tell them Kyle Nelson came after you. Maybe they'll find a connection between Kyle and Griff's murder."

"No." Sadie screwed up her face. "Kyle was weird and he—but murder?"

"I asked about him before, but is there anything else you remember?"

"Kyle couldn't have killed Griff. He was trussed up in my apartment when I made the call."

"You're right. But maybe he had an accomplice?"

"Let me think back. I first visited Hillcrest Church in July last year. Hannah's birthday. I'll never forget." Her soft words floated in the air before she cleared her throat. "I can't remember if Kyle was already attending, but my first encounter with him was several months later."

"How'd you meet?"

"He's a journalist working on a book. Something to do with cultural traditions. He took pictures all the time. I avoided him when he had his camera. But one day he cornered me after the church service and asked a bunch of questions. I think it was around Christmas because I remember holiday decorations on the door."

"What kind of questions?"

"You know, the usual. Kinda like the ones you asked. But I guess because he professed to be a

Christian, they didn't bother me as much."

"Was he persistent? Did he try to befriend you?"

"You mean like you did?"

The tone of those words wounded him. Bowen rubbed his chin and muttered, "I deserved that. I'm sorry."

"Forget it." She was silent for a few minutes. "I remember something else. A woman came with him recently. Kyle introduced her as his sister Lavonne." Sadie tented her fingers. "And you know what else, she—Lavonne—came into work a few times. She didn't speak to me, but I knew she watched me as she examined the plants."

The car ahead swerved, forcing Bowen's full attention back to the road. Wooden planks lay scattered across his lane and the road shoulder. He avoided the debris and checked his mirrors.

Red and blue lights flashed.

Bowen sucked in a breath.

18

"License and registration."

While Bowen complied with the state trooper's request, Sadie crossed her arms and hung her head. They'd made it safely to the outskirts of L.A. Would her flight end here, a few miles from Cal and Hannah?

The trooper examined Bowen's documents by flashlight. "Mr. Boudine, where you traveling to?"

"San Francisco. We're on vacation."

Sadie understood why Bowen lied, but it still disturbed her. Taking her cue from him, she relaxed against the seat while her gut churned.

"Your driving was a bit erratic back there, Mr. Boudine."

"I swerved to avoid debris in the road, sir."

"How much have you had to drink tonight?"

"None, sir. Nothing. I don't drink."

"Would you step out of the car, please?"

Sadie observed the trooper conduct a sobriety test on Bowen, nibbling on a nail the whole time.

Ten minutes later, Bowen returned to the truck, a ticket in his hand. "A warning for not signaling. Can you believe that?"

By the time he took the Highway 710 ramp, Sadie's heart had settled into a normal rhythm again. Her numb brain could barely string two words together.

After making a brief phone call, Bowen pulled into the driveway of a '50s style bungalow, replete with tidy lawn, two palm trees, and a black wrought iron fence.

As soon as Bowen switched off the engine, a lanky bald-headed man stepped from the shadows on the front porch. Highlighted by the streetlight, his sharp nose, prominent brow, and hollow cheeks reminded Sadie of a hawk.

Bowen gestured towards the house. "This is it, Sadie. Go inside, and we'll bring your things."

Hawk Man opened the passenger door and offered Sadie his hand, which she gladly took. Fatigue and anxiety had turned her leg muscles to mush. She staggered across the lawn to the small porch. Its three steps looked ten feet high. Joints complained as she climbed up and entered the house, Bowen's voice humming behind her.

A tall table lamp shed a soft yellow glow over the sparsely furnished living room. An old black and white movie played on a small TV set. Sadie dumped her purse on the blue plaid sofa and flexed her shoulders.

The men carried in the luggage, which they placed in the middle of the room next to a stained coffee table.

Hawk Man held out his hand to Bowen. "Give me your keys. I'll close the gate, and then move your truck."

Sadie couldn't place his heavy accent.

Bowen dropped the keys into the man's hand. "This way." He picked up her suitcase and pointed down the hall. "Do you want anything to eat or drink?"

"No, thanks."

Three doors led off the narrow space. Bowen stopped at the last one. "Here's your room." He set her suitcase and shopping bag on a straight-backed wooden chair. Deep lines etched the skin around his eyes and dark stubble covered his chin. His smile softened his features. "Sadie, I've got to repeat. Your life is in our hands—mine and Erik's. You must listen to us."

She nodded.

"First, get some rest. There's a bathroom through there." She lowered herself to the bed while he pointed out a door to her right. "Don't leave the house. Don't make any phone calls, and if anything happens to me, Erik will take care of you."

Wide-eyed, she stared at him, unable to comprehend his last statement.

Bowen sat next to her, taking her hand and stroking it as if she were three years old. "Don't worry. I plan on being around a long time. Now, before I go, any questions?"

A dozen sprinted through her brain, but she knew he meant questions about his instructions. "No. I understand."

With a final pat on her hand, he stepped to the door. "One more thing. Always be dressed to run out of here. Sleep in regular clothes, and when you shower, do so as quickly as possible. And have your things packed at all times." His dimple appeared briefly. "See you in the morning."

"Thank you for everything."

He gave her a nod and closed the door.

Sadie rose to her feet and glanced around. The room had heavily shaded windows, a double bed, a six-drawer dresser, and a lamp on a side table.

Tired, aching muscles called for rest. From the drugstore sack, she pulled her toothbrush and toothpaste. On the way to the bathroom, she removed the wig. She brushed her teeth and washed her face, and then shed her jacket and sneakers and tumbled into bed. Sleep descended immediately.

She awoke to the sound of male voices outside the window. For a second, she couldn't remember where she was, and then in the gloom she caught sight of the wig draped over her suitcase. Stretching tight muscles, she slid out of bed and peeked around the shade. Bowen and Erik conversed a moment longer before disappearing around the house.

Daylight. Today she'd see Cal, and maybe Hannah.

She showered and dressed in record time. With the wig securely in place, she packed her belongings. Checking her reflection in the mirror, she noticed an old-fashioned glass soda bottle with a yellow carnation on the dresser. Had it been there last night?

Erik stood at the stove, stirring a savory concoction that smelled like home cooking.

"Good morning."

He turned at her greeting and gestured to the counter. "Morning. There's coffee."

The aroma from the pan tickled her taste buds. She poured a mug of coffee, added an extra dose of creamer to the dark brew, and savored the first sip. "Where's Bowen?"

Erik set three plates on the counter. "Garage. He'll be back soon."

He shoveled his creation from the skillet onto the plates and pushed one to her. "Eat. It's good."

While he ran water into the skillet, she slipped around the counter and hunted for silverware. An odd assortment of knives, forks, and spoons rattled in the second drawer she opened. She gathered three sets, took her plate, silverware, and cup to the green Formica-topped square table, and sat facing the kitchen. Erik's dish of eggs, green peppers, and sausage was delicious. He ate standing at the stove while keeping an eye on her.

The morning light accentuated his sharp features. Rolled up shirtsleeves exposed faded tattoos. Deep crow's-feet etched the corners of his eyes. She guessed he had a few years on Bowen, although she didn't know Bowen's age.

The back door opened, and Bowen stomped into the kitchen. "Something smells good. Morning Sadie. Did you sleep OK?"

With her mouth full, she could only nod.

Bowen washed his hands, scooped up his plate and joined her at the table. "Hey, Erik, please bring me a cup of coffee, and come sit with us. She doesn't bite. I promise." He grinned and forked food into his mouth.

Carrying two mugs, Erik slid into a chair.

"Thanks." Bowen took a gulp of coffee.

One last bite and Sadie set her plate aside. "Did you get any sleep?"

"Not much. Erik and I had to finalize plans."

Erik drained his cup and nodded.

"Like what?"

Bowen took their empty plates to the sink and returned with the coffeepot and creamer container. He refilled the three cups and sat.

"Phone calls. Contacts. That kinda thing."

"I get the message. You'll tell me what I need to know." After shaking a liberal dose of creamer into her cup, Sadie sipped her coffee. "So, when are we going to meet Caleb?"

Erik checked his watch. "I'll make the call."

Sadie caught the glance Bowen sent Erik. The tall man stood and loped down the hall.

When he disappeared into one of the bedrooms, she asked, "Who is he?"

Bowen took another gulp of coffee.

"Where's he from? I don't recognize his accent."

When he ignored her questions, she scooted the chair back from the table and rolled up her sleeves. Might as well clean the kitchen. As steam rose from the sink, she concentrated on the chore and jumped when Bowen's breath heated her neck.

"Erik's from Bosnia. Now quit with the questions." He added his cup to the water. "Thanks for doing the dishes. We'll leave in ten minutes." His footsteps echoed down the hall.

Ten minutes. Soon she'd meet Cal, and they'd make plans to see Hannah. She glanced at her clothes. Blue jeans, pink and white striped top. Hurrying to her room, she shook her head. Crazy. She hadn't given a thought to her clothing in three years. Why start now? Cal wouldn't care. After all, he'd paid who knows how much for Bowen to locate her. After checking her room one more time to make sure all her things were in the suitcase, she collected her purse and faded denim jacket and headed to the living room.

Erik, a shoulder holster strap crossing his back, stood at the closed front door. He turned as Sadie entered.

Remembering Bowen's admonition, she refrained from asking questions, but she couldn't keep her gaze off Erik's weapon.

He yanked a brown suede jacket from the rack and pulled it on, effectively concealing the holster.

Sadie sank into the dark blue armchair and closed

her eyes. The day might hold all manner of surprises for her. Her stomach flip-flopped with nervous jitters. From out of nowhere a scripture floated into consciousness.

"Do not be anxious about anything, but in everything, by prayer and petition, with thanksgiving, present your requests to God."

Although prayer had been an integral part of her former life, she'd said few since Aaron died. But now, she found minute phrases in her soul budding to life. They grew and blossomed, until she crumbled forward and covered her face. *Oh, God, please forgive me. Come near and give me strength. I can't get through today without You.* She wasn't sure how long she sat there, but by the time Bowen interrupted, a shawl of peace covered her shoulders.

"Ready?" He sorted through jackets on the rack and chose a gray windbreaker. "Let's go."

In the driveway were two vehicles—a tan sedan and a black pickup, like the one Cal drove before she entered WITSEC.

"We'll use the car. Erik will take the truck."

"Where's your pickup?"

Bowen gestured to the detached two-car garage and opened her door. "Need to keep it hidden for now. Just a precaution."

His words knocked a small chink in her security blanket. She might be with Hannah soon, but her troubles were far from over.

Before setting off, Bowen inserted a device into his ear and set the microphone piece close to his mouth. "Testing. Erik, come in." He paused and then added, "Good to go. I'll wait for you to close the gate."

Although she'd lived in L.A. for many years, Sadie

had no idea where they were.

Bowen's set jawline and rigid posture squelched any thought of asking. His constant scanning to the right and left reminded her of their serious situation.

Erik followed close behind them.

She kept quiet until they turned onto Highway 101, and she caught a glimpse of the Hollywood sign. A light film of smog hovered over the city. Now she was in familiar territory. "Where are we going to meet Cal?"

"In the hills. Near Runyan Canyon Park. Erik will call and give him the exact location shortly."

"Why there?"

"Only one way in. Easy for Erik to monitor." His brusque tone and concise answer erected a barrier between them. No longer her driving companion, he'd morphed into her bodyguard.

"I know Erik carries a gun. Do you?"

"No." Bowen zigzagged through a neighborhood and then turned onto Runyan Canyon Road. They twisted up into the hills about a mile, with Bowen checking the rearview mirror every few seconds. He slowed and parked in a wide graveled area. With the vehicle facing the road, he tapped his earpiece. "We're here. Send him up."

Sadie glanced around. Where was Erik?

Bowen left the engine running and opened a window. With his hand on his earpiece, he looked at Sadie. "Erik's at the bottom of the road. He'll keep watch. Make sure no one followed Cal. Are you ready?"

A boulder-sized lump formed in her throat. She swallowed and nodded.

"I see his SUV now." As it drew to a stop, Bowen

opened his door. "Stay here until I call you. Understand?"

She twisted her purse strap and kept her eyes on the silver vehicle. "OK."

Cal climbed out and shook hands with Bowen.

Sadie's heart quivered and a gasp escaped her dry lips. Cal looked so much like Aaron. The same height, close to six-foot. Short hair a little lighter than Aaron's. Same square jaw. Hands on his hips, Aaron's favorite stance.

Bowen motioned to Sadie.

Without hesitation, she exited the car.

She ran and fell into Cal's arms.

He studied her face. "Sadie? You're so different." He wrapped her in a crushing hug. "I'm glad to see you."

"Hi, Caleb. Tell me about Hannah."

19

Sadie sat with Cal in his car while he repeated his story of finding Hannah. He added details to the conversation they'd had en route to California. Stepping out of the car, she beckoned to Bowen. "When can we see her?"

"We're working on that. But Cal won't be coming with us." Bowen was in charge.

"Will Cal and I meet again? We have so much to talk about."

"Maybe. Let's see what happens when we locate Hannah. We'll—hold on." He touched his earpiece, and then his brow scrunched tight.

"Get in the car. Cal, follow me out of here. We've got company."

Sadie jumped in the sedan and snapped her seat belt.

Jamming the car in gear, Bowen tore across the gravel. Cal followed close behind as they screeched around curves and raced up hills. Out the back window, Sadie glimpsed a dark SUV gaining on them. Erik's black pickup roared around the SUV. He maneuvered from side to side, preventing the SUV from passing him.

Sadie's thoughts worked overtime. Had someone followed Cal? Did that mean the Levasseurs knew she was in L.A.?

The grim set of Bowen's face confirmed her suspicions. By the time he turned onto Mulholland

Drive, he'd lost Erik and the SUV. Cal kept close as they drove down the 101, the Hollywood Freeway, to a café tucked away in a quiet neighborhood.

"I need to have a long talk with Cal. We're safe here. Erik will keep watch." He removed the ear piece. "Too easy to trace."

Face pale, lips tight, Cal joined them at the café entrance. "What happened back there?"

Bowen gestured to the café door. "Let's discuss that."

Once directed to a table close to the kitchen, Bowen pointed to the laminated menu. "Please order coffee for me. I need to make a quick call." He moved to the corner and held his phone to his ear.

Caleb ordered coffee for himself and Bowen, and Sadie chose hot chocolate. She had enough acid churning in her stomach.

Bowen returned a couple of minutes later and joined them. "OK, folks, here's the deal. It's obvious someone followed you, Cal. Did you adhere to all the precautions I gave you?"

"To the letter. Didn't tell anyone." Cal hiked his shoulders, eyes wide. "Took a circuitous route. Kept watch for a tail."

With his gaze fixed on the red tablecloth, Bowen pursed his lips. "And you've never called me on a landline—even from your office?"

Cal pulled his cell phone from his suit coat pocket and waited for the server to deliver their order. "This is what I use."

Bowen held out his hand. "Let me have it."

Before Cal could protest, Bowen located a tiny screwdriver on his key chain and popped the cover off the device. He examined the intricate innards, and then snapped the cover back in place. "No bug." He slid it across the table to Cal. "Start at the beginning and tell us what you did after seeing the child who looks like Hannah."

Mug in hand, Cal explained how he'd questioned the woman's neighbors and discovered she'd showed up with a child in mid-November. "They remembered it was the week before Thanksgiving, and I narrowed it down to the year of Aaron's accident."

"Did you tell anyone? How about your girlfriend?"

"My fiancée? No, I didn't tell Reyna or anyone else. That's when I decided to hire someone to locate Sadie."

She took Cal's free hand in hers and squeezed.

He acknowledged her action with a nod.

"I know I wasn't the first person you contacted. How did you find the others?" Bowen drained his mug.

"Let me think." Cal squinted for a moment. "When I entered my office the next morning, I asked my secretary to get me a list of private detectives."

"And you trust her?"

"I did, but she no longer works for me. She got married and moved to San Francisco a month ago."

"Did anyone overhear you ask her for the list?"

"There were probably three or four people in the reception area. Maybe—"

Bowen's phone rang. "It's Erik." While he listened, deep lines furrowed his brow. He shoved his phone back into his pocket and stood. "We've got to go. Erik ran the plates on the SUV. Turns out the guy works for Brady Holdings."

Struggling to catch her breath, Sadie rose and

searched Bowen's face for reassurance.

"The Levasseurs know you're in L.A."

"How?"

After slapping a ten dollar bill over the ticket, Bowen gestured towards the door. "Come on. We need to leave now." He ushered her through the parking lot to Cal's SUV. "There's one more thing I want to check." Bowen scooted under the vehicle. He moved around and then grunted, "Got it." He rolled out with a three-inch square black box in hand. "Tracking device."

"No! How long has it been there?"

"No telling, but this changes our plans." Bowen placed the devise on the ground behind the rear tire of Cal's SUV. When he straightened, he brushed the grit and dust off his shirt and pants. "The device will get crushed when you drive over it, but we've got to assume they've had it in place a while."

Hands shaking, stomach churning, Sadie pulled her sunglasses from her purse. "Do you think they know about the woman and Hannah?"

"I doubt it. The device was probably installed after Cal made inquiries about hiring someone to find you."

A low moan gurgled from Cal's throat and he slapped his palm against his forehead. "No, no."

"What?" Bowen and Sadie asked together.

"I've been back to the Adams's house several times. To get another look at the child."

Bowen grabbed Sadie's arm and motioned for Cal to follow. He opened the vehicle door and waited until she slid in. "I've got to get Sadie out of here. Cal, does your car have GPS?"

"Yes"

"Then take it home. Rent a car that has no

electronic tracking device."

"How about I use my old sports car?"

"That'll work. We'll have to run frequent checks for other tracking devices. When they realize this one has been destroyed, they'll try again. I'm gonna purchase two cheap cell phones. One for you, one for Sadie. We'll use them to communicate. Nothing else. Erik will get yours to you. Now go. Don't contact me until you have the new phone. Watch your back and don't go anywhere near Ms. Adams's house."

Cal climbed into his SUV, and Bowen joined Sadie.

"Will we have to move? Should we contact WITSEC?"

Wordlessly, Bowen navigated the neighborhood, eyes on the road or checking the mirrors. When they reached the safe house, he parked in the garage and closed the door. Only when they entered the living room did he answer her. "We're fine here for now. No one followed us, and Erik is keeping watch. Hold on. I need to call him." He moved down the hall and his voice drifted in and out.

She slumped onto the sofa and removed her sunglasses. When he returned she asked, "What about WITSEC?"

Bowen shed his jacket, a deep scowl marring his rugged face. "Not yet. There are too many unanswered questions about Griffin's death, Kyle's involvement, and now this deal with Cal. Wait a few days." Rolling up his sleeves, he entered the kitchen.

Sadie lost confidence in her ability to make sane decisions. She had to rely on Bowen for her safety and needed to trust his instincts. "When can I see Hannah?"

His voice carried from the kitchen. "You hungry? I

can make sandwiches."

"Maybe I'd better eat something." Still thinking of Hannah, Sadie plopped into a chair at the table.

Bowen selected canned sodas, packaged meat slices, lettuce, and a jar of mayonnaise from the refrigerator. He grabbed a loaf of sliced whole-wheat bread and assembled sandwiches.

They ate in silence until Bowen finished his sandwich. "When Erik gets back, we'll plan our trip to Santa Clarita."

The news hit Sadie like a punch to the gut. She leaned back in the chair and gulped in air. Hannah. She'd see her baby today.

Erik entered through the back door. "Boudine. Here's Sadie's phone. I already gave one to Cal. Close call, no?"

Bowen took the small cell phone. "Perfect. Have you—"

"All set. It's ready to go." Erik removed his jacket and hung it on the back of a chair.

After tapping keys on his own phone, Bowen handed the slim black cell to Sadie. "Only for calls I sanction. Promise you won't call friends or—"

"What friends? You think I'm stupid enough to call April or Sylvia?" Immediately she regretted her word. "Sorry, I know the drill."

"And I'm sorry too. It's…we're too close now to make a mistake. I've programmed your number into my phone. Erik has already entered our numbers into yours."

No mistakes. No mistakes. Sadie clutched the phone to her chest.

"Erik and I need to discuss our plans." Bowen cleared the table. "We'll be right outside. Sorry, there's not much to do. I think there are a couple of novels in the hall closet. I'll let you know when we can leave."

She slipped the phone into her jeans pocket and picked up her soda. "Don't worry about me. Hurry so we can see Hannah."

❦

Incessant banging roused Sadie. She tossed the romance novel aside, slid off the bed, and followed the sound to the kitchen.

Erik barged through the door, hammer in hand.

"What were you doing out there?"

"Securing the window screens. You want some tea?"

"Thanks. Where's Bowen? When are we going to Santa Clarita?"

After setting two mugs of water in the microwave, Erik selected a couple of teabags from a box on the counter. "Boudine had to leave. Have to wait for him to get back." Erik no longer wore his shoulder holster, but the weapon's handgrip stuck out his back waistband. A gun stowed at his back, mugs of tea in his hands—the contrast wasn't lost on her. His relaxed jaw softened the hard angle of his cheeks. He deposited two mugs on the table and sprawled opposite her.

They sipped in silence.

Would she see Hannah today?

Erik drained his mug and set it down with a thump.

Although her relationship with Bowen had changed irrevocably, Sadie figured she could pump Erik for information about him. "How long have you known Bowen?"

"Many years. Like fifteen."

"Did you know his wife?"

"Little bit. Boudine and I keep work and private life separate."

"Exactly what kind of work did you do together?"

"No, no. You'll get nothing more from me."

"Just one more question. How old is he?"

"I think he's forty-one, forty-two. Now I have more screens to check. You stay inside, OK?"

Sadie rinsed the mugs and scoured the hall closet. At the back, under a thick, musty old telephone directory, she found a Bible. As she carried it to the sofa, she thumbed through the well-worn pages. The frayed edge of the faded red ribbon bookmark dangled out, marking a spot in the middle. She opened to the page and found a scrap of paper torn from a magazine and a heavily underlined passage.

The words in Isaiah 40:31 tumbled from her lips. "But they that wait on the Lord shall renew their strength; they shall mount up with wings as eagles; they shall run, and not be weary; and they shall walk, and not faint." The force of the words surrounded her like a beam of light brighter than the sun. She'd read them before, but never had they held such a personal meaning. Wait on the Lord. Fly like an eagle. Run and not be weary. She was tired of running without the Lord.

The torn scrap of paper slipped off the Bible's slick pages. Sadie picked it up and read the caption. Ancient Dolomite Chant. Who had thought enough about the chant to tear it out and place it in this particular chapter? She read the words through once, but had to read them again, to absorb the full impact.

Not so in haste, my heart!
Have faith in God and wait;
Although He lingers long,
He never cometh too late.

He never cometh too late;
He knoweth what is best;
Vex not thyself in vain;
Until he cometh, rest.

Until He cometh, rest
Nor grudge the hours that roll;
The feet that wait for God
Are soonest at the goal.

Are soonest at the goal
That is not attained by speed;
Then hold thee still my heart,
For I shall wait His lead.

Stunned at the simple, yet profound words, Sadie sat back.

The scrap fluttered out of her fingers to land between the pages and she closed the Bible around it. Another lost prodigal may have need of its powerful sentiment.

Cold embers in her lukewarm soul stirred. With eyes closed, she let the words of the chant and the verse gel in the peace and quiet of the room.

Erik's booming voice shattered the silence. "Boudine called. We can't visit Santa Clarita today."

20

Arms loaded with take-out containers, Bowen banged open the back door and entered the kitchen. He dumped the containers on the table and opened them, revealing steamed rice, chow mein noodles, Kung Pao chicken, and Beijing beef.

"Let's eat. I'm hungry." Eric slid into a chair.

As Bowen piled noodles and beef on his plate, his phone rang. He left the room to answer it, returning a few minutes later. "That was Ginger."

"Who's Ginger?" Sadie asked.

"She's my...secretary." He glanced at Erik and shoveled noodles into his mouth.

Sadie finished her meal in silence, and then carried her plate to the trash. "Since everyone is so talkative, I'm going to take a long bath. Or rather a short shower."

At the click of her bedroom door closing, Bowen shrugged. "I didn't know what else to say. The name slipped out."

"Secretary. If Ginger hears you say that, you'll be in big trouble."

"I know. So you'd better not tell her." Bowen stood and stretched.

Erik moved his finger across his lips and twisted it at the side. "Sealed and locked." His grin lasted until Bowen slapped him on the shoulder.

"Hurry up. We've got to plan our strategy for tomorrow."

"Tomorrow?" Erik scooped up the empty containers and threw them away.

"Yup. We're going to stake out the Adams's house."

ംഃഛ

Bowen stood at Sadie's door and listened. What did he hope to accomplish? Be invited in? Convince himself she was safe? He tapped on the door and when he received no answer, opened it a little. He knew she'd follow his rule and be dressed.

A shaft of light from the hall triangled to the bed. She lay snuggled under the covers, all but her blonde curls hidden. The wig dangled over her suitcase.

He closed the door and retreated to his room across the hall. Once he'd shed his shoes and shirt, he flopped on the bed, hands behind his head, and stared into the darkness.

Tomorrow, Sadie would know. When she saw the girl, she'd know if it was Hannah. Crazy questions raced through Bowen's mind. Would WITSEC relocate them? Would Sadie grow her hair long? Would he ever see her again? He turned over and thumped the pillow.

They'd spent the evening watching TV, playing rummy, and talking.

Earlier, Erik had made a batch of cookies from a roll of frozen cookie dough. The oatmeal-raisin treats had been delicious, and a lingering hint of cinnamon drifted through the house.

Bowen crawled under the sheet and closed his eyes. The image of Sadie munching on a cookie and holding a hand full of playing cards danced in his head as sleep came to the rescue.

The next morning when Bowen entered the kitchen, Erik had fresh sliced fruit and blueberry muffins on the table. "Sleep well?" the chef asked.

Bowen poured a mug of coffee and sat. "No."

"Why? Worried about the stakeout?" Erik set plates on the table and sat next to Bowen. "We covered all angles last night."

After a few gulps of coffee, Bowen shook his head. "Not that."

"What then?" He raised his eyebrows and nodded slowly. "Ah, I see the problem."

Bowen flashed him a glare strong enough to sour milk.

"Boudine, I've known you long enough to hear what you're not saying. It's the woman, isn't it? It's Sadie."

Before Bowen could answer, Sadie entered the kitchen. "What about me?"

Bowen and Erik looked at each other.

Clearing his throat, Erik stood and pointed to the food. "Sit. Enjoy. I'll get coffee."

"Fine. Don't tell me what you were taking about, but please explain this elaborate breakfast."

Erik set a mug of steaming coffee in front of her, along with the creamer container. "Just because we're undercover, doesn't mean we have to eat from boxes and cans."

"I'm not complaining." She bit into a warm muffin. "Mmm, this is delicious."

"Erik's full of surprises." Bowen stood and refilled his mug. "Always provides great meals when he can. There've been times when we survived on crackers and jerky." Dark visions of being holed up in the mountains of Pakistan stabbed at his brain. He blinked.

Why taint the positive spin Sadie had added to the conversation? Bowen returned to the table. "He's the best."

Seldom a conversationalist, Erik eyed him and Sadie as he ate his fill.

By ten thirty they'd cleaned up the kitchen and Sadie departed to her room.

"Be careful, friend." Erik tapped Bowen's shoulder and lowered his voice. "You need your best game on. Can't have you—"

"I know. I know. I can separate my emotions from the task at hand."

"Her life depends on it." He spun around and picked up his shoulder holster.

Bowen stomped down the hall to his room. Every client's life depended on his professionalism. But Patricia had not followed the rules. Her husband had found her and... He yanked on his jacket, located his baseball cap and stepped into the hall.

Sadie stood by her door, eyes wide. "This is it, Bowen. I'll see Hannah today."

"If all goes as planned. Are you worried?"

"A little. It's been almost three years. Will she remember me?"

"We won't talk to her today. First you have to positively identify her."

Erik burst through the back door. "The boss called. I've got to go. Sorry, Sadie. Our trip has been postponed for a few hours. I'll return as soon as I can."

Sadie's face paled.

"If Erik says we wait, we wait. Be patient a little longer." He guided her to the sofa.

She snuggled next to him.

Words of solace and encouragement poured from

his lips.

After a while she excused herself and returned to her room.

His heart brimming with longing, he locked himself in his room and opened his laptop. Work, the antidote.

చిళ్ళ

At one o'clock Erik returned.

Bowen and Sadie had already had lunch and were still in the kitchen.

"The vehicles are ready," Erik said. Once outside, Erik slid into a dark green pickup, and Bowen pointed to a gray SUV. "This is our chariot today."

"Where are the vehicles from yesterday?" Sadie climbed in and fastened her seat belt.

Bowen adjusted the earpiece and set the tiny microphone by his mouth. "Can you hear me, Erik? Good. Let's go." He turned the key in the ignition. "We have a fleet of—"

"A fleet?"

"We have several cars to use in situations like this. Don't worry about the details."

She slipped on her sunglasses and faced the side window. A brief glance her way caught her dark lenses aimed at him. "What?"

"I've been thinking about you—"

"Really?"

"Not like that, you goof. About you and your organization. Are there others besides you and Erik?"

"The less you know the better."

"But all the—never mind. I'm trying to understand." She stared out the window again. "It must be costing Cal a tidy sum."

"No comment."

"Can you at least tell me the plans for today? I deserve that much."

He held up a hand to her and adjusted the microphone. "Got it. Thanks. Keep me updated. Erik says we made a clean run out of L.A. No tail. OK, here's the plan. When we get to Santa Clarita, I'll park down the street from Ms. Adams's house. There are binoculars in the back. We'll watch the house while Erik sweeps the neighborhood to make sure *we're* not being watched."

"And Hannah?"

"She's at school. Rides the bus home. That'll be your best shot at seeing her. I'll take pictures, too."

"That's a long time to wait. Why can't I go to the school and see her there?"

"Not a good idea. You need to stay—"

"What if the Levasseurs know she has Hannah?"

"No, no, Sadie. If they knew about Hannah, they'd have used her to lure you out of hiding long ago."

"I suppose you're right." She folded her arms. "You have been so far."

Bowen didn't acknowledge her statement but steered the vehicle through the thinning traffic. Erik's voice in his ear fed updates every ten minutes. All clear. He crossed the railroad tracks and drove down a tree-lined street. Stucco, stone, and clapboard houses, most with neat expanses of lawn, sprawled on each side. Bowen parked in front of a vacant house with a red and white *For Sale* sign stuck in the lawn. "That's her house, third from the corner, on the left. Pale green with darker green trim, shrubs along the sidewalk, blue car in the driveway."

Sadie removed her sunglasses. "I see it. So now, we wait?"

"Yup." Bowen snagged two pairs of binoculars from the backseat and gave one to her. "These are for you." He raised his and focused them on the house. "That car wasn't here yesterday."

"Was she at work?"

"No. She doesn't have a job. Our research revealed she inherited this house and a pair of duplexes several blocks over. I guess she lives on the rental income." He relayed the information about the strange vehicle with a rusted right rear fender to Erik.

Erik drove by twice, but they didn't acknowledge him. Other than a brown delivery van, no other vehicles moved in the quiet neighborhood.

At two thirty, the woman appeared on her front porch.

Bowen's stomach muscles tensed.

She examined plants in the two hanging baskets, and plumped cushions on a wooden swing while surveying the street.

Bowen slumped in his seat. "Careful, Sadie."

"I see her." Sadie scrunched down. "What's she doing now?"

"She's in the rocking chair. Staring at us."

21

"What now?" A vise of anxiety constricted Sadie's chest.

"That's not good." Bowen tapped his earpiece. "Hey, Erik, she's on the front porch. Don't drive by more than once."

Tension mounted like billowing storm clouds. The minutes ticked by at a glacial pace.

"What will we do if she stays on the porch?"

"I'll think of something. Wait, she's getting up and going inside."

Three years of grief lifted from Sadie's heart. *Don't get in the way of me seeing my daughter.* "If the girl is Hannah, what should I do?"

"Once you're certain, we'll leave and make further plans. We can't pick her up off the street and drive away."

"But—"

"Sadie, there'll probably be other kids around, parents waiting for them. Think of how Hannah might react to seeing you. She may not recognize you and resist. Or she might and...faint, scream, run home. Who knows? If she kicks up a ruckus it will draw too much attention."

Ten agonizing minutes ticked by.

Bowen straightened and focused on his side mirror.

"School bus."

The bus's lights flashed and the red stop sign arm

extended.

Sadie's heart raced and knots pretzeled in her stomach.

Six children exited. Two stayed on the right side of the street and four crossed in front of the bus. The big yellow vehicle pulled away and lumbered down the street.

Sadie focused the binoculars on the children.

Two boys headed their way and then entered a house at least four lots back. A tall girl stopped and waved to the other kids before running up her driveway.

Three others—a boy and two girls, one blonde, the other with shoulder length brown curls—chatted as they neared the car.

The boy slithered out of his backpack and threw it onto a patch of lawn. He picked up a bicycle and yelled something to the girls as he rode away down the sidewalk.

Bowen, now using a camera with telephoto lens, asked, "Is Hannah one of those girls?"

Eyes fixed on the brunette, she didn't respond. The child's movements prevented Sadie from studying her face.

The girls linked arms and skipped.

The binoculars slipped from Sadie's grasp, her breath caught.

The blonde skipped in a regular pattern, but the other girl had an extra little bob in her step. Hannah skipped that way. She couldn't master the fluid motion. The girls giggled and slowed.

Hannah. It had to be Hannah.

She needed to get closer. Sadie opened her door and climbed out. One face-to-face look and then she'd whisk Hannah away and never let go. As the girls came even with the SUV, she ran across the street. *Is it my child, my little girl?*

But Bowen threw his arms around her, his words a hoarse whisper. "Don't, Sadie. Don't."

As the wide-eyed girls passed her, Sadie held out her hand.

The blonde threw her a puzzled stare, while the brunette narrowed her dark eyes and glared.

Bowen half carried Sadie back to their vehicle while scanning to see if there were any witnesses. He remained by her door until she buckled her seatbelt. "That was not smart." His quick breaths stirred her hair.

"It's Hannah. Why can't I take her now?" Sadie's words caught on a sob.

"Remember what I said earlier. You'll need to confront her in a more controlled environment. Give her the opportunity to take in the shock of seeing you again."

Sadie kept her gaze on the girl who opened the front door and disappeared inside.

Bowen pulled away from the curb and focused on the traffic, body rigid, jaw muscles working.

She'd acted irrationally and had maybe even jeopardized their situation, but she couldn't sit there and watch the girl who looked so much like Hannah walk by. Tears trickled down her cheeks.

Bowen handed her a wad of tissues.

By the time they parked in the driveway, her eyes were dry. She entered through the back door and crumpled on her bed. Curled up, her heart aching, she closed her eyes. A skipping, giggling little girl filled her mind. In the relative quiet of the room, Sadie focused on one thought. At least Hannah appeared to be happy.

The stress had produced a jackhammer headache. She eased off the bed and searched her purse for Tylenol, but found none. Maybe Bowen had something she could take. On her way to the door, the makeshift vase on the dresser caught her eye. A pink carnation had been added. Was it Erik or Bowen? A small smile broke through the pain, and she opened her door.

Erik and Bowen were working at laptops on the kitchen table.

"Hey, Sadie. Hope we didn't disturb you." Bowen stopped tapping keys.

"Would you like tea?" Eric asked.

"What I need is something for my headache. And then tea, thank you." Neither of them mentioned the flower and with all the emotional chaos storming through her brain, she decided to leave it a mystery for now.

"Come with me. Let's see what's in the pharmacy." Bowen motioned for her to follow him.

They entered the bathroom he shared with Erik. It was the first time she'd been in there. They had given her the larger room with en-suite bath. Bowen opened a black vinyl bag, pulled out his electric razor, toothpaste, and two pill bottles. He picked one and shook it and then threw it away. "Empty. Let's check this one." Pills rattled in it as he handed it to her. "There're a few left. Hope they help."

She took the bottle. "Thanks. I'm sure it's a tension headache."

When they entered the kitchen, Erik had a box of assorted tea bags and a mug of hot water on the counter. "Just for you."

She tore into a packet of paradise mango and dropped the bag into the cup. "Thank you, Erik. It is very thoughtful of you."

Erik closed his laptop. "I have to leave. Come sit." He gathered a majority of the folders and carried everything down the hall.

Bowen returned to his place and focused on the screen.

"I can sit in the living room if you need to work." Sadie dunked the tea bag, the fruity fragrance rising on whiffs of steam.

"No, stay. I'm almost done with this report." He glanced at her over the laptop and then tapped the keys.

The soothing tea coated her throat, and the cup warmed her hands. With all the windows covered by blinds or curtains, she had no idea about the weather forecast, but the chill in the air nibbled at her toes. The hole in her heart didn't help, either. When she finished her tea, she took the cup to the sink and peeked through the mini-blinds. Sure enough, streaky gray clouds hid the sky. She hugged herself and shivered. Another cup of tea would help. She set the cup of water in the microwave and chose a cranberry-apple flavored bag.

Erik's footsteps clomped down the hall and stopped by the back door. "Be gone a couple of hours. Will you like lasagna for supper?"

"Sure. And tell Ginger I'm working on the report."

Erik mock-saluted and left.

The microwave dinged, and Sadie pulled out the cup, dunked the tea bag and waited by the trash can next to the sink.

A horn honked from the backyard. "What did Erik

forget now?" Bowen opened the back door, jumped down the stairs, and jogged to Erik's truck.

Bowen's open laptop sat all alone at one end of the table. Words on the white screen jumped out at Sadie. Evelyn Adams. Sadie tried to grab girl. Child is probably Hannah. The report detailed the stakeout. She took note of specifics. Bowen was e-mailing it to Holland395 at IRO dot org.

By the time he entered the kitchen, she sat on the sofa sipping her tea.

Bowen returned to his laptop. "I'll be finished in a minute or two."

Sadie's fingers itched to get a hold of a computer and check out IRO. And Ginger.

Bowen entered the living room. "All done. Mind if I join you?" He sat in the armchair before she could reply. "How's the headache?"

She drained her cup and set it on the table. "Easing off, thanks. Did you finish the report for Ginger?"

"I did, but how—of course, I told Erik. Ginger's a stickler when it comes to punctuality."

He'd confirmed Sadie's suspicions. He worked for IRO. Maybe he'd divulge more with a bit of prodding. "She must be a good secretary. Will I get a chance to meet her?"

"You have a subtle way of wheedling information from me. But no. Erik and I are the only staff you'll meet. That is, unless we run into problems." He lowered his gaze and clenched his jaw. "Speaking of problems, Sadie, we have to talk about this afternoon."

"I'm sorry, but I needed a closer look."

"And that's why I had to drag you out of there." His voice was gentle, and his hand brushed her arm.

The headache pulsed behind her eyes. Her empty

arms longed to hold her child.

"I understand why you ran after Hannah, but we can't—"

"How can you understand?" She swung around. "Have you ever lost a child and then found her again?"

"No. I don't know what you're going through." He opened his arms as though he wanted to hold her.

Her hands crept up his chest. His arms tightened as her whispered words of pain and hope sputtered out on each ragged breath. Somewhere in the outpouring of despair, the spicy scent of his cologne permeated her fog. His warm breath caressed her face as he placed soft kisses on her forehead.

His body tensed, and his breathing rate increased.

The safe cocoon within his arms felt so good…

A voice far away echoed in her brain. *It's a job. He lied.*

"Sam, I can't." She pushed away, forcing him to relax his hold.

"Sam?" His smoldering eyes, inches away, searched her face. "You mean Bowen."

For a moment, she'd been swept back to Austin, to Sam, and the idea of leading a normal life.

"I'm sorry, Sadie. That was unprofessional of me. I promise it won't happen again."

Why had she almost forgotten her vow to forget about him once he brought Hannah to her? "I'm sorry for my foolish actions this afternoon. From now on, I'll do whatever you say." She focused on his broad expanse of shoulders. "What's the plan?"

"Tomorrow we'll return to Santa Clarita."

"Am I included in the we?"

"Yes. Hannah's first grade class is going on a field trip to the Princess Cruise Line headquarters located in

Santa Clarita." A dark curl flopped over his forehead, partially covering frown lines. "Here's the tricky part. We—you and I—will take a tour at the same time. When safe, you approach Hannah, interact with her."

"But even if she remembers me, she won't recognize me."

"I've thought of that. On our way there, we'll stop and you can buy another wig to resemble your real hair color."

"Or I can dye my hair back to its natural color now. I don't want another wig." A shiver ran through her, and she wasn't sure if it was a chill or anticipation. "What if Hannah doesn't remember me? That's what I dread the most."

"I like the idea of dyeing your hair for this venture. You still need to wear the wig at all other times. I'll call Erik, and you can tell him what to buy. Now, is there an anecdote, or story, something that she might remember? Something special?"

Sadie thought back to Hannah's early years. Aaron wrote her a poem on her first birthday. They sang it to her every chance they got. It was their special song. Hope burned within. "Yes. A little song."

"Great. Here's the plan. When she's separated a bit from the crowd, quietly sing the verse when you're close to her. If she recognizes you, she'll probably get emotional. Erik will create a commotion to distract the other kids and adults while we spirit her out of the building to the car."

"What about security guards?"

"We have a contact who works at the location."

"Who?"

"I can't divulge the person's name at this time, but she and Erik will handle the guards and any adults who intervene."

Potential obstacles bounced around Sadie's brain. What could go wrong? "The teacher will notify authorities. We won't—"

"Sadie." Placing his hand over her tightly intertwined fingers, Bowen gave them a gentle squeeze. "We will take care of everything. The local police will be notified; there'll be no Amber Alert. All you have to do is convince Hannah you're her mother."

The warmth of his hand settled some of her jitters. She relaxed her fingers and glanced at him. "And then we'll call WITSEC?"

"Yes, and get you both under federal protection again. But if Hannah doesn't recognize you, then we'll have to take the long scientific route and get a DNA sample."

"Oh, heavenly Father, no. That'll take too long."

"Then let's hope she recognizes you."

Sadie paced to the door and back. "Can Cal come with me? He looks so much like Aaron. Maybe the two of us together——"

"No. Not a good idea. Although we've instituted precautions, I don't want someone following him. It could jeopardize you and Hannah."

"Will we bring her back here?"

"Don't worry about the details. We'll handle each and every contingency." He headed to the kitchen with her at his heels. At the back door, he stopped and pointed with his thumb. "I'm going for a workout in the garage. Erik should be back soon with supper. I'll call him right now, and you can tell him what hair product to buy."

"At this point I don't care what brand. Any dark

brown will do."

"I'll tell him. Don't fret. Use the time to practice your song." He jumped down the three steps. His punching bag would probably receive a volley of blows.

She wished she had something to punch.

᠅

Sadie dyed her hair after dinner. She patted the dark curls and grinned. It was good to be a brunette again. She joined the men in the kitchen.

"I've downloaded the pictures I took this afternoon. Want to see?" Bowen tapped a few keys.

"Of course."

He clicked on a folder and the two little girls, arms linked, skipped down the sidewalk. "I didn't take many because you jumped out of the car." Bowen clicked on the forward arrow. "This is an enlargement of the dark-haired girl."

"It *is* Hannah. My baby." Sadie caressed Hannah's image. Tears rolled down her cheeks in silence.

Bowen and Eric quietly got up and left the kitchen. The men were watching a movie when she finally entered the living room. At the conclusion of the movie, Erik retreated to his room and Bowen found a news channel. He and Sadie sat on the sofa, half-watching as they rehashed plans for the next day.

When the announcer mentioned a murder of a law enforcement officer in Texas, they paid attention.

Person of interest. If seen please contact. A picture of a sandy-haired woman flashed on the screen.

Sadie gripped Bowen's arm. "I know her. That's Lavonne, Kyle's sister."

22

Silence reigned when Sadie woke early the next morning. Today she'd see Hannah. Talk to her and bring her home. Dressed in brown slacks and a gold cotton sweater, she went down the hall to a deserted kitchen. Numbers in the microwave clock gave off an eerie glow in the corner. Seven thirty. Where were the guys? She made a pot of coffee, expecting Erik or Bowen to burst through the back door any minute.

Worry clawed up her spine as she knocked on Bowen's door. When he didn't answer, she entered. Bed made, suitcase closed. Erik's room was empty, too, except a laptop lay on the bed.

"Maybe they're in the garage." She ventured outside. The main doors were closed, but she found a side door, which opened with a hefty shove. Inside the dim garage she spied Bowen's pickup—the one they'd driven from Texas—and the tan sedan. Bowen's punching bag, suspended from a metal rod in the corner, twisted like a giant cocoon caught by a gentle breeze.

Back in the house, she dialed Bowen's number. No answer. She remembered his warning about leaving messages and hung up. She dialed Erik's number. No answer. Where could they be? Could their absence be connected to the news item they'd watched the previous night concerning Lavonne, Kyle's sister?

Sadie poured a cup of coffee and made a slice of toast. If the guys returned with breakfast tacos or

Danish, she'd kick herself for worrying. The routine activity of making breakfast and eating kept her from an all-out panic attack.

By eight thirty, the what-ifs sank the full force of their talons into her. The men had been involved in a car wreck; Cal was in trouble; the Levasseurs knew about Hannah.

Sadie jumped up from the sofa and shuddered as fear swarmed. What should she do? Run? Stay? Back in her bedroom, she clutched the Bible to her chest and paced while reciting, "Wait on the Lord. Wait on the Lord." When the jitters settled, Sadie sank onto the bed. How could she occupy herself until the men returned? She had to believe they would return.

With eyes closed, she rehearsed the possible scenario awaiting her. Drive to Santa Clarita. Locate Hannah among the other school children. Quietly sing the song to her. Aaron had set the poem to the tune of "Jesus Loves Me."

Sadie sang it in a halting voice and then belted out the words again.

We love Hannah, yes we do.
She loves her Mom and Daddy, too.
Hair and eyes of chocolate brown,
Out little princess wears a crown.

Yes, she is precious,
Yes, she's our princess.
Yes, she is precious,
Our Hannah is the best.

Very simple words, but Hannah had cooed and laughed at them. When she'd gotten older she joined in the verse. Aaron or Sadie sang it to her every night before tucking her in. Memories shattered when her cell phone rang. She held the phone to her ear.

"Hi, Sadie." Bowen's voice sent a shower of relief over her.

"Where are you?"

"I've got bad news. The field trip's off."

"Excuse me?"

"We won't be going to Santa Clarita today. Evelyn and Hannah left last night. They're gone."

"Gone?" She clutched the Bible tighter and slid to the floor.

23

How could everything have caved so quickly? The only explanation Bowen and Erik had come up with was Cal had a leak in his office. The other explanation, too unpleasant to contemplate, spiked his ire. IRO had a major breach. Bowen dreaded facing Sadie. Her daughter had disappeared under his watch. He charged to the back door. It opened wide before he reached the top step.

"What happened?" Her dark, red-rimmed eyes sought answers. She breathed heavily as if she'd run a marathon.

Bowen tried to look anywhere but at her stricken face as he brushed past her into the living room.

"Bowen Boudine, don't walk away from me. Where's Hannah? And why didn't you answer your phone?"

He longed to take her in his arms and comfort her but hung up his jacket instead. He faced her. "Come sit. I'll tell you everything I know." He sank onto the sofa.

Sadie settled as far away from him as she could.

"First, I couldn't answer my phone, and I apologize for that. Erik and I were in a situation where—"

"You said either you or Erik would always be available. What if I'd been in real trouble?"

"We couldn't talk on the phone."

"You said you'd tell me everything."

"Within reason. There's a major leak somewhere. We think it's in Cal's office."

Her eyes widened.

"You asked once about our organization. There are other operatives. We've had Evelyn's house under periodic surveillance and were alerted last night to unusual activity."

"Is that when she left?"

"Yes. About four this morning. Evelyn and Hannah took off. Unfortunately, they eluded the chase car, but we have…"

She deserved the full picture.

"We have sources that will tap her phone and place an alert on her credit cards. We'll find her."

"I can't believe we were so close. Why didn't you let me rescue Hannah yesterday?"

"We discussed that already."

Shoulders slumped, Sadie stared at the carpet.

"There's more. Lonnie knows about her."

"Lonnie knows?" Her voice cracked.

"Yes. He knows where Evelyn Adams lives. We have to discover how Lonnie found out."

"Who cares how he found out?" she cried. "How do you know all of this?"

"After Evelyn took off, we left one guy at her house, disguised as a gardener. A few hours ago, Lonnie showed up, asking if Mrs. Adams lived there."

"What now? Am I safe here?"

"Yes. Our surveillance team gave us the OK."

Bowen touched her arm, hoping she'd turn around. His voice softened. "We'll find Hannah. You'll be with her soon."

Erik barreled through the back door, diffusing the tension. He set bags from a fast food joint on the table.

"Brought lunch. Anyone hungry?"

Taking advantage of the interruption, Bowen rested his arm across Sadie's shoulders. "Let's eat. You look kinda pale."

They ate in silence for a few minutes.

"That's all I can manage. I don't feel well." Sadie folded the wrapper around her half-eaten burger.

"Are you sick, or is it the situation?"

"Another headache. Tension, anxiety. Who knows? I'm going to my room."

"I'm worried about you." Bowen escorted her to her bedroom door.

"I didn't sleep much last night." Sadie yanked off the wig, fluffed her curls and flopped onto the bed.

Bowen closed her door and returned to the kitchen. He missed his loft apartment. Would he ever be able to take Sadie to see it?

Erik lowered himself into the lone armchair, his elongated frame dwarfing the old recliner. "I've got news."

"What?"

"I had a long visit with Cal."

"Where?" Bowen stretched out on the sofa.

"No chance we were overheard. Santa Monica pier." Erik straightened his legs, crossing one boot over the other. "I think I know why the Adams woman ran. Cal said he has a photo of Hannah on his desk. Taken at Disneyland. Reyna and her daughter, Francesca, visited him at his office and commented on it. Francesca loved the blue princess dress Hannah wore."

"How does that result in Evelyn leaving?"

"I'm getting there." Erik rolled up his sleeves as he talked. "Reyna told Cal this morning that Francesca recently attended a slumber party. Hannah was also a guest. The girls played dress-up, and you guessed it. One of the costumes was a blue princess dress. When Francesca saw Penny, um, Hannah in it, she said she'd seen her in it before. Told her about the photograph her future stepdad had on his desk."

"Hannah must have told Evelyn, and Evelyn panicked. That answers why she ran." He slouched and folded his arms. "But we still don't know how Lonnie found out about her."

"We're working on it. I hear a car outside." Erik eased out of the chair and peeked through the drapes. "It's Ginger."

24

Low voices from the front room carried down the hall, interrupting Sadie's concentration on the Bible. She flipped to the book of Psalms and snuggled back on the pillows. Truths welded into her soul years before clamored for acknowledgment. No matter how hard she tried to bury them, they kept rearing their blessed heads. Subtle stirrings of spiritual awakening had begun before she'd met Bowen, but she'd been too stubborn to realize it. Attending Hillcrest Church had slowly become a joy instead of a chore.

The Dolomite Chant released the old restraints that held her soul in bondage.

Now she couldn't let the disappointment of Hannah's disappearance drag her back to that dungeon of despair. Hope had gained a foothold and she wouldn't allow it to die again. She read Psalm 121. It had always been a favorite. *Lift up your eyes*. It was hard to be despondent when gazing on hills of hope.

Something about the voices in the living room changed. Sadie slid off the bed, combed her hair, and then set the wig in place. She walked down the hall, shoulders squared, ready to face the men and their guest.

The woman's cropped red hair—a color no dye job could imitate—softened her square face. A sprinkle of freckles sparred for space on her pale skin. Brows too full to be fashionable arched over large, wide set eyes. Packed into a burnt orange suit, her tall, svelte shape sent a stab of envy to Sadie's heart. Even the towering brown stilettos shouted superiority.

Without taking his eyes off the woman, Bowen motioned for Sadie to join him on the sofa. Erik sat in a chair taken from the kitchen. He held a can of soda to his lips, his gaze flicking from Bowen to Sadie.

Usually self-assured and confident, Sadie felt both strengths drain from her. If this was Ginger, Bowen's secretary, why did they exchange such an intense look crackling with tension?

The woman broke the awkward silence. "Hi, Sadie. I'm Ginger." She reached out a hand to shake.

Her fingers were warm and soft. "Hi. You must be Bowen's secretary."

Ginger placed her hands on her hips, raised her eyebrows, looked at Erik, and then at Bowen. "Something like that." She sank into the recliner and extracted a thick folder from a leather portfolio. "Mr. Boudine, you and I need to have a little chat later."

He slipped his left arm along the back of the sofa, his fingers lying lightly on Sadie's shoulder.

"Sure, Ms. Holland. Anything you say."

Ms. Holland rolled her hazel eyes. "Until then, we have work to do." She tapped the folder. "I brought information that may provide answers to several of our problems."

"I told you to check her out." Erik set his soda can on the floor.

"I know, and I'm sorry we didn't follow your hunch." Ginger opened the file and handed Sadie an eight by ten headshot. "Do you know this woman?"

Short, black hair cut in a bob framed an oval face. Her clear olive skin and dark eyes added to her beauty.

Sadie studied the photograph. Her breath caught

as a memory drawer slid open in her brain. Covering the dark hair with one hand, she viewed the face and nodded. "She looks vaguely familiar." She covered more of the hair and blinked back images from the past.

Bowen removed his arm from the back of the sofa. "She's Irene Grayson, Cal's former secretary. He told us she married and moved to—"

The memory flashed in neon. "No. I've never met Cal's secretary. This is Vicky Randolph. I remember her name because I had foster parents named Victor and Sue Randolph. The coincidence stuck with me." A cold hand strangled her heart. "Vicky worked for Duke Levasseur when Aaron and I..."

Two seconds of stunned silence before Bowen reacted. He yanked the picture from Sadie and examined it. "Are you sure?"

"Yes. Vicky had light brown hair. But that's her. I'm positive. Let me see it." Sadie took the photo. "Here's something else." She covered the black hair again. "Bowen, look at her nose and eyes. Add a few years and a mustache and you have Kyle."

"Doggone it. You're right." Jabbing a finger at the picture, Bowen frowned. "She has to be related to Kyle Nelson."

"The man from Austin?" Ginger opened the folder and held out her hand for the photograph. "Then we have work to do."

"So Irene and Vicky are the same person? That'll be easy enough to check." Erik rubbed his chin.

"Get on it right away and see if you can find a connection to Kyle." Ginger placed the picture in the folder. "Bowen, you—"

"Wait." Sadie scooted to the edge of the seat and

frowned. "I remember something else about Vicky. She had a mole high on her cheek. It's not in that photograph. So either she had it removed, or she has…a twin."

"That's possible," Bowen said.

"I know Cal." Sadie twisted her hands in her lap. "He would never hire someone who'd worked for Brady Holdings. So it stands to reason these are two different women."

Ginger nodded and turned to Erik. "Check on it."

Still on the edge of the sofa, Sadie jiggled one knee up and down. "If you give me access to a computer, I can find out. Remember, I worked on Brady's systems."

Erik and Bowen focused on Ginger. She pursed her lips and shook her head. "No. Our guys will handle it."

"Can I at least talk to Cal?"

They exchanged another glance that excluded Sadie.

"Considering the leak and Evelyn's disappearance, I think not. Communication with you can't be traced if there is none." Bowen patted Sadie's arm. "I know it's hard, but for now we have to keep you isolated."

Sadie slouched onto the overstuffed cushions. A few forays into cyber space would confirm her suspicion that Irene and Vicky were Kyle's sisters. Although she understood the need for caution, being tucked away in a safe house was getting old. She ached to use her skills to provide answers that would bring Hannah back to her and keep Lonnie away forever.

An awkward silence followed.

Ginger stood and straightened her jacket, smoothing her hand over her flat stomach and slim hips.

Erik eased out of the chair and grabbed his jacket. "I'll go to the office and investigate Irene and Vicky."

"I have to leave, too. Sadie, nice to meet you. Next time, I hope Hannah's with you." Ginger picked up her leather purse that matched her shoes and raised her eyebrows at Bowen. "I need to see you."

Bowen followed Ginger outside. Sadie tried to eavesdrop, but they stood too far away from the house beside Ginger's sleek, metallic gold car at the curb. About the same height, their faces were inches apart. They chatted, getting closer and closer. Sadie's heart clenched. *I like redheads. I like redheads.* Bowen's words when she bought the wig burned like a repeating branding iron in her brain.

Bowen bounded through the front door. "Hey, Sadie. You hungry?"

"Sort of. That burger—"

"Let's go out. There's a terrific restaurant down the block."

She studied his face. Eyes bright, worry lines gone, and dimple tweaking his cheek. That conversation with Ginger must have been quite encouraging. "Sounds good. I'll get my jacket and purse."

Bowen followed her down the hall.

In her room, Sadie picked up her jacket and purse from the worn dresser. At least the soda bottle vase and flowers added a bit of cheer to the dreary surface.

"Hey."

Startled to hear Bowen's voice, she swung around.

"I need to do laundry. How about you?"

"You read my mind."

"We can stop at a laundromat before going to eat." He left, mumbling something about garbage bags.

Sadie sorted through her suitcase and dumped dirty clothes on the bed. Bowen returned with two black plastic garbage bags. "When you're ready, bring them to the kitchen. I'll get my things."

While stuffing the bag, Sadie thought of everything she'd left behind in Austin—clothes, a car, friends. April's sweet face, Julian's concern for her promotion, Pastor Patterson's sermons, Kyle's...was he really related to Vicky and Irene? Is that how he located Sadie?

The Bible still lay open on the bed. She slipped it into her purse. Waiting in a laundromat might be the perfect time to reacquaint herself with more of her favorite scriptures. It would also keep her mind from dwelling on her precarious circumstances.

Bowen met her at the end of the hall. He hefted her bag of clothes and opened the back door.

"Do you have detergent?"

"We'll use the vending machines there."

While driving, Bowen hummed as if they were going on a picnic.

"You're in a good mood, considering the bad news we received today."

He turned into a gravel lot and parked at the end of a row of vehicles. "We missed Hannah this time, but we found a connection between Cal's company and Brady Holdings. Plugging that leak will be major. I'm confident we'll get a lead on the Adams woman soon. Let's get our clothes in the washers, have a good meal, and forget our problems for a few hours."

How she wished she could forget.

The Kleen 'N Brite Laundromat, to the left of the lot, had one door boarded up. Bowen pulled open the other one and waited for Sadie to enter. Floral scents from a dozen brands of detergent and fabric softener mixed with chlorine to swirl in the warm humid air.

They found three empty washers. Sadie and Bowen combined their dark clothes into one, and then used the other two washers for their separate loads. No way did she want his private things to mingle with her shirts and underwear.

Bowen deposited coins in a dispenser to purchase miniature boxes of detergent. When water surged into the washers, he took Sadie's arm. "The restaurant's right next door. I figure we have about forty-five minutes."

They enjoyed the authentic Mexican food—beef fajitas with the works. Bowen kept the conversation light and impersonal, sharing amusing anecdotes of his time with Erik.

When they returned to the laundromat, the washers were finished. They sorted clothes into two dryers, one for Sadie's lightweight articles, and the other for thick, bulky items, and then chose seats along the front wall. Two young women chatted as they folded clothes. A toddler pushed a yellow plastic truck on the floor, making engine noises as he scooted back and forth. A TV mounted high on the wall blared Spanish. Since Sadie had limited knowledge of the language, she pulled out the Bible while Bowen appeared to be engrossed in the TV drama.

Sadie located the book of Philippians and started at chapter one.

When Bowen lost interest in the TV show, he slid his arm across the back of her chair. His head inched closer as he eyed the white pages. "What you reading?"

"Philippians. The words of Paul the Apostle have

a special significance to me." Other than Bowen's visit to Hillcrest, she knew nothing about his religious beliefs. "Do you know who I'm talking about?"

"I do." His gaze left the pages and roamed the interior of the pale green room.

Sadie couldn't tell if he wanted to continue the conversation or not. With the faded ribbon marking her place, she closed the Bible and tapped Bowen's leg with it. "What do you remember?"

"I remember a lot. My mother took Charlotte and me to church every Sunday. Dad joined us when he could. Good memories." His voice cracked, and he stared outside.

"So what changed? I get the impression you don't attend anymore, that going to Hillcrest was a ruse."

Bowen pointed to the wall of dryers. "I think your clothes are ready."

The dryer with her delicates and lightweight tops had stopped tumbling. She slipped the Bible into her purse and held it out to him. "Hold this a minute."

At the dryer, she pulled out the warm items and dumped them on another table near the two women. Surely Bowen had seen women's underwear before, but having him watch as she folded hers sent heat creeping up her neck. To distract from her actions, she asked again, "What changed?"

Holding her purse under his arm like a football, he opened the other dryer door and felt the clothes inside. "Not dry." He closed the door, jabbed the button, then raised his gaze to the TV. "I don't know. Life, I guess. Work, marriage. Everything tugged me away."

The women loaded their piles of clothing into plastic baskets and left the laundromat with the toddler dragging his yellow truck behind them.

With Sadie's clothes neatly stacked on the table, she moved to a chair closer to the dryers. Her jeans and dark shirts tumbled and dried with Bowen's things. She watched them make their circular dance. They mimicked her jumbled thoughts.

"How'd you handle it?"

She reclaimed possession of her purse. "Handle what?"

A deep frown lined his brow. "The trial. Aaron's death. Loss of everything. How'd you keep your faith?"

"I didn't." She hugged her purse to her chest. "I blamed God for everything. How could He treat me that way when I'd served Him for so long? How could He take my family?" Even now the accusations struck a chord of truth.

"How'd you overcome that?"

Memories of her nights of anguish clouded her focus. She stared at the stained concrete floor. "I'm not sure exactly. I turned my back on God, but after a while, my knowledge of the scriptures knocked down the wall I'd built, brick by brick." She glanced at Bowen. "Reece Patterson's counsel helped, too. I realized God wasn't responsible for the Levasseurs' actions. We each have freedom to choose good or evil. God doesn't force us to make that choice, either."

A dryer buzzed, but they both ignored it.

"But if we've chosen evil, will he take us back?" Bowen searched her face.

Although he didn't use the words *I* and *me*, she sensed from his tone and the intensity of his gaze that this issue was close to his heart.

"There's a verse in the Book of Revelation. It says Jesus stands at the door and knocks. It is up to each individual to open the door. He is always ready to forgive the truly repentant."

An arm's length away, he whispered, "Even me?"

Although she still struggled with a weak faith herself, his question strengthened her resolve. "Even you, Bowen Boudine."

25

Using the guide in the front of the Bible, Sadie leafed through the books of Luke, Ephesians, and Colossians. She read aloud scriptures on forgiveness while Bowen listened, fully focused.

But then he withdrew and seemed to fight a self-contained battle. While he folded his clothes, he scowled at an elderly man who entered with a plastic tub overflowing with laundry.

"Do you want me to read more?"

He turned his frown on her. Lips tight, jaw firm, he slapped his clean jeans on the table and forced out the wrinkles with his forearm. "No." He shoved the folded pants into his bag and hefted it over his shoulder.

She picked up her bag of clothes and followed him to his truck.

Accepting Bowen's silent treatment, Sadie stared out the side window as he drove. By the time they returned to the safe house, the stress lines had eased off his brow and his jaw muscles relaxed.

She went to her own room and deposited the clothes on the bed. When she came out, she passed Bowen's bedroom.

He slumped on the bed, head bowed, hands clenched, his bag of clothes in a heap at his feet. He glanced up. A ghost of a smile flickered across his face, and he raised a hand as if in defense. "I have work to do. You're on your own for the rest of the evening.

Have you seen Erik?"

Her arms ached to hold him and ease away the demons their laundromat conversation had roused. But she pointed towards the kitchen. "He's in the backyard."

On cue, Erik tromped down the hall. "Have a good meal?" He sidled by Sadie and entered the bedroom. "Boudine, I've got information on the sisters."

"Can I listen in?" Sadie asked.

"Sure." Bowen picked up his clothes and dumped them on the bed. "I'll pack these things away, and then we'll meet in the living room"

Sadie returned to her own room and folded her clothes neatly into her suitcase. In the kitchen, she heated a mug of water, chose a tangerine passion teabag, plopped it in the mug, and then sat on the sofa with her legs tucked underneath her.

Erik brought a pink bakery box from the kitchen. "You want a cookie?" He opened the box and held it for her to see. Aromas of cinnamon and spices escaped the assortment of chocolate chip and oatmeal raisin rounds.

"No, thanks."

He took a handful and set the box on the side table. The recliner creaked an objection as he sank into it and extended the footrest. His black boots dangled over the end. "Hurry up, Boudine." One cookie disappeared into his mouth.

When Bowen entered, he took several cookies and sat on the other end of the sofa. "What did you discover?"

Erik curled one arm behind his head, looking more like a sunbather than an agent ready to divulge information. "You were right, Sadie. Vicky and Irene are twins. Vicky's married and still works at Brady Holdings. She's in the accounts receivable department. Irene lied to Cal. She never moved to San Francisco. Lives here."

"She could still have ties to Cal's company. We need to warn him. Ask him about her friends." Bowen slipped another chunk of cookie into his mouth and nodded to Sadie. "I know you want to visit him again. Maybe we can arrange a meeting in a day or two."

"I'd like that." She set her empty mug on the side table. "Did you find out if Vicky and Irene are related to Kyle?"

Erik chewed the last of his cookie. "You have a good eye. They're his sisters. He used to work for the L.A. Times but got fired when they downsized a year ago. He's writing a book on ethnic celebrations around the country. Taking photographs—"

"That's it. That's how he found me." Sadie set her feet on the floor.

"How?" Bowen asked.

"Early last December, Rhodes supplied potted plants for the Travis County Holiday Festival. Glenna and I were in charge of decorating the stage and meeting hall. A reporter kept taking pictures, and I hid my face whenever he came near." Sadie closed her eyes, sending her memory on a journey to the past. The reporter's face and physique came into focus. "It could have been Kyle. I met him a week or so later at church."

Bowen moved along the sofa, closer to Sadie. His large hand stilled her tapping fingers. "That's probably when he contacted Vicky and she, in turn, told Lonnie. As a reporter in California, he knew all about the trial.

Maybe sat in the courtroom."

A shudder that started deep within raked Sadie's body. She turned, her knees meeting Bowen's, and let the warmth of his hand calm her nerves.

"Kyle's book is legit?" Bowen asked.

"Yes. He has a contract with Treehouse Publishing," Erik said.

In control of her emotions again, Sadie freed her hands. "I guess as a reporter-photographer he must have a keen eye and recognized me." She folded her arms and focused on a bare patch in the rug. "But why didn't he do something, then? Why wait until he saw the photograph of me with Aaron and Hannah?"

"Maybe he—"

"I think I know." Erik tapped his temple. "It's money. How much you want to bet, Lonnie offered him money, and Kyle was waiting for the price to go up?"

"Why? What else did you discover?"

"Our friend Kyle is a gambler. Likes the ponies. He's up to his armpits in debt."

"Hmm. None of this came up when I researched him in Austin." Bowen glanced at Sadie.

She raised her eyebrows.

"After I met him, I checked him out."

Erik released the footrest and lumbered out of the recliner. "I'm needed at the office. Be back before midnight." He grabbed his jacket and left through the kitchen.

Sadness trickled into Sadie's mind. Kyle's interest in the puppet ministry had nothing to do with helping children. He orchestrated the whole business, including the use of the Hands for Hannah website to engage her. She eased off the sofa and stepped to the front window. "Is there anything we can do about Vicky, Irene, or Kyle? Contact the police?" Her gaze drifted back to Bowen.

"No. We've got no concrete evidence. Other than Kyle pulling a gun on you, what have they done? Once you and Hannah are safe, maybe we can prove their connection to Lonnie." Bowen joined her at the window.

At the mention of Hannah, Sadie's stomach knotted again.

Bowen's hands squeezed her shoulders. His warm breath fanned her neck.

She dared not turn around.

"Sadie, I don't know how much longer I…we can keep you safe. We have all our resources working overtime."

Tiny zaps of electricity traveled down her arms as his fingers eased the tight muscles.

"Maybe it's time you contact WITSEC and—"

"No." She turned, her face inches from his. "Not without Hannah." She searched his eyes and found sympathy, along with a glint of passion.

Her pulse rate quickened; she could barely breathe.

He held her shoulders again and lowered his head, his eyes on her mouth.

No, screamed a part of her heart. *Yes, yes*, shouted another. She forced her gaze from his face to her hands on his chest. They rose and fell with his breath. She scrunched her eyes tight and shook her head. No. She couldn't let his compassion and his all too masculine form tempt her. Once she found Hannah, he'd move on to another assignment, and she'd never see him again.

She pushed away and headed to the hall. "Good-bye, I mean good night."

๛

The next morning, Sadie's somber mood continued.

After breakfast, Bowen slung his jacket and computer case over his shoulder. "I'll be gone about three hours." He tapped Sadie's arm. "Erik will stay with you."

Erik set up his laptop on the table.

What could she do? What else—the dishes.

The old house had no dishwasher, so Sadie scrubbed and wiped, aware of Erik's murmurs and mutters as they drifted from the table.

His next words got her attention. "Sadie. Come look. News of Hannah."

26

Bowen rubbed his temples again and focused on the computer screen. His e-mail messages blurred. A phone rang in the next cubicle. Voices mingled with traffic sounds from the street below his office window. He rolled his desk chair backward right into the divider. With coffee mug in hand, he stomped to the small kitchen and picked up the coffee pot.

Other IRO personnel milled around the office, but he ignored their chatter. He took a gulp of the stale coffee with no expectation of a hot brew this late in the morning.

Ginger strolled past and then stepped back and eyed him. "What's up? You look like you lost your best friend."

He took another gulp and gave her a wide grin. "Is that better?"

"You can't fool me. Is it this job?"

"You could say that." He refilled his mug and attempted to leave the kitchen, but Ginger blocked the doorway.

"It's a job, Boudine. Remember that. I need you to wrap it up quickly. I've got a major project in Columbia that needs your expertise. I also need Wesner. I have to reassign him in a day or two. He won't be with you much longer."

Bowen returned to his desk. Which operative would take Erik's place? Maybe Ginger would assign one of the women. He hoped it would be Lela Ortiz.

He plopped into his brown leather chair and rolled it back to his desk. Wrap up the job quickly? How he wished he could locate Hannah and get her and Sadie to safety. Find something criminal to connect to Lonnie so he'd be out of the picture and Sadie could resume her normal life.

The screensaver patterns swirled bright colors. Only a job. How often had he repeated those words? Sadie was no mere job.

Last night at the laundromat, he'd opened his soul to her. He hadn't realized how deeply he'd been affected by his visit to Hillcrest Church. Or how images of his early church days had remained stuck in his memory.

Charlotte hadn't lost her way. She lived her beliefs, and attended church regularly.

Rocking back and forth, Bowen gulped the last mouthful of coffee and picked up the photograph on his desk. Mother, Dad, Charlotte and him, taken the year he'd graduated from college. So young, so full of dreams.

Sadie had read scriptures about forgiveness. Would God really forgive him? What would Sadie think if she knew the sordid details of his past?

He recalled her words of rejection in the pickup on their way out of Texas. He couldn't blame her for reacting to his cover story of lies. But last night in the living room, she had responded—if only for a second.

A *ding-ding* from the computer signaled a new e-mail message.

Bowen replaced the picture, set his cup on the desk, and touched the keypad, dissolving the screensaver. The message came from Erik. He opened it and the words sent blood speeding through his veins. *Have you read Smitty's report? Good news, no?*

Smitty was one of the operatives tracking Evelyn Adams. Bowen searched through his unopened messages and clicked on the one from Preston Smith. After reading the first sentence, a jolt of excitement kicked in.

Without too many details, Smitty reported evidence that Evelyn had returned to her house briefly. Had withdrawn the child from school, informing authorities she'd be home schooled. The best news— Evelyn had used her credit card at a market in Santa Clarita, which meant she hadn't moved far. Smitty would follow up on her whereabouts.

Bowen let out a low whistle and rocked in his chair. If Smitty located her, then Sadie and Hannah...

He typed quick replies to Erik and Smitty and responded to his other messages. With that task accomplished, he called Cal and told him about Irene, reminding him to treat every conversation as if it was being monitored. Bowen also arranged for a technician to repeat the electronic bug scan of Cal's office and home.

Just before noon, he logged off and packed up his laptop. He stopped at Ginger's office. "I read your message about testifying in the Ullman trial. Do you know when they'll call me?"

She stood at an open file cabinet drawer. "No, but I'll have someone on standby to work with Sadie. Is that all?"

"Yeah. Thanks."

On the way back to the safe house, Bowen stopped to gas up the SUV. In the strip mall next to the gas station he found a florist. He parked in front and bought one carnation. Then at drugstore, he purchased a toiletry bag for Sadie. He drove around back and entered the house through the kitchen. All clear. Sadie's and Erik's voices drifted from the living room. In her room, he placed the white carnation in the vase with the others and then set the toiletry bag on her bed.

She hadn't mentioned the flowers, but he hoped they cheered her.

Once in the living room he found Sadie and Erik at the coffee table playing a game of chess on a small, travel-sized board.

"Want a bowl of soup?" Erik pointed to the kitchen. "It's on the stove. Sandwich stuff's in the fridge."

"Sure. I'll join you in a minute." Bowen headed to the kitchen where he prepared a ham and provolone sandwich and poured a bowl of minestrone soup. He placed it all on a tray which he balanced on his lap as he sat on the sofa.

Erik moved his bishop and wagged a finger at Sadie. "See if you can counter that. Glad you're back, Boudine. I need to check on the other house. They need my help."

Bowen swallowed a spoonful of soup and gave Erik a mock salute.

"Sorry, Sadie. Maybe Boudine can finish this game with you." Erik left through the kitchen, the door banging shut behind him.

Without the wig, Sadie's face seemed fuller. Although the fake hair gave her a sophisticated air, he preferred the natural look.

"Did Erik give you the good news? About Evelyn still being in Santa Clarita."

He almost missed her small nod.

"What's wrong?"

"One minute I'm ecstatic to be here, the next, the tension is about to drive me insane."

"Drive you? I thought you were—"

"Quit making fun of me." A brief twinkle in her eyes took the edge off her words.

"I didn't know you played chess."

"You never asked." She rubbed her temples. "But I don't want to finish the game right now. I'm going to my room."

"I have a surprise for you. A toiletry bag. It's on your bed."

"Thanks."

Bowen drained his glass and then scanned the chessboard. If Erik had continued the game, Sadie would have won.

Bowen despised this waiting game. He took the tray to the kitchen and then flopped into the recliner and turned on the TV.

Later, Sadie joined him and settled on the sofa, where she hunkered by the armrest, her legs folded beneath her. Her body language warned him to stay away.

"Want to watch a movie?" He flipped through channels

"There. That's a good one."

Bowen raised the footrest and relaxed, content to be in the same room with Sadie. What emotions must be warring within her? He had no idea what is was like to lose a child, find her, and lose her again.

After ten minutes or so, her eyelids fluttered and her head sank onto her shoulder.

He eased out of the chair, pulled the blanket off his bed, and covered her. With the TV off, he tiptoed to his room and opened his laptop. His phone buzzed before his e-mail account opened. "Hello."

"Boudine, it's Hernandez. I have news about that U. S. Marshal in Austin."

Bowen sat up straighter, his heart racing. "Go on."

"The woman arrested has several aliases. The one she used in Texas was Lavonne White."

"And?"

"She's a professional hit man, uh, hit woman. Rumored to be contracted by someone in L.A."

If Sadie had remained in Austin, would she have been Lavonne's next target?

27

Sadie's disjointed emotions eased as she shared the evening meal with Erik and Bowen. The men discussed Smitty's report and Sadie latched on to the positive news. "When will we return to Santa Clarita? Can we go there and drive around? We may see Evelyn's car."

"We're not going anywhere near that place," Bowen said. "Smitty checked the other houses Evelyn Adams owns and is on the lookout for her car. You need to stay right here."

"I can't get far without wheels, anyway." Sadie picked up her plate and carried it to the sink.

Bowen filled the sink and rolled up his sleeves.

A tiny sigh puffed through her lips. With his muscled forearms deep in suds, he looked nothing like a bodyguard. Images of future domestic bliss warred with her resolve to forget him once she found Hannah.

The evening dawdled by.

Bowen and Erik worked in the bedroom for hours, talking on the phone or tapping computer keys. Sadie watched TV, read an old magazine, paced up and down the hall, and listened in on snippets of cryptic conversations.

Resigned to spending the rest of the evening alone, Sadie took a longer than usual shower, dressed in jeans and a black shirt, and snuggled among the pillows on her bed. With the Bible opened to the book of Psalms, she read until her eyelids drooped. She fell asleep to the gentle patter of raindrops on the window.

But her dreams were anything but gentle. When a three-armed Lonnie attacked her, she awoke with a scream echoing in her head. She jumped out of bed and collided with Bowen at the door.

"What's wrong?" He took a firm grip of her shoulders and flipped on the light.

"Lonnie. Dream."

"A dream? That's all?" Anxiety coated his words.

"What's going on?" Erik stood in the doorway.

"Sadie had a nightmare." Bowen cradled her close to his chest and whispered in her ear, "You're fine." He led her to the bed. "Sit, Sadie."

When they were both seated, he raised her hand to his lips and kissed her fingers. A little shiver scampered down her arm.

"Sorry you had a scare."

"I thought Lonnie had found me." She stifled a nervous giggle that almost dissolved into sobs. She would not break down in front of Bowen. Tears were a mere heartbeat away.

"I have a little more work to do in my room. Erik, will you say with her?"

"Sure." He moved aside as Bowen left. "That was a big shock. Hot tea will be good, right?"

What an unusual man. He was as much at home in the kitchen as behind the wheel of a surveillance vehicle. His concern for her welfare touched her heart.

Erik worked by the pale light above the stove. When the microwave dinged, he pulled out two mugs of hot water and set them on the counter next to the box of tea bags.

Sadie selected a mint and chamomile bag, hoping the combination would settle her nerves. Swishing the bag up and down, she carried her cup into the living room.

"Don't turn on the light." She plopped on the sofa, legs up, next to the green blanket that had covered her while she napped earlier. She knew it was Bowen's——it still carried his body scent.

"OK." Erik sank into the recliner. The faint illumination from the kitchen cast eerie shadows. Erik's dark shape dominated a corner of the living room.

They sipped their tea in silence for a while.

Sadie asked, "Do you have any family?"

"Wife and children were killed during the fighting in my country." His deep voice cracked, and he stood up quickly. "Don't want to talk about it. Must go now." He set his mug in the sink with a clatter and tromped down the hall.

She slid her off the sofa to apologize, but Bowen entered the living room.

"There you are." His outline loomed behind the sofa. "Are you going back to your room?"

"Is Erik all right?"

"What do you mean?" Bowen joined her on the sofa.

She described Erik's behavior.

"He won't talk much about his life before coming to America. I've known him a long time, and he hasn't shared many details with me."

"I'm sorry if I upset him."

"He's a very private person. I'm ready to close up shop for the night." He glanced at his watch. "Almost midnight. I don't want to turn into a pumpkin."

"What?"

"You know—Cinderella, pumpkins."

"You silly guy." She chuckled. "The pumpkin turned into her coach. Mice turned into her footmen. A…" Her voice trailed as visions of the story flooded her mind. Cinderella was one of Hannah's favorite fairytales. A sharp pain pierced her heart and took her breath away. She sank back and raised her feet onto the seat, hugging her knees.

"I'm sorry, Sadie. We will find Hannah." He stood and held out his hand. "You'd better turn in and get some rest."

"I don't want to go back there."

"Why not?"

"I don't want to be alone." She remembered the jolt of fear the nightmare produced.

"OK. I have an idea." Minutes later he returned with pillows and another blanket. "You sleep on the sofa. I'll take the recliner. Will that suit you?"

"Thank you." She snatched up his green blanket.

He fluffed two pillows and laid them on the armrest. "Come on. I'll tuck you in." He straightened the blanket over her, exaggerating the motion of tucking it around her legs. "Is that satisfactory, ma'am?"

She stifled a giggle. "Yes. Can we leave the stove light on?"

"Uh-huh." He threw the other blanket onto the recliner. "I'll take a quick shower and be right back."

Alone in the small living room, she snuggled into Bowen's blanket. She didn't know if it was the tea or the comfort she leeched from his familiar scent, but she fell asleep before he returned. She awoke with the nightmarish sensation of not knowing where she was. But a quick glance at Bowen sprawled in the recliner brought the evening's events into focus.

Quietly, Sadie sat up and rubbed her eyes. A hint of daylight peeked through the drapes.

Bowen's foot twitched, and he groaned. His face, relaxed in sleep, looked so boyish, except for the shadow of dark whiskers.

Sadie gathered up her pillows and tiptoed out of the room. By the time she'd freshened up and applied a bit of makeup, the strong pungent aroma of coffee drifted down the hall.

Erik had prepared french toast with blueberry compote, which he set on the table. "Good morning. Come help yourself."

She poured a mug of coffee and stirred in a dose of powdered creamer. "You're up early."

"Always. I like to see the sun rise." Erik straddled a chair and added several slices of toast to his plate.

Bowen stomped down the hall, whiskers gone and damp curls tamed for the moment. "Morning all. Sadie, you sleep OK?" He poured a mug of coffee and sat.

"The sofa's quite comfortable."

He stabbed a piece of toast and glanced at Erik. "You tell her yet?"

"No."

"Tell me what?" Sadie scanned their faces. "What's wrong?"

"I'm leaving today." Eric held up his mug in a mock toast. "Been nice getting to know you, Sadie,"

"Where are you going?"

"Been reassigned." He gulped down the last of his coffee.

"Another operative will join us." Bowen set his fork down on the empty plate. "Don't know who yet."

"I've got to go." Erik thumped Bowen on the

shoulder and doffed an imaginary hat at Sadie. "Good-bye." His steps echoed down the hall, returning a minute later. He carried his computer case and a large, black duffle bag. "See you." The back door slammed behind him.

"I'm going to miss him. He's an unusual guy."

"He's one of the best." Bowen stood and stacked plates.

"What are the plans for today? When can I see Cal?"

Bowen ran water into the sink and swished the suds. "We'll see if we can arrange something for tomorrow, but right now—" His phone rang. Without drying his hands, he pulled it from his pocket and checked caller I.D. "It's Ginger. Hi, what's up?"

Sadie motioned for him to move aside. As she washed the dishes, she listened to his part of the conversation.

"Ten o'clock. Fine, I'll hold on." He held the phone a little away from his mouth and leaned against the refrigerator. "I've got an appointment." Then he uh-huhed a few times. "Yes. Erik left about thirty minutes ago. Who's coming to replace him?"

Sadie released the sink stopper and dried her hands.

A scowl settled on Bowen's face. "No. Why him? Where's Lela Ortiz?" He raised his eyes to the ceiling as if pleading for mercy. "Fine, I'll leave when he gets here." He hung up.

"You don't seem too happy with Erik's replacement. Who is it?"

A knock on the front door stalled Bowen's answer. He checked the peephole. "He's here." Bowen squared his shoulders and thrust his chin out before opening the door.

Adonis walked in.

Sadie couldn't take her gaze off the man's muscled arms and chest straining inside a tight-fitting black T-shirt. His wavy blond hair complemented his lean, tanned face.

He ignored Bowen and strode straight to Sadie, hand extended. "Hi. I'm Preston Smith, but you can call me Smitty."

Sadie's knees turned to mush as she gazed into the handsome face. She didn't remember holding out her hand, but next thing she knew, he clasped it in both of his and drew her close. "We're going to have so much fun."

Behind Smitty, Bowen rolled his eyes and threw up his hands.

Amused at this reaction, Sadie arched her eyebrows. "Exactly what do you have in mind?"

28

Surrounded by hordes of vehicles, Bowen inched his way to the downtown courthouse. Why'd he been called now? Forced to dress in a suit and tie added to his already dark mood. And to top it off, his testimony might not be needed. While keeping a wary watch on the traffic around him, his warring thoughts marshaled into dual flanks of attack: Sadie and Smitty at the safe house and a strange longing to heal the gaping gash in his soul. His head ached from deep concentration. Bowen removed his sunglasses and rubbed a spot between his eyes.

Regrets populated his mind like dark unfriendly planets. He'd always been able to corral them and move on. But sometimes, like this morning, the aliens swarmed out of the swamp and snarled at his heels.

A butter-yellow sporty convertible passed him. The driver's blonde hair whipped around her face and streamed behind her like a pale flag in a Santa Ana wind. The hair reminded him of Sadie. If she rode in a convertible wearing her wig, the hair would act that way.

Images of Sadie bombarded his brain. One refused to budge: Sadie and Smitty sharing admiring glances.

What chance did he have against the Golden Boy, Preston Smith?

Especially when Sadie had made it clear she'd sever all ties once she was safe with Hannah. Although Sadie's words rebuffed him, her eyes sometimes betrayed her. He'd thought more than once that she had feelings for him. The way she responded to his touch, the softness in her gaze.

Would he ever have a chance to convince her that his acts of affection in Austin were genuine? Bowen knew his cover story lies would rear back and bite him one day. He never figured the wound would involve his heart. Meeting Sadie had thrown his ordered world into chaos. He could no longer keep his professional life and personal life in separate compartments.

By the time Bowen found a parking space, his jaw muscles ached. Relax, relax. He rolled his shoulders and loped to the courthouse where the assistant district attorney cautioned him his testimony may not be needed.

Bowen unzipped his briefcase and pulled out his Bible. A hint of printers ink still clung to the new golden-edged pages.

She'd made him buy it, although Sadie didn't know it. After their discussion on forgiveness in the laundromat, Bowen had purchased the Bible. He used the concordance to locate the scriptures she'd read to him, and as he devoured them late at night, he found other gems he remembered from his youth.

There was a small church close to the safe house. Bowen wanted to ask Sadie if she'd like to attend. As her bodyguard, he'd offer to accompany her. He wasn't ready yet to discuss his interest in redemption.

Bowen opened the Bible and suddenly remembered the small one his parents gave him on his tenth birthday. Where was it? The last time he'd seen that Bible was the night his father held it to his chest and pleaded with Bowen to change his ways. At seventeen he had been so sure of himself and had replied, "I don't want your God in my life."

"Even when you reject God, He still wants you." His father fought back tears.

A tsunami of guilt flooded him. His father had died six years ago without mentioning Bowen's wayward lifestyle again. What would he have said to the resurgence of Bowen's interest in God now?

A picture of Sadie cradling the old Bible in the laundromat drifted through his mind. He attributed his awakened interest in his soul to her. If she could overcome her doubts and return to her faith, why couldn't he? Getting a handle on God forgiving him was one thing. But could he convince Sadie to forgive him, too?

Even reading his favorite passages from Acts couldn't banish Sadie from his mind. Bowen returned the Bible to his briefcase and paced to the window. What was his problem? Why did the idea of Smitty spending time with Sadie feel like a dagger plunged in his chest?

29

"How much farther?" Hope effervesced inside Sadie.

They were on their way to Santa Clarita. Smitty had received word that Evelyn Adams's car had been spotted near one of her rental houses.

"Ten miles. Plenty of time for you to tell me about your time with Boudine. Does he ever lighten up?"

"What do you mean?"

"We all know he's an uptight kinda guy. Serious, no fun. I wager he's spent more time on his computer than he has with you."

Images of Bowen bringing her a rose on their first date, the warmth of his smile and gentleness of his touch floated through her mind. But then she remembered their hours together in the safe house. How many reports did he make, anyway?

"I knew it." Smitty traced the emblem on the steering wheel. "The look on your face says it all. But you're with me now. Get ready for a wild time."

Sadie studied his profile. Movie star gorgeous, he had a dangerous curve to his mouth that warned her to keep her distance. "The only wild time I'm planning on is celebrating with my daughter."

"I understand. I'm not making fun of your situation." The teasing tone left Smitty's voice. "Trying to lighten things up a bit."

They traveled in silence through the city center and out to the suburbs.

He pulled to a stop and parked along the curb.

"Which house belongs to Ms. Adams?"

"Down a ways. Let's get out and take a peek."

They stepped onto the cracked sidewalk.

"See those stone duplexes with red flowers in the window boxes? They belong to Evelyn."

"I hope she's there." Sadie's heart fluttered.

"She may have parked in back."

They neared the duplexes but could see no cars on the property.

Smitty punched in a number on his cell phone.

The front door of the first unit opened.

"Who's that?"

He terminated the call and whispered, "I guess the tenant." He squared his shoulders and cocked his head. "I have an idea."

Sadie followed him up the sidewalk to the house.

A tiny silver-haired woman met them at the porch steps.

"Good day, ma'am." Smitty's white teeth gleamed in his golden face. "We have a little problem and need your help."

The woman adjusted a hearing aid with skeletal fingers. "What is it, deary? Speak up now."

"We're looking for Evelyn Adams. We believe she owns these houses. Is that right? We have good news for her but don't know how to reach her."

"She owns them, but she don't live here. Lives over yonder." She raised a withered arm and pointed. "Evelyn's having her house fumigated. Came by and told me this morning. Said she's staying in a motel over on The O—" Her watery blue eyes widened as far as the droopy lids allowed.

"Which motel, ma'am?"

The woman backed away, her slipper-clad feet shuffling as if performing an awkward dance step. "Not supposed to tell. Sorry. I've got to go." She limped to the door and retreated into her house.

"So much for that." Smitty took Sadie's arm and led her down the sidewalk. "At least we know Evelyn's in a motel, and the old girl gave us a good hint. The Old Road, I think she started to say. Let's get back to the car and check my GPS."

The navigational system indicated four motels on The Old Road.

"All we have to do is cruise the parking lots and look for Evelyn's car. You hungry?"

As the robotic GPS voice guided them through the area, Sadie's stomach rumbled reminding her that she hadn't eaten since her early breakfast. Even so, right now she had no interest in food. "No. Let's find Hannah."

They checked two motels without success. But at the third motel, they found a blue sedan with a rusty right rear fender angled into a parking spot near the vending machines.

Smitty maneuvered his car across the lot where they had a clear view of the rooms, reversed in, and then opened the windows. Tempting smells of burgers and fried chicken from the nearby restaurant floated in on the slight breeze.

Sadie swallowed and kept her eyes on the motel. Was Hannah in one of those rooms? Maybe the one with the yellow *Do Not Disturb* sign dangling in the breeze. Was she watching TV? Eating lunch?

A pickup entered the lot. Another vehicle roared out. The door with the sign opened.

"It's Evelyn Adams." Sadie sat up straight

The woman scurried to her car. She dropped the keys, almost fell over when she bent to pick them up, and struggled to unlock the door. As she drove past them, she rubbed her temple as if massaging away a headache.

"She looks terrible. Is she ill?" Sadie rubbed her own brow in sympathy.

Smitty set his key in the ignition.

"What are you doing? Hannah might still be in the room." Sadie opened her door. "You can chase that woman, but I'm going to check." She rushed to the building and knocked on the door.

Smittty joined her as she knocked again. "Don't call her Hannah. Remember she goes by Penny."

Heart racing, Sadie pounded on the door. "Penny. Penny Adams, are you in there?"

A man popped his head out of a doorway two down and scowled. He retreated after making a rude gesture.

"Maybe Evelyn told her to ignore anyone at the door."

"Each room probably has a window around back. You stay here while I check it out." Smitty crept around the corner.

Listening at the door a moment longer, Sadie closed her eyes. "Please, God. Let me find Hannah."

Back in the car, she stared at the door of Evelyn's room.

Ten long minutes later, Smitty strolled around the building as if he had nothing better to do. He slid behind the wheel.

"What did you find?"

"I got in through the bathroom window. No Hannah, but there's plenty of evidence that she's been there—girls' clothing and toys, school books."

"What now?"

Resting his muscled forearms on the steering wheel, Smitty glanced at her. "You may not be hungry, but I'm starved. Let's find a place to eat where I'll relay this information to the office. We'll return later and see if Evelyn's come back. I think it's time we confront her and take the child."

Sadie had no intention of leaving the motel. "There's a restaurant across the way. I'm going there to eat where I can watch the parking lot."

"But there's probably nothing healthy on their menu."

"Suit yourself. That's where I'm going."

They entered the Blue Hills Café and asked for a booth by a window. After a brief wait, they were seated and given menus.

Sadie scooted across the smooth turquoise vinyl until she could see the whole motel parking lot. "They have a bunch of salads, Smitty. Is that healthy enough for you?"

"I guess, as long as they don't fry them."

While they waited for their order, Smitty texted a long message, his thumbs flying across the tiny keys. He slid his phone into his pocket. "I told them everything we've discovered. Another operative will keep watch if we don't see Evelyn again today."

After their food arrived, Smitty griped about the poor quality of lettuce.

Sadie ignored his comments until she noticed the twinkle in his eyes and the twitching of his lips. How did she miss his teasing note? She kicked his foot under the table.

"What? I'm eating, aren't I?" His grin softened the

tone of his words. Then he bumped Sadie's foot. "It is pretty good." He tapped her foot again. "Any movement at the motel?"

Unnerved by his playing footsie, Sadie glanced outside. "Evelyn hasn't returned. How long are we going to stay here?" She shifted in the seat and moved her foot. Was she imagining his flirting or was he teasing again?

"We can stay another hour or two. I have to get you back to the safe house before dark. Are you ready?"

As they neared the lobby, he slid his arm across her shoulders. "We could rent a room and keep watch from there. Have fun while we wait." He wiggled his eyebrows.

Sadie decided to beat Smitty at his own game. She could tease, too. "Here? Are you kidding? I require a five star hotel."

His jaw muscles clenched, and the gleam dissolved from his eyes.

Ha. Gotcha.

She flounced to the restroom, convinced Smitty wouldn't try another pass at her. A feast for the eyes for sure, but nothing in his character attracted her.

Returning to the lobby, Sadie took Smitty's arm. "Let's wait in your car."

Once outside, he drew her under a tree. Frown lines formed a V between his eyes. "I'm sorry. I didn't mean to—"

"Don't worry about it." Touched by his sincerity, Sadie squeezed his arm. "Let's get back to the motel."

Walking to the car, Sadie spotted a man cross the parking lot. His gait and build tugged out a memory. She slowed. With her hand still on Smitty's arm, she pulled him to a stop and used his massive body as a shield.

"What's up?"

Words formed in her brain but lost connection with her mouth.

Kyle.

A sinkhole opened in Sadie's heart. What was he doing here?

Smitty tensed. "What is it?"

"There's a man going to the motel. It's Kyle. From Austin."

"Kyle? Here?" He glanced over his shoulder. "Is that him in the navy warm-up suit?"

She nodded, clutching Smitty's T-shirt. "Call the cops."

"We can't involve the authorities. What would we accuse Kyle of? All we can do is keep watch."

Smitty guided Sadie to a cluster of trees. With the trunks as cover, he made a call to the office.

Sadie never let Kyle out of her sight. He sidled slowly past Evelyn's door but didn't stop. "He has to be here because of Evelyn and Hannah. If the local cops can't help us, I'm going to call WITSEC."

"That's a good idea. Let me get a secure connection for you." Smitty made another call using Bravo Tango words as Bowen had done. Sadie paid no attention until he handed her the phone. "Do you have the L.A. number?"

Flipping through a little notebook she pulled from her purse, she stopped at a dog-eared page. "Here it is."

"We're far enough away from Kyle. Put the call on speaker."

She dialed, identified herself by name and case

number, and waited a few seconds before Elia Valdez spoke.

"Sadie Malone. We've been looking for you. What happened in Austin?"

"Do you know the details of my case?"

"I do, but let me hand this over to my partner. He has a special interest in your situation. His name's Jake Quillian."

A click, elevator music, and then a deep voice. "Hi, Sadie. This sure is a pleasure. How can I help you?"

"You're familiar with my case?"

"Of course. Where are you? You need to come in."

"I don't have time to discuss that. My daughter's alive, but I don't know exactly where she is right now. There's a man here from Austin. His name is Kyle Nelson, and he discovered my identity. He's found the place where my daughter's been living."

"Is Kyle still there?"

"No. I think he drove away."

"Sadie, you did the right thing calling. We'll handle everything."

Grabbing her notepad, Smitty scribbled and pointed to the words. *Don't tell him too much.*

"Mr. Quillian, what do you want me to do?"

Smitty covered the phone and whispered, "How can he handle everything when he doesn't know where you are?"

An iceberg slammed into Sadie's chest.

"Sit tight," Jake said. "Don't go anywhere. I'll be in Santa Clarita before dark."

The phone slid from Sadie's grasp. Smitty's warning blazed in her head. How did Jake Quillian know she was in Santa Clarita?

30

The satisfied expression on the attorney's face as she approached heralded good news for Bowen. "Thank you for your time, Mr. Boudine. Your testimony is not needed. You're free to go."

Bowen thrust his briefcase under his arm and yanked off his tie. Snippets of scriptures he'd read ministered to his soul as he threaded his way through the parking garage to his car. Come Sunday, with or without Sadie, he'd attend the community church.

His phone hummed—a text from Smitty. What did the Golden Boy want to brag about now?

However, the words Bowen read twisted a dagger into his gut. *We found Evelyn. No Hannah. Trouble. Kyle here and problem with WITSEC.*

Bowen's heart dropped even as he replied. How had they gotten in so much trouble in so short a time? His phone beeped.

Sadie's with me. Safe.

"Of all the lame brained, stu—" Bowen roared out of the parking garage. He had to see for himself that Sadie was safe. Although a good operative, Smitty sometimes allowed his bravado to cloud his judgment. Bowen slowed his racing thoughts, trying to work out how they could recover the situation.

Smitty had located Evelyn. Good. Where was Hannah? Unknown. Kyle was in Santa Clarita? Bad. What about WITSEC? Not good. Not good at all.

"God, please keep Sadie and Hannah safe." Unfamiliar words came out of Bowen's mouth. Did one little sentence constitute a prayer? A spark of heat flared in the center of his chest. He liked the sensation.

Vehicles clogged the freeway. It would take over an hour to reach Santa Clarita, but to keep Sadie safe, he'd endure all the traffic on the continent.

Another text. He couldn't afford to stop again. Knowing it was against the law, he read the message, anyway.

Evelyn returned. Going to confront her.

31

"Evelyn's back in her room." Sadie lowered the binoculars.

"Let me handle her."

Smitty popped the glove box and pulled out a holster with a long strap. He wound it over one shoulder, adjusting it so the gun fit snuggly under his left arm. Next, he slipped into a windbreaker and opened his door. "Let's roll."

He knocked on the door and waited, his right hand under the left side of his jacket.

The door creaked open and Evelyn wavered into view. Thin gray skin covered her haggard face. Her eyes were dark caverns.

"Evelyn Adams?" Smitty lowered his arm.

The small woman raised her head in the direction of his voice but focused on a point in the distance.

"Ms. Adams, are you all right? Where's Penny?"

"I don't know." A shiver raked her slender frame, almost knocking her over.

"What do you mean you don't know?" Hysteria cranked Sadie's tone up a notch. "Was she here with you?"

"He took her."

Sadie clutched the doorjamb for support. Icy fear gripped her heart. She brushed past the woman and entered the room.

Evelyn sank onto one of the unmade beds.

Smitty closed the door. He pulled up a chair.

"Who took the child?"

"Who are you?" Evelyn stuck her hand into the pocket of her dark brown skirt.

Smitty moved his hand to his holster and then dropped it when Evelyn extracted a rumpled tissue.

"I don't have a child. What are you talking about?"

Sadie yanked a coloring book off the dresser. "Then why do you have this? Come on, Evelyn. We know a child was here." Sadie pointed to a box in the corner and opened the closet. "We see her toys, and these are probably her clothes." Anxious and angry, she stormed back to the bed. Grabbing the frail shoulders, she yelled, "Where is my child?"

Evelyn crumpled. Sobbing hard, words stammered out. "The man took her. The man with...with the moustache took her."

"When? We were watching all afternoon? When did he have the chance?"

Smitty held up his hand. "Ms. Adams, when did he take her?'

"At...at noon."

"Noon? That was before we arrived." Smitty stood and paced in the small room. "Then why did he come back?"

Evelyn did not answer.

Unable to keep her lunch down, Sadie dashed to the bathroom and threw up. No. No. Kyle could not have Hannah. She wiped her mouth and slumped to the cold tile floor. The distorted words of Smitty's questions and Evelyn's answers reached her ears as roaring static. Would she ever see Hannah again? Gray mist clouded her vision. She longed for oblivion.

"Come on, Sadie. Up you get." Smitty took her

hands and helped her stand.

"Why did Kyle take her?"

Evelyn's hand trembled as she stuck it into her other pocket and withdrew a slip of yellow paper. "Earlier today I got a ransom call."

Blood whooshed out of Sadie's head. Little dots of light floated. She swayed and landed on the bed.

"How much do they want?" Smitty asked, his voice hard.

"He didn't ask for money. A garbled voice told me to go to Creekview Park and wait on a bench next to the big tree at the south end."

"And?" Sadie's voice sounded hoarse even to her own ears.

Evelyn stood and turned to Sadie. "Penny has your eyes."

Shards of pain pierced Sadie's heart. "You know who I am?" She shook off the implications of Evelyn's words. "What happened at the park?"

Evelyn shuffled towards the door. "I found a note there."

A quick step and Smitty reached the door first, barring her way. "What did the note say?"

Evelyn threw the little square of paper at Sadie. It landed on the olive green spread. Her words sliced through the stuffy air. "Read it for yourself."

Sadie snatched the paper scrap. She struggled with the folds and finally, dark scrawled words snaked across the wrinkled yellow square.

I don't want money. Go home. I'll contact you at 7. I want the child's real mother.

32

Sadie fumed with rage and collapsed onto the bed.

Evelyn withered and shrank into the shadows.

Still guarding the door, Smitty tapped keys on his phone. "I've reported this latest development to the office. Now we need to call the local police."

Sadie catapulted off the bed and grappled for Smitty's phone. "No. They'll find out who I am and notify WITSEC."

"We must report the kidnapping. And WITSEC already knows you're here somewhere. Boudine and I can't handle this alone."

Contact the police and give up her freedom? Risk calling WITSEC again and hope she reached Valdez instead of Quillian? Kyle's note said he'd contact Evelyn at seven, ninety minutes away. Would she be safe here until then?

"Please don't call the police until Kyle contacts Evelyn. Can you give me that much time?"

"OK, Sadie. I understand your reluctance to involve the authorities, but I'll have to call, eventually."

Turning back to Evelyn, Sadie's voice took on a new authority. "Since you know who I am, please tell me how you found Hannah."

"What are you going to do to me?"

"Your fate's not in my hands. Tell me what I need to know. Please."

"I found her beside the Santa Ana River. I was

241

walking my old dog and saw a little bundle on the embankment, a piece of wood near the child's hand. She must have used it to stay afloat."

Sadie covered her mouth.

"She was battered and bruised but alive. I took her home. At first, she had no memory of the accident or who she was. I called her Penny and after a while she stopped asking about you and her daddy."

"You knew about the accident?"

"It was in the papers the next day."

What kind of sick person would keep a child from her mother? "Why didn't you contact the authorities?"

Evelyn raised her eyes to the ceiling, her lips quivering. "I read about the trial and saw you on TV. That man threatened you. I thought he would kill Penny. I wanted to help her and keep her safe." She sniffed and dabbed at a tear. "I've treated her right and I wasn't lonely anymore."

Sadie stumbled into the bathroom where she tore off the wig, and threw cold water over her face. Slamming the door shut, she swiped at her wet face with a wad of tissues. Her baby had been in that cold, dark water all alone. Had she suffered? She must have been so scared. But Evelyn had taken care of her, kept her safe. Sadie's anger and grief were tempered with the knowledge that this woman had saved her child. Like Moses and the Egyptian princess, her baby lived because someone saved her. Still, Sadie wanted to wail, to cry to heaven at the loss of those precious years in Hannah's life. Alone in WITSEC, Aaron dead, Hannah would have eased those long, lonely years.

A phone rang in the bedroom. Sadie checked her watch. Five forty-five. She picked up the wig and opened the door.

Evelyn mumbled into the phone. She turned and covered the mouthpiece, eyes widening at Sadie's changed appearance. "Your name is Sadie Malone, isn't it?"

"Yes."

Evelyn held the phone out to Sadie. "It's for you."

She couldn't move.

Smitty placed his hand on her back and whispered, "Hold the phone so I can hear what he has to say."

Sadie took the receiver, her hand and voice shaking. "Hello."

"Sadie?"

"Yes."

"It's been a long time." Lonnie Levasseur's voice hadn't changed.

"What do you want?"

"It's not what I want that matters. It's what you want." He let the words sink in before adding, "I have something, no sorry, someone you want."

Smitty caught her when her knees buckled.

"Tell me, Lonnie."

"Ha. So you know it's me. I'm flattered."

"Just say it."

"I have your daughter, and if you want to see her alive again, you'll meet me in L.A."

33

Until he could see Sadie, hold her, and know she was safe, Bowen would have to trust Smitty. He glanced at his phone when it buzzed in the dashboard holder.

Smitty sent another text.

Bowen squinted at the words.

Returning to L.A. Call me.

Bowen eased over and took the first exit. A quick turn, and he parked in an empty lot where he punched in Smitty's speed-dial number. He answered right away.

"We'll be there in less than an hour."

"What happened? Do you have Hannah?"

Smitty gave him the scant details of Hannah's abduction, outlined their confrontation with Evelyn, and Sadie's conversation with Lonnie.

"Lonnie has the child. How—?"

"We don't know how he found Hannah. Kyle's the one who took her."

Rage blackened Bowen's vision.

"Boudine. You still there?"

"Yeah. What exactly did Lonnie say?"

"Not much, but I assume he'll trade Hannah for Sadie. He gave her a phone number and wants her to call at nine, tonight."

"That'll give us time to make plans. How is she? Can I talk to her?"

Muted voices traveled through the airwaves.

"Hi, Bowen." A hitch in her voice ripped a chasm in his chest.

"Sadie, how are you holding up?" He wanted to comfort her.

"I'm numb, but I know you guys will help me survive this."

"We will. Let me talk to Smitty again. And Sadie, I...I prayed that God will keep Hannah safe."

Smitty returned to the line, and the job took precedence. "We need to muster the troops."

"I've already alerted the boss."

Bowen drove to the safe house and called Ginger.

"Erik and Lela are on their way, with operatives on standby." A crisp, take-charge tone infused Ginger's voice.

"This could get ugly. Is Lela bringing the gear?"

"Yes, she is. Vests, night vision scopes, listening devices. Everything you'll need. I'll take over Erik's case for now, so use him as much as necessary."

"Thanks."

Smitty's vehicle roared into the driveway.

Bowen bolted to the car and helped Sadie out.

Her wan complexion matched the color of her wig. She managed a ghost of a smile and held onto his arm as they entered the house.

Bowen had not expected his heart to somersault at the sight of her. He led her to the sofa.

"Boudine, when will Erik and Lela arrive?" Smitty asked.

"Smitty and I need to talk." Bowen touched Sadie's arm. He signaled Smitty to follow as he marched down the hall. "They're on the way. You relayed everything that happened in Santa Clarita?"

"Seems there's a problem at WITSEC. The guy

Sadie spoke to knew she was in Santa Clarita."

"So my decision not to contact them right away was sound."

"One more thing. It looked like Evelyn planned to run. I notified the local cops—"

"You did what?"

"Don't worry. I kept Sadie's name out of it. Evelyn was in no hurry to talk so that should buy us some time before she implicates us."

"Go on."

"I asked how Kyle found her. She said the day after she vacated her house, she returned to pick up a few items. Before she left she checked her e-mail. There was a message from a high school acquaintance asking for her address and phone number. Evelyn remembered the person and sent the information. She has since discovered that the woman she knew passed away last year. She figures whoever sent the message used the information to locate her."

"Sounds logical." Bowen peeked through the blinds. "Someone's here. Probably Erik, by the sound of the vehicle."

They returned to the living room where Bowen sat next to Sadie. "Erik's arrived. When the other operatives get here we'll strategize." He glanced at his watch. "We still have thirty minutes before you need to call Lonnie. Can I get you anything?"

"Please. Hot tea."

"Coming right up." Bowen entered the kitchen as Erik opened the back door. They shook hands. "Good to have you here."

"You couldn't keep me away." Erik gave Smitty a slap on the back and then shrugged out of his jacket. Entering the living room, he spread his arms wide.

"Sadie, girl. I've come to save the day."

The sweet sound of Sadie's chuckle sent a wave of warmth over Bowen as he set a cup of water in the microwave and selected a tea bag.

Erik and Sadie chatted on the sofa. If Erik's daughter had lived, she would be close to Sadie's age. No wonder they got along so well.

The microwave dinged, interrupting Bowen's thoughts. He dunked the tea bag and carried the cup to Sadie. "Madam, your tea is served."

"Thank you, kind sir."

Smitty peered through the drapes. "Lela's here. I'll help her with the equipment." He slipped outside.

Bowen wiped off the table. "We need another chair."

"There's one by my dresser," Sadie said.

"I'll get it." Erik had already started down the hall.

With Sadie's chair in one hand, Erik returned to the living room. "Pretty flowers, Sadie."

Although Bowen watched for Sadie's reaction, she seemed to ignore Erik's comment. Lela and Smitty entered the house and dumped duffle bags by the door.

Bowen introduced Lela to Sadie, and then the five of them settled at the table. "OK, guys. We assume Lonnie is going to ask Sadie to meet him." He glanced at her. "You tell him you'll meet on one condition—if you designate the time and place. Understand?"

She nodded, cheeks hollow and lips tight.

"Get the L.A. map, Lela. Let's check out possible venues." He rubbed his chin, his fingers shaking. What was wrong with him?

"Boudine, we need your laptop. I didn't bring mine."

"Sure." He hurried to his bedroom to get it. Erik followed.

"Listen, friend. I don't think you should lead this operation."

Bowen unzipped his computer case. "Why not?"

"You're too close to her. She's way more than a job to you and has been for a long time." Erik placed his giant paw on Bowen's shoulder. "Sadie is not like Patricia. She'll follow orders. Let me handle this."

"Fine."

They returned to the table, and Bowen opened the laptop. "Erik's going to be alpha on this one. Give him your best, guys."

Once seated, Erik pointed to the map. "Lonnie's office is in Santa Monica, and he lives in Bel Air, so let's choose a venue far from either place."

"How about Griffith Park?" Smitty suggested.

"Pretty far for us and the size of the park could present a major problem." Bowen turned the map and stabbed a finger at a small green section. "How about Lynwood City Park? Close to us, smaller, easier to monitor comings and goings. Plenty of lights in the park."

"I like that idea. A good meeting spot would be near the tennis courts. Easy access from Spruce Street." Erik ran a hand over his bald pate. "We select the site now. Send our backup guys to scout the area so by the time Lonnie hears about it, we're already in place. All in agreement?"

The three operatives nodded. Sadie focused at the map.

"I'll do an Internet search on the area." Bowen tapped keys, all the while struggling to keep from panicking. How could they so cavalierly send Sadie out knowing a killer waited for her?

"Here it is. The aerial map gives a good perspective." Bowen turned the computer so the others could see the screen.

"Has any one else been there?" Erik scanned the group.

Lela, who hadn't said a word yet, held up her index finger. "I grew up in the neighborhood. Practically lived at the park."

"Good. You'll head the advance group. Smitty, take a good look at the aerial shot." Using the same forthright tone, Erik addressed Sadie. "Here's what will happen, Sadie. Lonnie will probably want you to come alone, but you won't. We'll surround you. You'll wear a vest—"

"Huh?" she asked.

"A bulletproof vest. We'll have you in our sights at all times and you will wear a wire and an ear bud."

"So we can communicate with you and hear what's going on around you," Smitty said.

Sadie's dark, cavernous gaze met Bowen's.

Everyone else receded into the background as he rested his hand on her vibrating leg. She closed her hands over his. Erik might be alpha, but Sadie wasn't looking at Erik. In that moment, Bowen sensed her soul reach out to him. He would not fail her.

Under the table, Erik nudged Bowen's foot. Jerked back to reality, Bowen folded the map so the Lynwood section showed in the center. He wrote on the corner of the map. "Here's the address if Lonnie doesn't know the location."

"I think that's it for now. Lela and Smitty, you know what to do. Need anything before you take off?" Erik crossed his arms

They both shook their heads.

Lela stretched out of the chair like a panther on the hunt. "We'll set up and wait for your call. Come, Preston. We'll take my truck. I don't like your driving."

"Yeah, yeah, yeah. Don't like my driving. But you do like my—"

"Kids! Enough." Erik softened his reprimand with a smile. "Be careful out there."

Lela and Smitty executed sharp salutes and left the house.

Bowen slid his arm along the back of Sadie's chair. "I know this is terrifying for you, but you must study these pictures. See, here." He tapped the screen. "This is where you'll enter the park. One of these structures will provide a good shield. We'll be set up here, here, and here. Erik will give you instructions through your ear bud. It's a good plan. I've got your back, Sadie. I won't let anything happen to you."

"You guys will have everything ready at the park, but what if Lonnie won't meet me there?"

"Believe me. He will. He wants you. If you asked him to meet next door to the FBI building, he'd agree."

"But what about Hannah?"

"Let's sit on the sofa. Want more tea?"

"No, thanks." She pushed back from the table. "I want this to be over." Sadie curled into a ball with one elbow on the sofa armrest.

Bowen ignored her body language and sat close, taking her hand. "One more thing. When you talk to Lonnie, ask for proof of life."

Her fingers tightened. "What?"

"We must know that Hannah is still alive."

This time her squeeze cut off circulation to his fingers. He could barely hear her whispered words.

"What if she's not?"

The anguish in her voice shoveled salt into the wound already gaping in his chest. What could he say to calm her? What if she was right? His voice conveyed confidence he didn't feel. "As I said before, Lonnie wants you, and he can't risk hurting Hannah because then he'd have no leverage." He had to believe that. "Hannah is alive, sweetheart. She is."

Sadie slid sideways and rested on his shoulder. Although the circumstances were dire, Bowen relished her closeness.

"It's almost nine," Erik interrupted. "Sadie, use your phone. Our device will block any trace he tries to use."

"Whatever you say." She went to her room and returned with the phone and the slip of paper. Her hands shook. "I need to sit." She dropped onto the sofa, her face paler than it had been all evening.

Squatted in front of her, Erik held a legal pad and pen. "Use the speaker, but don't acknowledge us. We're assuming Lonnie doesn't know who's helping you. If you have questions look at us, and we'll tell you what to say, or we'll write it out for you to read."

"Are you ready?" Bowen quirked an eyebrow. He had the map with the address in his lap.

She consulted the piece of paper, punched numbers on the slim phone, and then held it close to her face. Her eyes were wide, her lips quivered. "Lonnie? Where's Hannah?"

His nasal tone punctuated each word. "Patience, woman, patience. I sense you are not in the mood for small talk. Meet me at—"

Bowen stabbed a finger at the map.

"No. No, Lonnie. You want to meet me. It will be

where I say, when I say." Her voice strengthened. "Do you hear me? *I* will name the place and time."

"Whoa. Calm down. Fine, I'll grant you the place, but I call the time."

A quick look at Bowen and Erik. They both nodded, but Erik wrote on the pad.

She read the words. "I accept that, but you name the time first."

Lonnie took a few moments to reply. "Um, let's say midnight."

The men nodded.

"Midnight is good." Sadie took the map from Bowen. "We'll meet at Lynwood City Park. Near the tennis courts off Spruce Street. Do you know where that is?"

"Say the name of the street again."

Sadie repeated it as Bowen grabbed the pad and scribbled.

"One last thing, Lonnie." She read. "I want to talk to Hannah. I won't come if you don't let me talk to her."

Bowen mouthed, "Good job."

Her fingers cold and stiff, Sadie slid her hand into his. This was the moment he'd dreaded. What if Lonnie refused?

Garbled words came through the line and then a small voice said, "Mama, this carpet is scratchy. I'm scared. Please come get me."

The call ended with a loud click.

Sadie's phone slithered to the floor, and she slumped on Bowen's shoulder.

34

Bowen cradled Sadie's upper body. "It's gonna be OK, Sadie."

She straightened and rubbed her eyes. "I'm not dreaming, am I?" Her face was as white as an over-bleached sheet.

"No. Hannah talked to you." Bowen reluctantly moved his arms. How he wished he could take her place so she didn't have to venture out tonight.

Erik searched one of the duffel bags and yanked out a vest and night vision goggles. "I'll join the others at the park. Boudine, you get Sadie prepared. Everything you need is here." He pointed to the bags. "Head to the rendezvous point at eleven thirty."

"Roger that. See you then." Bowen accompanied Erik to the door.

Sadie's steps echoed down the hall. He followed, but she entered her bedroom and closed the door.

Bowen understood her need to be alone. He searched the refrigerator and produced the makings for an omelet. He whisked the eggs, chopped tomatoes and green pepper, and heated the pan. Sadie's wan face, never far from his mind, clouded his vision. His stomach responded to the smell of onions sautéing. Maybe Sadie hadn't eaten recently. No matter her state of mind, her body needed nourishment, especially to face the dangers ahead. He whisked more eggs and made an oversized omelet. Even if she ate a few bites—

"That smells great. Is there enough for two?"

Bowen's spirits lifted at the sound of her voice. "Sure." He turned off the burner and divided the omelet onto two plates. Bowen joined her at the table and took in her appearance.

She had dampened her hair, the curls tamed and soft, and she'd applied makeup. Her eyes, still hauntingly dark, held a quality he couldn't name.

Placing her hand over his, she said, "Before we eat, I want to do something I've neglected for far too long."

"What's that?"

"We used to pray before eating. Do you mind if I do that now?"

The idea jolted a memory. As a kid he'd done his share of listening to his dad say a blessing. "Go ahead."

She bowed her head, but he couldn't bring himself to close his eyes. Instead, he focused on her profile as she spoke.

"Father God, thank You for this food and the many other gifts that surround us. Keep us in the palm of Your hand tonight and for the rest of our lives. In Jesus name. Amen."

The words came from her heart and conveyed more meaning than any grace he'd ever heard before.

"Why are you looking at me like that?"

"You surprise me, that's all." Was he ready to open his soul to her? No. Stick with the obvious. "When you left the living room I thought you were going to sleep or—"

"I figured I wouldn't be able to accomplish anything tonight if I keeled over. To boost my spirits I did my makeup, readjusted my attitude by praying for strength, and now I'm as ready as I'll ever be to meet Lonnie."

They small-talked while they ate, with Bowen's

apprehension diminishing as he absorbed her calmness and confidence. He also figured out what he'd seen in her eyes—the mother-daughter connection. She'd find Hannah tonight, one way or another.

Bowen washed the dishes with Sadie drying and putting them away. For a brief few minutes, he fantasized about a life where he and Sadie shared household chores, planned for the future, loved.

With an hour before time to leave, Bowen invited Sadie to join him in the living room. He fitted her with the wire and gave instructions on the operation of the ear bud. Next, he found the smallest vest and helped her strap it on. When he'd secured his vest and communication device, he sent her to the bedroom and they practiced listening and talking to each other.

Now they were ready. They sat on the sofa. Sadie scooted close, which thrilled Bowen despite the circumstances. Whatever Sadie had done to prepare for the night, it showed on her face and in her body language. No one watching would ever conclude she was about to face her daughter's kidnapper or that she'd finally reconnect with her long lost child.

He took her hand and rubbed his thumb in circles on her soft skin. "Do you have any questions?"

She moved a little closer. "Yes. One. But first let me say, whatever happens tonight, I want you to know how grateful I am for all your help. So before we leave, please tell me about IRO. What exactly do you guys do, besides make people wear wigs?"

He grinned at her jab. How did she know the name of his organization? Too late to worry about that. "International Retrieval Organization. That's who we are. A worldwide company and as the name suggests, we help extricate people from difficult situations. Then we keep them safe until their problems are resolved."

"Who exactly is Ginger? I know she's not your secretary."

"She's my boss."

Silence settled between them for a moment. Then Sadie leaned towards him. "Is she anything to you besides your boss?"

Admitting the truth felt good. "No. She's my boss. Nothing more."

She edged closer still.

He released her hand and embraced her.

She clung to him a long time and then raised her head. "One last thing. Thank you for the flowers."

Her lips inches from his, he lowered his head. He gazed into her eyes, asked for permission. Receiving her consent, he pulled her close.

Her soft, sweet lips responded to his kiss and Bowen sighed, deep in his soul. This was where he belonged.

35

Standing at the dresser mirror, Sadie gently touched her lips. What had come over her? In the warm, safe harbor of Bowen's arms, kissing him had seemed the most natural thing to do. Still determined to sever ties with him, she stared at her reflection. Is that really what she wanted? If she survived the night, she'd contemplate her future. But she couldn't plan anything until she had Hannah safe in her arms.

Her denim jacket wouldn't snap over the vest. She had no other, so it would have to do. After inserting the ear bud, she picked up her purse. The bulky, brown fake leather bumped her hip. Too much. She withdrew her slim billfold and squeezed it into her jacket pocket.

Ready or not, the time had come. Sadie took one last sniff of the carnations before walking down the hall on surprisingly steady legs.

Bowen waited at the back door, his vest adding inches to his chest. "Take your pick. The SUV or Smitty's car."

"I'll take the SUV."

He gave her the keys and folded his fingers over her hand. "Remember the route?"

She nodded.

"It's time, then. Let's go." On the way outside, Bowen's phone rang. He kept hold of her hand while he answered it. "Hello." He listened and then said, "I expected as much. Thanks for the call."

Holding the car door open for Sadie, he gave her the gist of Ginger's conversation. "She has notified LAPD, the FBI, and WITSEC. Somehow she convinced them to let Erik remain in charge. We'll have all the backup we need."

Sadie drove away first, keeping an eye on Bowen's lights in her rearview mirror. Close to the park they disappeared and Sadie felt his loss as if he had physically abandoned her. She parked, slipped out of the car, and crossed to the building alongside the tennis courts. By the SUV's clock, she had fifteen minutes to wait for Lonnie—assuming he'd be punctual.

Quiet chatter in her ear reassured her that Erik had his crew in place and her in their sights. Occasionally Bowen added a word of support.

At five minutes before twelve, Smitty announced a vehicle's approach. He included the time for her benefit. But the car drove away without stopping. Sadie shifted against the wall and scanned the tennis courts. Movement near the fence surrounding the courts caught her attention. She whispered concern.

"We're aware of it," replied Erik. "Careful, Sadie. Stay in the shadows. Remember to ask for another proof of life when you talk to Lonnie."

But it turned out to be a large dog that loped off into the night.

Anxiety attacked her insides like an erupting volcano. Whatever composure she had at the house oozed out and vaporized in the night air. Why did she ever agree to this? *Lord, give me strength. Please…*

A flurry of words in her ear. Person on the scene. Sadie stiffened and searched the courts. Yes. At the far end. A man took a few steps onto the paved surface and stopped. Tall and beefy. It had to be Lonnie.

He puffed on a cigar and spoke at the same time. "Hello, Sadie. Show yourself."

"Over here."

"Come closer. Let me see you. Are you alone?"

"Yes." Not exactly a lie, as she was alone at the fence. "Where's my daughter? I want proof she's alive."

Lonnie ambled to the net stretched across the court. "All in good time. You sure have been hard to find, Ms. Malone."

A voice in her ear reminded her that their conversation was being recorded. "How exactly did you find me?"

"Ooh. Now wouldn't you like to know that?"

"I would if you can make it brief. I want to take Hannah home, and it's getting late."

Drawing on his cigar, he allowed the smoke to drift away. "I have my sources. Money will buy anything if the amount is high enough."

"Like Kyle?"

Lonnie chuckled, the sound falling short of mirth. "Kyle's been helpful. But I have other, more official sources."

She stepped closer to the fence. "Please, Lonnie. Where's my daughter?"

With his gaze on her, Lonnie dropped the cigar and stomped on it, crushing it into the concrete surface. Was that what he wanted to do with her?

Instantly, a loud crack shattered the silence and a hard projectile slammed into Sadie's chest. She flew backward and landed with a thud against the wall, winded as if a load of bricks had been stacked on her chest. She couldn't breathe. Her legs gave out, and she slid down the wall. On the ground, she opened her eyes. What happened? Dropping his cigar must have been Lonnie's signal to a hidden shooter. Thankful for the vest that had saved her life, Sadie gasped for air and winced as she placed her hand over the impact site.

Shots whizzed through the air around her, voices cursed, moaned, shouted. This could not be happening. Two bodies lay on the tennis court. One she recognized as Lela, the other in a dark uniform.

Lonnie squatted beside the net. As he withdrew a pistol from under his jacket, he teetered backward and landed on his plump derriere. Bowen forced his torso down and jabbed his boot on Lonnie's thick neck. He aimed his gun at Lonnie's head.

It's over. Where's Hannah? Struggling to stand, Sadie scanned the court. The uniformed person on the far side moved. Lights illuminated sandy colored hair on his upper lip. Kyle. He brought his hand up and fired twice.

Bowen staggered and fell, hitting the ground hard. He groaned.

Sadie rushed around the fence towards him.

Blood seeped from Bowen's body.

36

Piercing pain. Bowen blinked at the bright lights.

People prodded and poked his body. Asked him questions. Someone removed his vest, tore his shirt. Fire ripped through his gut. His upper arm throbbed.

Focusing on Erik's face, Bowen tugged at his jacket. "Help me up."

"No. You need to keep still." Erik applied pressure to Bowen's right bicep. "Heard two shots. One hit your arm. Are you hurt anywhere else?"

"Gut." Bowen grabbed Erik's hands. Wet. Gooey. He glared at his blood-covered fingers. "Who?"

Crouched next to Bowen, Erik jerked his head towards the far end of the court. "Kyle."

Still dazed by the unexpected shots, Bowen attempted to sit. "I've got to help find Hannah."

"No you don't. You need to get stitched up."

৵৵

Shooed out of the way, Sadie chewed on her lower lip while Erik and Smitty tended to Bowen. Men and woman in uniform swarmed over the tennis courts. Lonnie slumped near the fence, his wrists bound in flexi-cuffs. Two officers escorted a woman in handcuffs and forced her to sit by the fence several yards from Lonnie. Nicole? She was in on it, too?

For a second no one paid the slightest attention to Sadie. Since Bowen didn't need her help, she focused on locating her daughter. She grabbed Lonnie by the shirt collar. "Where is Hannah? You're going to join your father in prison so why not tell me?"

An officer pulled her away.

"I must find my child. Don't you know he kidnapped her?"

"Yes, ma'am," the young officer said. "We're scouring the park."

Lonnie's smirk hit Sadie like a poisoned dart. Somehow he figured they wouldn't find Hannah. What had he done to her?

"Where is she? Have you hurt her?"

Arching an eyebrow, Lonnie indicated with a quick nod that she should step closer.

The officer had his back to her. Sadie bent down and sucked in quick breaths as the wounded area in her chest throbbed.

"She'll be dead before they find her," Lonnie's whispered words jabbed at Sadie's heart.

Glacial ice flowed through her veins as she backed away. She never had the chance to ask for proof of life. Claws of fear ripped her insides. What now? Glancing at Lonnie, his words echoed in her brain. *Before they find her.* So Hannah had to be close. The officers were searching everywhere, their flashlights bobbing around the park like giant fireflies.

Overcome with panic, Sadie clung to the fence and banged her head against it. The words Hannah uttered to her on the phone played over and over in her mind. *I'm scared, Mama. I'm scared. The carpet's scratchy.*

Sadie stopped. Carpet? What carpet? Old memories surfaced.

Hannah had exceptionally sensitive skin. She did not like certain carpets in their home, and she hated to be in the back of their SUV when they watched a fireworks display or used the area as a table while at the beach.

There certainly was no carpet around here. But there were cars. She must be in a car. Where was Lonnie's vehicle? While waiting for him, she recalled seeing headlights on the other side of the park. Everyone had expected him to arrive via Spruce Street. What if he parked on the other side?

Oblivious to the sharp pain in her chest, she dashed through the trees. One thing occupied her mind—find Hannah. *Please, God. Let me find her.*

As two law enforcement officers ran past her, one said to the other, "They've cleared Levasseur's vehicle."

Sadie increased her speed and caught up with them. "What? Where's his car? Please. I know my daughter is in it."

They slowed, and the female officer asked, "You're Mrs. Malone?"

She nodded.

"Come with us. The bomb squad examined the vehicle and found no evidence of explosives."

A cold chill iced Sadie's heart, and she gasped, unable to breathe. That possibility had never entered her mind.

They approached a dark SUV parked under a large tree. Officers brandishing high-powered flashlights surrounded it.

"Lieutenant, Mrs. Malone is here."

A robust man in a gray suit glanced at Sadie.

What were they waiting for? Polite introductions? Panic fueled her muscles. She ran to the vehicle and set her forehead against the cold glass. "We're coming baby. Hang on. Don't worry." She grabbed the door handle. Locked. "No. No. Break into the car. My child's in there." Sadie yelled at the officers as she clawed at the window.

One of the men used his flashlight to smash the driver's side window, and unlocked the doors.

Sadie wrenched open the back hatch and found her little girl, wrapped in a drab olive green coverlet. She tore away the motel spread and scooped her up, wailing as the child's limp body hung in her arms.

∽∾

EMTs secured Bowen onto the gurney. As they wheeled him into the hospital, a nurse asked his name.

"Bowen Boudine."

An elevator ride. Masked people moved him.

"Bowen, you're going to have surgery on your arm." Medication added to his I.V. "You'll start to feel drowsy real soon."

While he waited for the drug to kick in, the horrific night replayed like a nightmare on a looped tape. Sadie down, but OK. Lonnie smirking. His foot on Lonnie's neck. The furnace-hot anger roiling through him as he aimed the pistol at that monster's head.

Then missiles had struck his gut and arm.

One bullet hit the vest over his abdomen and the other pierced his arm. The vest saved his life. Saved him. Why did those words hold a double meaning? Before he could process the thought, a welcome blackness descended over him.

37

A medical technician inserted an I.V. into Hannah's arm. Another monitored her pulse rate, blood pressure, and ran numerous other checks. One thing he said Hannah had going for her—she could breathe unassisted. Instead of intubating her, he placed an oxygen mask over her face.

Thank You, Lord.

Sitting with Hannah in the back of the ambulance, Sadie tried to stay out of the way but couldn't resist holding the small, clammy hand. It was so cold and gray. Escorted by the siren's wail, they soon reached the hospital. Sadie followed the gurney into the ER, her heart aching with worry.

Asked over and over if she knew what Hannah had ingested, Sadie explained for the umpteenth time that her child had been kidnapped. She didn't know anything. At the ER doctor's, request, she signed permission forms for a gastric lavage if necessary or the administration of activated charcoal. Anything to help her child. Agonizing at the quick jab, she watched a bespectacled young man draw vials of Hannah's blood. Although an empty bottle of over-the-counter sleeping pills had been found in Lonnie's pocket, test results would determine the type and amount of drug in her system.

During the agonizing stint in a small waiting room, Sadie spent the time on prayers for Hannah and Bowen. She jumped when Dr. Obregon, the ER doctor, returned.

"Good news, Mrs. Malone. We won't have to do the gastric lavage." The doctor continued as they entered Hannah's cubicle. "We've started her on the activated charcoal. It will bind the drug in her stomach and intestines."

"How long will she be unconscious?"

"Hard to say. We'll monitor her vitals. Right now her blood pressure and heart rate are down. Temperature is a little low, but we should see an improvement in the next hour or two." He checked the digital readout on the machines hooked up to Hannah.

While the doctor worked on Hannah, a slim, olive skinned woman entered. She held out her hand. "Hi. I'm Elia Valdez. We spoke on the phone. I'll be working with you."

It took Sadie a couple of seconds to figure out who the woman was. She'd forgotten about WITSEC. "What's going to happen now?"

"We'll talk in detail later. Just wanted to make contact."

Sadie kept an eye on the nurse taking Hannah's pulse.

"I won't stay long, but when you're ready to leave, give me a call." Elia removed a business card from her shirt pocket. "Here's my direct number."

"I do have one question."

"What is it?"

Sadie indicated they step away from Hannah's bed. "Now that Lonnie and Nicole are in custody, do I still have to be in the program?"

"No decisions have been made yet, but from what I know, it looks like you'll be free. The evidence from tonight's little shindig will probably lock them up for a long time. There's no Levasseur crime family to worry about, and from what the FBI shared with us, Lonnie's staff is not exactly itching to go to jail on his behalf. "

Despite being in the ER with her drugged daughter, relief lightened Sadie's mood. "It's nothing personal, but I can't wait."

Elia pivoted and said over her shoulder, "Give me a call."

An hour later, Dr. Obregon returned. "We have the test results. Hannah ingested enough medication to sedate her for a number of hours. But we've begun the treatment in time, and she is responding. I want to admit her tonight so we can continue to assess her condition for the next twenty-four hours. If her oxygenation status and vitals are satisfactory you should be able to take her home late tomorrow or the next day." With a nod, he left the cubicle.

Her thoughts veered from Hannah to Bowen. Had he also been brought here?

After a long while, Hannah was taken to a room. Sadie pulled a chair right up to the bed and watched her daughter.

Every so often, Hannah stirred. Her lids fluttered, and she opened her eyes for a second. But she continued to sleep peacefully. Her breathing seemed normal and the color had returned to her skin.

Sadie shrugged off her jacket and removed the flack vest. She unbuttoned her shirt and realized why her upper chest ached. The shot had left a large, round bruise, extremely tender to the touch. She buttoned up again and took Hannah's hand, now warm and dry.

Words of gratitude blossomed and overwhelmed her. She trusted the Holy Spirit would do as the Bible promised and transport her thoughts to the Father.

Resting her head near Hannah's knees, she closed her eyes. The night played over and over in her head like obnoxious summer reruns. Although she had her baby back, a wound still pieced her heart. Where was Bowen? Last she heard he needed surgery to repair his arm. When Hannah woke up, she'd contact Erik and find out about him, but right now, she had to wait for her baby to regain consciousness.

☙ ❧

"Sadie, I have news." Erik whispered in her ear.

She jerked awake and blinked unwanted dreams away. Releasing Hannah's hand, Sadie stood and stretched. "Hi, Erik. Let's step outside."

In the hall, Erik propped himself up against the wall. His gray eyes, underlined with strain and fatigue, held her gaze. "Came to report on Bowen."

Her stomach sunk on the elevator of fear. "Is he all right?"

"Yes. They repaired his shoulder—the bullet went straight through. His vest prevented the other slug from doing damage. His gut will be tender for a while." Yawning, Erik slid down the wall.

Sympathy tightened her throat and Sadie joined Erik on the floor. "Where is he?"

"Here. He's lost a lot of blood. By the way, we're all donating in his name. Can you?"

"Sure. When Hannah's awake. After I've had a chance to explain what's happened, and I have someone to stay with her. I can't leave her right now."

"Understand. I'll check on Bowen again and then come back."

"You're one of the few I'd trust with Hannah."

Sadie took his arm and snuggled next to him, laying her head on his shoulder.

They sat there a while in silence. When Erik stood, he yawned again. "Better check on my buddy. I'll keep you posted."

He helped Sadie stand and wrapped his long arms around her.

"Thanks for stopping by. I was worried about him."

With a nod, Erik tromped down the hall.

Sadie returned to Hannah's bedside. No change. She settled in the chair and folded her arms. So much had transpired in the last few hours she could barely wrap her mind around the details. At least Hannah was safe, and Bowen…did she have to say good-bye to him?

She'd threatened never to see him again once she had Hannah safe, but why? He claimed his affection for her was no lie. Could she believe him? A glimmer of hope tickled her heartstrings. He had shown that he considered her more than a job. Was it time for her to lower the drawbridge of her heart and destroy it forever? Why not give love another chance? When Hannah awoke, she'd visit Bowen.

Content with her plan, Sadie took her daughter's small hand, and in a soft, soothing voice sang the song Aaron had written for her. Over and over she repeated the sweet words until her own lids drooped and her head rested on the bed again.

Every time nurses checked on Hannah, Sadie awoke. Her intermittent sleep left her with bleary vision and a headache. At dawn she eased out of the chair and rolled her shoulders. In the small bathroom, she fixed her hair and dabbed at her face with a damp towel.

A murmur in the room startled her. Was Hannah awake? Sadie opened the bathroom door. Hannah's little body stirred under the covers. At her bedside, she hesitated to take her child's hand again. What if she awoke and screamed at the stranger beside her bed?

Hannah's eyelids fluttered. She raised her thin hand and wiped her hair off her cheek. Her eyes opened, and she stared around the room. She plucked at the I.V. inserted in her arm.

Sadie gently removed her hand. "It's all right, sweetie pie." Would Hannah remember this pet name? "You're in a hospital, and that tube is giving you medicine."

"Who are you?"

What could she say? *Sing Aaron's song.* "We love Hannah, yes we do. She loves her Mom and Daddy, too. Hair and eyes of chocolate brown. Our little princess wears a crown."

Hannah's frown deepened. Her mouth quivered. "I know that song." She blinked and blinked, and then swiped one hand across her eyes. "Why are you singing that song?"

Leaning close, Sadie took her hand. "We used to sing it to you every night."

"You look like my mommy. My real mommy." Her voice tapered off and she gave a half sob. "My real name is Hannah." The words were a mere whisper.

"I am your real mommy, sweetie pie." Sadie answered. "And yes, your real name is Hannah."

With a gasp, Hannah jerked her hand away and covered her eyes. "Where have you been?"

How much more could her heart take before it shattered in pieces? "I've been looking for you."

"Do...do you want me now?"

"I've always wanted you. What do you mean?" Sadie sank into the chair.

The little head moved on the pillow. Dark, questioning eyes examined Sadie's face. "Mama Evelyn said I had to stay with her because after my daddy died, my real mommy didn't want me anymore."

38

Bowen shivered. He tried to tug the covers around his shoulders, but his arm didn't cooperate. He opened his eyes. His blurred vision slowly cleared. Hospital. Surgery. No wonder he couldn't get the sheet—his right arm was immobile, bandaged to his chest.

Propped against the pillows, he assessed his situation. Arm operated on, but whole. Bruised area just below his ribs. That would heal. So far, his life appeared to be back on track. So why did he have a niggling ache, like someone prodded a sore spot in his brain?

A nurse bustled in.

"Good morning, Mr. Boudine. My name's Robin. How you doing?" She wrapped a blood pressure cuff around his left bicep and then thrust a thermometer into his mouth. "Under your tongue, please."

The cuff tightened. Relaxed slowly. The machine beeped results.

Robin removed the cuff and the thermometer. "Blood pressure is a little high. Temp is normal." After scribbling notes on a little pad, she checked his bandage. "The surgeon will come by later this morning. Need anything? Hungry?"

"No. Yes. When can I get out of here?"

"Ask the doctor. On a scale of one to ten, how's your pain right now?"

Closing his eyes, Bowen shrugged. "OK, but I'm cold."

Another cover dropped over his body, but he didn't open his eyes. Where was a good cup of hot coffee when he needed it?

He drifted off to sleep again and woke to find Erik dozing in the chair. The guy could sleep anywhere.

Erik's eyes snapped open as soon as Bowen stirred. "Hey, friend, how you feeling?"

"OK, I guess. Want to go home."

Covering a yawn, Erik rolled his shoulders. "No need to hurry."

"Why don't you get some rest? You don't look too good."

"Speak for yourself, buddy. Just came to check on you and tell you about Sadie."

Bowen didn't want to think about her. Now that she had Hannah, she didn't need him in her life. She'd made it abundantly clear. But he had to ask. "Where is she?"

"Second floor. Room 267. I checked on them before coming here. She wants to see you."

"No. Tell her not to come. Please." How could he be in her company and not long for something more?

"You're back to your usual pigheaded self. Good. After I chat with your nurse, I'll go home. See you later."

Although Erik's words sounded harsh, Bowen sensed his compassion. How many hours had he been sitting by his bedside? Only a friend would do that.

Rattling carts moved up and down the hall. Breakfast. Nausea visited his stomach at the very idea of food. Another round of vitals left Bowen longing for the peace and quiet of his own bedroom. He'd almost fallen asleep again when a doctor wearing an oversized lab coat bustled into the room.

The petite, dark-skinned woman, no bigger than his thirteen-year-old niece, gave him a big smile. "Good morning, Mr. Boudine. I'm Doctor Loudermilk. Let's see how your arm is doing." Wire-rimmed glasses set on her dainty nose, she drew the covers off his torso and ran her hand over the bandaged area. "No swelling. Good. The exit wound resulted in a lot of damaged tissue which I had to remove. You're a lucky guy. A couple of centimeters to the left and the bullet would have shattered the bone. You should regain complete use of your arm."

"*Should* regain complete use?"

"I wish I could be more specific, Mr. Boudine. But for now, your body needs time to heal." She slipped her glasses into her pocket and glided to the foot of the bed. "Any questions?"

"When can I go home?"

"We'll reevaluate your situation tomorrow. The human body is a remarkable machine. You need to rest. Is that clear?"

He nodded, but none of it was OK. What if he lost the use of his arm?

"Later the staff will get you up. I'll see you tomorrow." Dr. Loudermilk nodded and exited the room.

Robin, who'd been hovering in the background, tucked the covers around Bowen's torso. "Ring if you need anything, Mr. Boudine."

Left alone at last, Bowen stared at the wall. What would he do if he couldn't work for IRO? Without the job he enjoyed and the woman he loved, what would happen? Would his lies deprive him of happiness with her?

A muscle spasm shifted his focus to his right arm.

With effort, he moved his index finger, sending a welcome twinge up his arm. He tried again. Definite movement. He closed his eyes. "Thank You, God."

Grabbing the bed rail, he sucked in a breath. Pain shot through his bicep. The short prayer had prodded the tender spot in his brain. The flack vest might have saved his body. But what would it take to rescue his soul?

39

Catching up on three lost years of Hannah's life thrilled Sadie. In between short naps, her daughter chatted about school, friends, and Evelyn. Sadie didn't care. Right now, she just needed to reconnect. The latest blood test showed that the drug had almost vacated Hannah's body. She could be discharged from the hospital the next day.

While Hannah lounged in bed watching cartoons on TV, a steady stream of officials debriefed Sadie. The LAPD, the FBI, and WITSEC had called on her at different times, conducting their interviews in the hospital wing's staff kitchen for privacy. They understood her need to be near Hannah, and agreed she could make formal statements sometime later.

She worried about Bowen but didn't want to leave her daughter's side.

When Elia Valdez visited, a counselor came with her.

Cuddly and rosy-cheeked, Mary Irving's soft hazel eyes twinkled as she greeted Hannah. "Hello, young lady. I want to talk to you. Will that be all right?"

Hannah glanced at Sadie, brown eyes seeking direction.

The tiny action sent Sadie's heart fluttering. She nodded. "It's all right, sweetie pie. Mary's here to help us."

Mary asked a series of general questions, establishing rapport, and then motioned for Sadie to step into the hall.

Elia produced a box of crayons and a coloring book, eliciting squeals from Hannah.

"Mrs. Malone, what is your assessment of Hannah's emotional state at this point?"

"To be honest, I'm surprised and relieved. When Hannah regained consciousness, she recognized me——you don't know how I'd dreaded that moment." Sadie's throat tightened. "Anyway, she asked if I wanted her. Apparently, Evelyn told her I didn't want her because her daddy was dead. That worries me. But so far, Hannah appears to be a normal, happy, well-adjusted child. I've not seen or heard anything else from her that concerns me, and I've been watching."

"Has she mentioned anything negative about Evelyn?"

Listening to her daughter's quiet chatter, Sadie frowned. "No, but she said something a while ago about her bicycle and wanting to visit a friend down the street. I'm afraid she thinks she's going back to Evelyn's house and..." The words locked in her throat.

"Possibly. Have you ever heard of Stockholm Syndrome?"

Oh Lord, please not that.

"Classic symptoms. The victim develops an attachment to her kidnapper. It's a survival instinct. This is where therapy might help. Here's my card." Mary pulled one from a little pocket in her beige sweater. "When you're settled, we'll schedule a series of visits. Do you want me to stay here while you tell her she's going home with you?"

Sadie hadn't thought that far ahead. Where was she going to live? No need to return to the safe house, but would IRO let her live there a while? She'd have to add that to her prayer list. "I can manage, but thank you. I will call for an appointment as soon as I can."

"From the short time I spent with Hannah, I've determined she is emotionally stable. You can help her adjust by keeping things as normal as possible. Have the authorities collect her clothes and toys from the house. Allow the visit to her friend."

These ideas hadn't occurred to Sadie. "Are you sure?"

"Uh-huh. If Hannah had negative experiences there, it would be different. But it doesn't seem she did. If you have no other concerns, I'll be on my way. I mainly came to introduce myself and do an initial assessment of Hannah's emotional state."

Mary nodded to Sadie and then entered the room and said good-bye to Hannah.

Elia gathered the loose crayons and handed them to Hannah. "Go on, Mary. I'll meet you at the elevator. Sadie, come over here a minute."

At the window, Elia whispered, "Jake Quillian's been arrested. He was on the take and supplied information to a variety of people, Lonnie Levasseur included."

"So that's how he found me?"

"Yes. I have to go now, but we'll be in touch."

Sadie returned to the chair. When would be a good time to tell Hannah? She seemed so content. Her hair could do with a wash, but her little cheeks glowed and her inquisitive eyes took in every detail of her surroundings. Sadie chose to tell her now.

"Sweetie pie, remember a while ago when the nurse removed your I.V. and the doctor came? He said you could go home tomorrow."

Hannah stopped coloring and nodded.

"When we leave here we won't be going to Mama Evelyn's house."

"Why? Did the bad man hurt her?"

Whoa. She hadn't expected that. "No. The bad man took you, but he didn't hurt Evelyn." Anxiety clutched her throat muscles. "Did the bad man hurt you?"

The purple crayon stilled. "He...he covered my face with a yucky cloth and I went to sleep. When I woke up he gave me applesauce to eat. I slept again. He didn't hurt me, but I don't like his carpet." She inserted the purple crayon into the box.

Anger at Kyle and Lonnie darkened Sadie's vision for a second. How dare they take her baby and force her to eat doped applesauce!

"Why can't we go back to Mama Evelyn's house? She said the bad people were after us, and we had to hide. Are we going to hide?"

With the bad people in jail, Sadie hoped she'd never have to hide again. "No, sweetie pie. No more hiding. You're going to come and live with me."

Hannah folded her arms and pouted. The coloring book slipped off her legs to the floor. "I know you're my mommy, but I want Mama Evelyn, too."

Maybe that was enough for now. She'd try again another time. Sadie picked up the book and set it next to Hannah. "Why don't you rest? They'll be bringing your lunch soon."

With Hannah's head turned away, Sadie couldn't see her expression, but she sat among the pillows like a rigid doll. Sadie lowered the bed. When Hannah didn't protest, she entered the bathroom.

Whew! That was hard. Sadie had expected Hannah would want to live with her. But maybe, as

Mary suggested, Hannah had no negative feelings for Evelyn. Sadie had to give Evelyn credit. This child still had the sweet disposition of the four-year-old Sadie had lost. Hannah respected adults, had good manners. All of that and so much more could have been destroyed by a terrible experience with Evelyn.

A gentle knock. When Sadie reentered the room, Erik gazed at sleeping Hannah, a soft expression playing on his face. He motioned for her to join him in the hall and carried out two chairs. They sat with the door ajar.

"Did you sleep some?"

He yawned. "*Some* is the operative word."

"How's Bowen?"

"Waiting to see if he gets full use of his arm back. Other than that, he's his usual stubborn self."

Her bubble of relief at Hannah's progress burst. Bowen, incapacitated. "I want to see him."

Erik settled his arm across her shoulders. "Give him time. Maybe later today."

"OK. What about Lela and Kyle?"

"Lela is fine. The bullet grazed her thigh. Kyle is dead. He—"

"What?" Sure, she'd despised him, but she'd never wished anyone dead.

"He fired the shot at you, and he shot Bowen. His police uniform got him past our surveillance. Good thing you wore that vest."

Goose bumps prickled down Sadie's arms as she rubbed her chest—right over her heart. Without the vest she'd be dead.

"Our official contacts relayed that Lonnie is under indictment for murder—he hired Lavonne White to kill you, and Miles Griffin got in her way."

Gentle Griff. He died saving her.

"Of course, add kidnapping, extortion, et cetera. Nicole will also be out of the picture for a long time. The feds are investigating Brady Holdings again. Our friend, Evelyn, will be indicted for kidnapping."

For a moment, Sadie snuggled on Erik's shoulder. "That's kinda sad. I mean I know she kept Hannah, but she saved her life and provided what appears to be a pretty normal existence for the past two and a half years."

"Maybe so, but she knew about the accident. She could have turned Hannah over to the authorities. Hannah would have gone with you into WITSEC."

Erik's words sat like a boulder on Sadie's heart. He was right. Although Evelyn had kept Hannah safe, she'd stolen nearly three years of their lives together.

"One more thing. Vicky has been arrested. She initiated the hiring of Lavonne and contacted Evelyn pretending to be a high school chum."

"What about her sister, Irene?"

"They can't pin anything on her yet. She might have eavesdropped or pumped information from Cal's staff, but until they have something illegal on her, she'll probably skate. She's not even in custody."

Sadie stretched her legs. Muscle stiffness had become a constant companion. "So that accounts for everyone."

"Pretty much. I'm going back to Bowen."

"I appreciate you coming. With the bad guys behind bars, I can be Sadie Malone again."

Erik lumbered out of the chair and pointed down the hall. "Speaking of the Malones, here's your brother-in-law."

Cal and a slim, dark-haired woman approached.

She carried a small duffle bag.

Erik greeted the visitors and then continued to the elevator.

"Cal." Sadie fell into his arms. "Thank you. Thank you for sending Bowen to find me."

"Praise God for a successful outcome."

They held each other for a while before he released her. "I want you to meet my fiancée, Reyna Perez."

Sadie extended her hand, but Reyna dropped the bag and wrapped her in a hug. "So nice to meet you. How's Hannah?"

"She recognized me, which is wonderful, but she also wants to be with Evelyn."

"It'll take time." Cal nodded towards the door. "Can we see her?"

"She was asleep. Let me check." Sadie peeked around the door and whispered her name. Snuggled under the covers, Hannah didn't budge.

"Don't wake her. We'll chat out here." Cal picked up the bag and motioned for Reyna and Sadie to sit. "We have a proposition for you."

Sadie glanced from Reyna to Cal. "What's on your mind?"

"IRO has kept me abreast of your situation. What are your plans?" Cal knelt on one knee beside Reyna. "No need to worry about finances, because I will provide whatever you need."

Another trait Cal had in common with his brother—generosity. Her emergency stash wouldn't take her and Hannah very far. "Thank you. I'll need help until I can find a job. My immediate problem is where to live. The counselor told me to keep things as normal as possible for Hannah, but I don't know how to do that."

Reyna blinked luscious dark eyes. "That's what we want to discuss. Cal and I have set a wedding date for August. Until then I will continue to live in Santa Clarita. I have an extra bedroom." She touched Sadie's arm. "I'd like you and Hannah to live with me."

The idea flew through Sadie's mind connecting the dots. A safe place to live. Hannah would be in a familiar community. It was an answer to prayer. "Are you sure we won't be an imposition?"

"Not at all. I wouldn't have offered otherwise. Hannah and Francesca are already friends and will attend the same school. Although it will be a different school for Hannah, she'll know some of the kids from soccer." Reyna nudged Sadie with her elbow. "You can help me plan my wedding."

The mention of a wedding date hadn't registered before. "Congratulations to you both. This is exciting news." Family. How she'd missed a family. "Thank you, Reyna. I accept your wonderful offer."

Cal slapped his thigh. "Great. When will Hannah be discharged?"

"Tomorrow. The counselor advised us to get her belongings from Evelyn's house. I guess I'll ask Elia Valdez to take care of that. Maybe Erik or Smitty can bring my things from the safe house."

"Then it's settled. You can use my SUV. I kinda like driving the old sports car again."

Reyna pointed to the bag. "Since we didn't know how long you'd be here, I brought you a change of clothes and a few toiletries, along with an outfit for Hannah."

Holding back tears, Sadie squeezed Reyna's hand. "Thank you so much."

"Erik says Bowen's doing well." Cal stood and

offered his hand to Reyna. "Have you seen him yet?"

"No."

"We can stay with Hannah if you'd like to visit him now."

Sadie fingered the zipper pull on the bag. "I don't want to leave Hannah while she's asleep."

"I understand. When you do see Bowen, tell him I said he really earned his money last night. But he doesn't get paid extra for getting shot." His quick grin softened his words. "We'll be on our way. Let you get some rest." Cal slipped his arm across Reyna's shoulders. "Call when Hannah is ready to be discharged and we'll come get you."

"How can I ever thank you enough for uniting Hannah and me?"

"My reward is seeing you together and happy. We're family."

"Answer one question. How did you know I was in Texas?"

Cal harrumphed. "Remember Chuck and Trisha Coleman?"

"Sure." The couple served in her wedding party.

"A year or so ago, they vacationed in Texas and saw someone who looked like you. They'd been told you passed away but mentioned it to me over dinner one evening. Trisha recalled overhearing the woman give her address to a clerk at the mall. She remembered Monterey Oaks Boulevard because her mother lives on a street with that name in Sacramento."

Sadie nodded. "Must have been when I first moved there, before I cut and dyed my hair."

"You know how scatterbrained Trisha is. She couldn't remember the city. I guess that's why it took Bowen a month to find you."

"I will always be grateful to you. And Trisha." She squeezed Cal's hand and tilted her head towards Reyna. "You've landed a good guy."

"I know."

Sadie waved as they headed to the elevators.

Her mind still reeling from the perfect solution to her problems, she entered the room and tiptoed to the window. She stood there a long time.

Before returning to the bed, she glanced down at the crowded parking lot and spied a familiar woman exit a taxi. Squinting against the setting sun's glare, Sadie studied the figure. Surely her eyes deceived her. Could it be Irene?

40

Liquids. What a meal! Bowen discarded half of it on the tray and turned on the TV. Several stories were about violence around the country. A shudder rippled through his body as he relived the rush of anger that surged in his chest when he'd aimed his weapon at Lonnie.

He turned off the TV and slid off the bed. Enough. He'd call Ginger and resign. He would never carry a gun again.

But he didn't have to call.

Ginger entered his room carrying a bouquet of balloons. "Good evening, Mr. Boudine. How are you?" Dressed in jeans and a fluffy pink sweater, she still exuded authority.

"I'm doing pretty good." He settled in the chair, glad Erik had brought him a pair of sweat pants. "You're just the person I need to talk to. I'm going to resign—"

"Before you do anything rash, listen to my proposal." Ginger draped herself in the other chair, crossed her legs, and set the balloons on the table. "I know all about your situation. Erik has kept me informed. James Greene is retiring. How would you like to take over his slot as head of the San Diego office?"

Bowen's jaw gaped, but he closed it with a snap. "San Diego?"

"Yes. I know you need rehab, et cetera. It's a desk

job, directing the agents in the area. Take time to think about my offer." Ginger uncrossed her legs and stood in one fluid motion. "I'll be in touch. I have one more visit to make, which may result in a nice surprise for you."

Before Bowen could react, she placed a light kiss on his cheek and left the room.

Bowen rubbed his whiskered chin. Head of the San Diego office. That was a job he could do even if he didn't gain the full use of his right arm. His gaze drifted to the balloons. And to the Bible he'd been reading earlier.

Ginger had rescued his career.

Now he needed to do something to rescue his soul.

৵৽

Short of breath from the long walk, Bowen sat in the back of the quiet, peaceful chapel.

A nurse settled in a pew a few rows over and bowed her head.

Bowen shifted on the seat and focused on the stained glass panels in the front of the chapel. One depicted Jesus standing, arms outstretched to a swarm of children. Today he identified with those children.

In the somber, but reverent, atmosphere, Bowen remembered his desire to visit the community church near the safe house. Would Sadie have gone with him?

Studying another glass panel of the crucifixion, Bowen cringed at the nails through Jesus' hands and feet. The Savior had suffered physical pain, but also the spiritual anguish of bearing the sins of the world.

Bowen blinked away unfamiliar moisture building in his eyes. He'd spent several hours that afternoon reading the Bible, absorbing its truths, and learning how to talk to God. He located the scripture Sadie mentioned in Revelation 3:20. *Here I am! I stand at the door and knock. If anyone hears My voice and opens the door, I will go in and eat with him, and he with Me.* Bowen recalled a picture in his first Bible—Jesus standing beside a door with no outside handle, knocking.

After the nurse left, Bowen took a deep breath. Here he sat in the chapel, convinced of what he needed to do. Would a mid-week commitment to the Lord count the same as one given on a Sunday? He stared into the face of Jesus on the cross and knew the answer.

Bowen balanced the Bible on his lap and opened to the bookmarked page. Aloud he read I John 3:9. "If we confess our sins, He is faithful and just and will forgive us our sins and purify us from all unrighteousness."

Closing the Bible, Bowen stood and took a few steps forward to the stained-glass portrait of a shepherd surrounded by sheep. He'd read Psalm 23 and recognized the shepherd as Jesus.

Since no one else had entered behind him, Bowen bowed his head. "God, I don't know how to do this, but the Bible says I need to confess my sins. OK, I'm doing that. I've done a lot of things I'm not proud of. Some were pretty bad. Will you even forgive those actions?"

He waited, not sure what to do next until an idea struck him. "And, God, just to remind You, when I was ten I gave my life to you. Sorry I didn't stick with the plan. But now I want to follow You. I want to serve You, so help me with the decisions I have to make. What should I do about Sadie? Please keep her safe and give her happiness. And thank You that I can move my fingers. Amen."

An overwhelming sense of peace covered him like a warm cloak. Was it relief at his load of guilt lifting, or God's presence—or maybe both?

Emotionally exhausted, Bowen sat, absorbing the healing atmosphere.

Minutes later, several people entered.

Bowen exited via the side aisle and made his way to the elevators. Movement down the hall caught his eye. A woman ducked past a group of nurses. Bowen did a double take. She sure looked suspicious. And she reminded him of someone. His stomach knotted.

What was Hannah's room number?

41

With Hannah tucked in for the night, Sadie settled in the recliner and covered herself with a blanket the nurse provided. Words of thanksgiving swirled through her heart. She had Hannah. A place to live while her daughter recovered. And a job.

Ginger's visit had caught Sadie off-guard. When the woman tiptoed into the room, Sadie's first response had been to glance down at her borrowed clothes. No match for Ginger's designer jeans, but at least the slacks and blouse from Reyna were clean.

Adding to the surprise, Ginger offered Sadie a technical analyst position with IRO in San Diego. After the words sank in, Sadie said the move would depend on Hannah's progress. Ginger gave her until June to decide—two and a half months—and left the room chuckling to herself.

Sadie eased out of the chair and stepped into the bathroom. The door automatically closed behind her. She stared at her reflection. No question she wanted the job, could do the job. But move away from L.A. and Bowen?

Tomorrow she'd visit him. Test the waters. See if he—

A muffled moan came from the room. Was Hannah awake?

Sadie yanked the door open and screamed.

A woman held a pillow over Hannah's face.

42

Lightheaded from the exertion, Bowen stood outside room 267. A couple of deep breaths and his head cleared.

From inside the room, Sadie yelled something unintelligible, but the panic is her voice registered.

Bowen shoved open the door. Sadie had a nurse in a headlock. The woman in scrubs struggled to keep a pillow over Hannah's face. The child squirmed under the covers.

He charged towards the bed. With all the strength he could muster in his left arm, he tore the suffocating pillow from the woman's grasp. The nurse shot him a dagger glare. In that instant he recognized her. Irene, Kyle's sister.

Forcing both Irene and Sadie backward, Bowen gritted his teeth. A bolt of fire shot through his arm. He ignored the pain, even as Irene pounded the bandaged area. He shoved her towards the bathroom, and with super-human effort, pushed her inside and slammed the door. He grabbed the handle in a tight grip.

Irene rattled the handle and then began pounding on the door.

Bowen held it with sheer will. "Call the nurses, security, 9-1-1!"

☙❧

Sadie mashed the nurse's call button, ran out to

the hall, and screamed for security, and then took out her phone and dialed 9-1-1.

As people ran towards her, she told the dispatcher what was happening and gave the hospital name. "I have to take care of my daughter, now," she yelled into the phone.

"Ma'am, stay on the line until an officer gets there."

"I will, but I can't talk."

Hannah's wide-eyed stare and sobs ripped a swath through Sadie's heart.

She slapped the phone on the table and hugged her child. Sadie muttered words of comfort and rocked her daughter as if she was an infant.

A bloody stain spread over Bowen's gown covering his right arm. Sweat beaded on his forehead and a grimace marred his handsome face.

She wanted to rush to him but couldn't leave Hannah.

"Stay with her. I'm OK." His words came out in a hoarse whisper.

Two nurses and a security guard entered.

Sadie explained what had happened, and handed her phone to one of the nurses.

The security guard snapped handcuffs around Irene's wrists while the nurses pried Hannah away from Sadie to check her vitals.

Assured that Hannah had suffered no physical harm, Sadie took her daughter into her arms again. "Thank You, Lord."

The nurses directed Bowen to the chair. One untied his hospital gown and let it fall around his torso. The other snapped on gloves.

The taller nurse said, "We'll have to remove the

bandage. See if you've popped your stitches. What's your room number? "

"I'm not going anywhere." Bowen's gaze never left Sadie's face.

"Thank you," Sadie mouthed to him.

"Mr. Boudine, I'll get a wheelchair and take you to your room." The taller nurse flicked his hospital ID bracelet.

"No, ma'am. Whatever has to be done can be done right here."

"Please, nurse. Let him stay. He's…a friend and he saved my daughter's life. I need him to stay." A surge of warmth flowed through Sadie. Did that mean she was ready to give her heart to Bowen? Would Hannah love him as she did?

43

The police left at midnight. Hannah slept, and Bowen had a fresh bandage on his arm now nestled in a black sling.

In the aftermath, Sadie had thanked him a dozen times and had learned why he showed up at Hannah's room. After he described his experience in the chapel, she bowed her head and said a prayer of thanks. Bowen added his words of praise.

Reveling in the company of this new Bowen, Sadie scooted the straight-backed chair closer to his recliner. In a clean gown over his sweat pants, and wearing hospital issued gray socks, Bowen produced a lopsided grin.

"Are you smiling because the pain meds kicked in?"

"Nope. Yes, I am pain free, but I'm content to be here with you."

His comment warmed her heart. Without his intervention, she could have lost Hannah and never known contentment again. "After they arrested Irene, you were gone for a long time."

"Had to make a phone call."

"So late?"

"The person I called didn't mind." Bowen took her hand. "Sadie, I've got to get this off my chest. While we were in Austin, I realized you were more than a job to me. I tried to convince you but obviously didn't succeed. During our time in L.A., I took you at your word and didn't pursue a relationship—although that would have been strictly against the rules. But you know what I mean."

She lowered her head, sure the intensity of his stare would burn her corneas.

"No matter what I try, I can't get you out of my mind. There's no way around it. I love you, Sadie Malone."

Those were the words she longed to hear. Was she ready to make a commitment? Her heartbeat raced as the drawbridge disintegrated into a fine dust. She raised her gaze to his and blinked at the strength she read in his eyes.

About to reply, she stopped when a soft tap at the door interrupted.

Bowen eased out of the chair. "I think it's for me." He blew her a kiss and closed the door behind him.

Snippets of whispered words teased Sadie.

Then Bowen peeked around the door. "Close your eyes. Don't open them until I tell you."

Intrigued, Sadie complied. "What's going on?"

"Keep them closed."

He set something on the floor.

"You can look now."

She scanned the dim room and noticed nothing different. Except the quizzical expression on Bowen's face as he knelt in front of her. "What are you up to?"

From behind the recliner he withdrew a soda bottle holding a long-stemmed red rose bud. "Life's too short for a lengthy courtship. Sadie, will you marry me and let me help you raise Hannah?"

Sadie had contemplated a variety of explanations for Bowen's strange behavior, but a proposal had not been one of them. She took the vase with one hand and moved the other over his firm chest until her fingers intertwined with the curls at the nape of his neck. "I love you, Bowen. Yes, I'll marry you."

Encircled by his good arm, she surrendered to the demands of his kiss, sweet and warm, arousing a passion familiar yet new.

Suddenly she pulled back. "I have to tell Ginger."

"What does she have to do with this?"

Taking the rose bud from the bottle, Sadie pressed the soft petals against her lips. "She offered me a job with IRO in San Diego."

Bowen slapped his thigh. "So that's what she meant. When she visited me earlier today, she offered me the lead position in San Diego. She must have come to see you next." He shook his head. "That woman is full of surprises."

"Yes, she is."

Bowen settled into the recliner. Sadie nestled as close as her chair would allow. Hannah's relaxed breathing soothed her soul. Contentment dribbled over her like warm honey.

Sadie let out a deep sigh. "I am thankful to Kyle for one thing."

"You're kidding."

"Without his interference you might never have suggested we pretend to date."

"Sadie, sweetheart, I would have found a way." He tugged her closer. "When will you marry me?"

"When Hannah has fully recovered. But I have one request."

"Name it."

"At the reception I want soda bottles with roses on every table."

He nuzzled the top of her head with his chin as a

nurse entered. "We have company."

"I don't care. I want the world to know I love you." Sadie pulled his face towards her, parted her lips, and lost herself in his kiss.

Thank you for purchasing this Harbourlight title. For other inspirational stories, please visit our on-line bookstore at www.pelicanbookgroup.com.

For questions or more information, contact us at customer@pelicanbookgroup.com.

Harbourlight Books
The Beacon in Christian Fiction™
an imprint of Pelican Ventures Book Group
www.pelicanbookgroup.com

May God's glory shine through
this inspirational work of fiction.

AMDG